Peter Crossings
And The Gate of Abaddon

To: Harrison, Noah, Liam, Tristan

May Tehus Guide You!

James Andrew Wilson

[signature]

Copyright © 2004 by James Andrew Wilson

Peter Crossings And The Gate of Abaddon
by James Andrew Wilson

Printed in the United States of America

ISBN 1-594673-99-3

All rights reserved by the author. The contents and views expressed in this book are solely those of the author and are not necessarily those of Xulon Press, Inc. The author guarantees this book is original and does not infringe upon any laws or rights, and that this book is not libelous, plagiarized or in any other way illegal. If any portion of this book is fictitious, the author guarantees it does not represent any real event or person in a way that could be deemed libelous. No part of this book may be reproduced in any form without the permission of the author.

Table of Contents

Chapter One
Shadow Stalkers 13

Chapter Two
Bullies, Shells, Freckles, and Friends 35

Chapter Three
The Hall of Faces 51

Chapter Four
The Flight to Edeneth 65

Chapter Five
An Un-welcome Welcoming 77

Chapter Six
A Meeting with the Master 99

Chapter Seven
The Hidden Shores of Patmos 123

Chapter Eight
A Vision From Beyond 143

James Andrew Wilson

Chapter Nine
Many Things are Revealed 165

Chapter Ten
The Unexpected Visitors 189

Chapter Eleven
Aracon City 207

Chapter Twelve
Into the Heart of Abaddon 227

Chapter Thirteen
Nefarious 247

Chapter Fourteen
Farewell to Friends 265

Chapter Fifteen
It's Only the Beginning 287

Peter Crossings And The Gate Of Abaddon

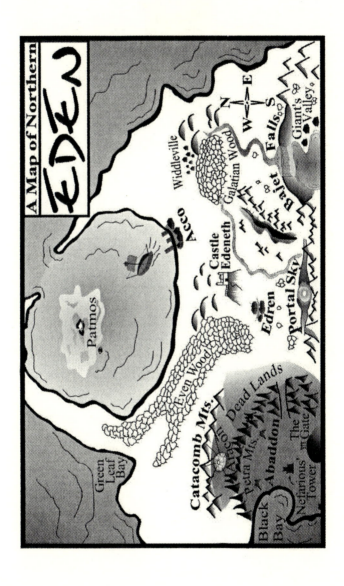

This work is dedicated to my Grandmother,
who always knew I was meant for more
than just breathing our God given air,
and who gave her last breath in prayer for that.

See you soon…

And so, it begins…

Chapter One

Shadow Stalkers

The strange creaking noise echoed through the house again. Peter A. Crossings sat straight up in his bed and swiped the flashlight off the nightstand into his quivering fingers. Like the beacon of a lighthouse searching for treacherous rocks, the light illuminated everything it touched. Peter scanned over the rows of neatly stacked books, the dresser with a stray sock hanging out the top drawer, and across the lazy curtains covering the window. The creaking sound echoed again… footsteps. Someone, or worse yet, *something* was in the house!

Visions of monsters and spiders flashed through his mind. He imagined a large drooling creature sniffing around his house looking for an eleven-year-old boy to devour. The footsteps magnified as though each step the creature took pounded through his head and echoed through his bones. He held his breath and clenched his fists in hopes that he could will it away.

The footsteps become louder. The fourth stair-step down to his room groaned under the weight of the creeping creature. He had marked that certain step's sound in his mind for just such an occasion as this. Four more steps and it would be to his room! Peter waited until the last step sounded, then all was silent.

Maybe he was just imagining it all. His parents never stopped telling him that "Someday you're gonna wake up in the middle of the night scared out of your mind because of all those weird stories you always read."

He breathed in the darkness and waited. Nearly a minute must have gone by, but it seemed more like an hour. Nothing happened. *"Alright Peter, get a hold of yourself,"* he tried to calm himself down. *"Just climb back under the covers, turn off the flashlight and go to sleep."* He reluctantly obeyed his conscience. *"There, see, nothing to worry about. Those foot steps you heard were just your mind playing tricks on you."* He grunted, now he was sounding just like his parents.

Peter pulled the covers up and sighed. Lightning cracked outside flashing a white light through the room. During the brief seconds of the revealing light from the sky, Peter saw something horrifying. Standing just inside his door was a tall, thin, entirely black shape.

"Peter Crossingssss…" something in the darkness hissed.

The sky cracked again revealing the ghostly shape once more. Peter was terrified to see that the shadowy creature had moved closer to his bed! It was reaching out a slender hand with long black fingers that moved like spider legs. There were two blood red eyes that seemed suspended in mid air above him. "Peter...Crossingssssss..." the shadow hissed once more.

Peter suddenly froze. He felt an icy touch on his arm. The fingers crawled along his skin toward his neck. He couldn't move! The fingers tightened around his throat. He couldn't breathe!

WHOOSH!!! The curtains were blown aside as a wind rushed in from the opened window. Peter strained his eyes to see what had happened. How had the window opened? He could hear a steady rain pouring, and felt the cold wind. Then a bright light spilled into the room. The shadow creature loosened its grip and shrieked back, shielding its eyes. Peter watched as a shaft of light that resembled an arrow, shot across his room piercing the shadow in what would have been its chest if it had a body. The shadow screamed, then shrieked and whirled, and then, it disappeared.

After he finally caught his breath, Peter looked up and realized that the window was now closed. For a second he doubted his sanity, then reassured himself of what had just happened. Cautiously he reached to the nightstand where he had returned the flashlight, grabbed it, and clicked it back on. His room appeared normal as far as he could tell. Slowly he shone the light at the door. It was still closed, and it didn't appear to have any damage. He scanned across his room to the window. The curtains had settled down and once again hung lazily concealing him from the sight of the rain, which he could still hear. Everything looked normal, like nothing out of the

James Andrew Wilson

ordinary had ever happened—but Peter knew, he knew that something from another world had visited him. And he was determined to figure out why…

* * * * *

Peter awoke to the insistent *tap, tap, tap* upon his door. When his body caught up with his mind, he hurled himself forward gasping for breath. It was morning, a bit of light was shining through the window to the carpet.

"Time to get up Peter," a voice came from the other side of the door. "Peter?" It was his mother. He imagined her for a moment: curly brown hair packed neatly around her ears, blue eyes gleaming. She was either wearing stripes or a solid colored shirt, and she most likely had her usual pair of blue jeans and old people shoes on.

"Peter, you're gonna be late again if you don't get up!" his mother said with her voice slightly raised. Peter didn't remember ever seeing her angry, but from time to time she was stern.

"I'm up, I'll be out in a minute," Peter moaned.

"Well hurry up. Breakfast *is* on the table." He heard his mother march back up the stairs.

Peter stretched, then reached over to his nightstand and grabbed his watch. Through his blurry morning vision he could read the illuminated numbers: 7:17. At the top of the small screen he noted the date: Sept. 12th. The date didn't seem too important to him. He thought about the shadow monster that had entered his room in the night, and then how the window had burst open and the arrow had pierced the shadow. Did it really happen, or was he making it all up? It seemed so real, it must have been.

Then it hit him, somebody had been outside his bedroom! He swung back the covers and ran to the window. The yard was bathing in the morning sun. His mom's flower garden was dying, and the fence desperately needed an extra coat of paint. Everything looked normal. *Wait! What was that?* One of the bushes beside his window rustled, and then a white piece of fabric flapped into his vision, but quickly disappeared toward the corner of the house.

Peter wasn't sure if he should be scared out of his wits, or too excited to breathe. He ran over to his nightstand, slid on his watch, and then darted to his dresser. In thirty seconds flat he was out of his pajamas and into a pair of worn blue jeans, a yellow collared shirt, and his favorite pair of sneakers.

The window complained about being opened, but Peter was finally able to pry it enough to slide through. He crawled out of his small window and crept to the corner of the house. Like a spy, Peter poked his head around to see the other side of the house. *Nothing.* He continued sneaking until he had gone all the way around the house. There was nothing, nothing except dad's perfectly mowed lawn, and mom's failures at gardening. The yard, the house, everything, everything was normal, and boring.

Disappointed, Peter pulled himself up the steps to the deck that was in the back of the house. He slid open the door, brushed back the blinds and scooted into the dining room.

James Andrew Wilson

As he made his way across the kitchen floor, his parents watched him curiously. No one said a word until Peter had sat down and started poking at the food prepared for him.

It was his father who finally spoke up, "Peter, why did you come in through the deck?"

Peter looked up to his father. He found it amazing that his dad could hide behind the paper every morning, yet still hold a conversation as if he were looking right at you. "I was outside, so I just came in through here instead of going around."

His parents looked to one another oddly, and then went back to their usual morning motions. Peter ate slowly, but he kept feeling as though his parents were watching him like vultures. He peeked up from his plate in time to see his father's eyes dart away from him and back to the paper. His mother though, just continued to stare.

"What?" Peter asked with half a scrambled egg in his mouth.

His mother hesitated, "Um Peter...do you remember what day it is, son?"

Peter thought for a second, shrugged, and then almost choked. He looked quickly at his watch. The little green lights revealed it to him once more: Sept. 12th. It was his birthday! Any "normal" boy Peter's age might have jumped for joy, but Peter Crossings was hardly "normal." He had developed a disliking for all kids at a very young age in his life. As soon as he learned to read, he delved into all sorts of stories, and rarely ever left them. He found excitement and companionship in his books, but he considered his life very boring, and especially disliked his birthdays. This wasn't because he became older, but because his parents always tried to throw a party for him. And birthday parties always meant kids, other kids, and lots of them. He said nothing, but shrugged and continued eating.

"Today is your birthday son!" his father exclaimed peeking over the headlines.

"Oh yeah, that's right, I guess I just forgot," Peter mumbled.

"We were thinking, if you'd like, that we could invite some of your friends from school over and have a birthday party this evening. How does that sound?"

Peter grunted, "Mom, first of all, I don't have any friends, and even if I did, I still don't want to celebrate it. I think other kids are just annoying."

"But Peter," his mom tried.

"Mom, I don't like them!" Peter said stabbing his fork into another egg and slopping it into his mouth.

"Son, I don't want you talking to your mother like that. Now tell me, *why* don't you like the other kids?"

"Like I said, they're annoying. They're all just, just weird!" Peter knew this was not the best excuse he had ever come up with, but it was true!

The newspaper lowered and Peter knew that he was going to get it: The Speech. "Weird? Son, they are boys and girls just like you. If you never go out and play with them, then you will never make any friends, if you never make any friends then you will never go anywhere in this world, and if you never go anywhere in this world, then you will end up as some bum under the bridge. I have gone very far in this crazy world, and if I hadn't known some of the people I do, I would never have become the president of my business!" His father sighed. "Son, we want the best for you, and we just think that you would be happier if you had some friends, that's all."

Peter was silent for a moment. He had heard the speech before, and could almost recite the whole thing, but it hit deeper this time. "Well... I guess that maybe..." What was he doing? He was about to say that it was fine for a bunch of strange kids he didn't even like to be running through his house. He couldn't do it. "No! I don't want to!"

"Well what *do* you want to do?" his mother asked.

"I want—" Peter stopped in mid sentence. His gaze was fixed on the glass doors that led out onto the deck. There, peeking in between the blinds stood the largest person Peter had ever seen. He was wearing mostly white, except for a few bits of blue and gold. He had a long blue cape that was secured neatly to his back. His features were smooth, his eyes were a sharp hazel, and his hair was a dark brown that curled just above his broad shoulders. At his side was a very long scabbard with gold carvings, and a long bowstring was strung across his chest connecting to the golden bow at his back.

Peter's father waited with baited breath while Peter just continued to stare without saying a word. His parents followed his gaze until all three people in the Crossings household stared out the window.

Peter couldn't believe his parents reaction. They

Peter Crossings And The Gate Of Abaddon

just turned back around with utter confusion scratched across their faces. Didn't they see him?

"Peter? Peter?" His father waved a hand in front of him.

"Wha—oh huh?" Peter looked to his father for a second.

"Are you okay son?"

"Yeah I'm fine." He looked back to the window. The man was gone.

"Peter, your birthday? Son, what do you want to do for your birthday?" his mother asked.

Peter dropped his fork and stood to his feet, still staring out at the empty deck. "Oh, nothing mom, thanks." He walked toward the sliding glass doors. "May I be excused?" But before he had an answer, he was out on the deck, and the door closed behind him.

For a minute Mr. and Mrs. Crossings watched their son as he looked anxiously all over the deck, and then ran down into the yard and searched through all the bushes, and even crawled up and looked over the fence into the neighbor's yard. Finally Mr. Crossings closed the blinds and threw the paper down on the table.

"I can't take it anymore Martha! This boy is driving me crazy!" He started pacing around the kitchen.

"Honey, please sit down," Martha tried.

"How can I? I mean look," he pulled apart the blinds. Peter was sneaking around one of the arborvitaes. "What is he doing? What is he looking for?"

"I don't know Phillip, maybe he's...maybe he's—"

"Maybe he's what?" The veins in Phillip's neck

James Andrew Wilson

were starting to pulse.

"Maybe he's going through a stage or something."

"A stage?" Phillip grabbed his forehead and tried to calm down. "Martha, he's twelve years old now, why, that used to be the age of an adult!"

"But things are different now."

"Yeah, I'll tell you what's different, our son! He's different."

Martha held her sides and started to sob. "I don't know dear. But he is our boy, and we need to try to understand."

Phillip breathed deeply and then sat back down. He mumbled something and then grabbed the paper back up and resumed reading.

* * * * *

When Peter came back into the kitchen his mom was alone at the table and she was crying. "Mom, mom where's dad?"

Martha stood up immediately and went to the sink. "Your father went to work early, go and get ready for school."

Peter left it at that and headed for the bathroom. He hated it when this happened. His parents had been fighting more and more lately, and he couldn't help but feel like he was the reason.

It wasn't long before Peter found himself opening the door to the white minivan. He sat down and buckled himself into the front passenger seat. A song droned on the radio and the air-conditioning cooled the entire van. The seats smelled new, and supported a light gray color with dull blue stitches. It was a family van, even though Peter had no siblings. His mother shifted into drive and the vehicle nudged forward.

What Peter didn't know was that a muscular man in white clothes was watching him from atop his roof. As soon as the van started down the road, the man crawled to the edge of the roof and leapt off. He landed, almost like a cat, in the front yard, then ran quickly right out into the road and started after the vehicle.

A slight hum sounded, and the van gently vibrated as Martha maneuvered the morning traffic. She peaked at Peter in between straight-aways. He shared her dull green eyes, and skinny nose. His hair though, was the sandy brown of his father; it inched down his forehead, but never quite reached his eyebrows. She was surprised to find that he wasn't reading. Rather, he sat still, clutching his backpack and staring out the window.

Martha finally asked, "Son, is everything okay?"

Peter looked up at his mom and then back out the window. "Yeah, I guess."

"Peter, your father and I—"

"Mom, stop the car!" Peter exclaimed. Martha slammed on the brakes. The car behind them swerved out of the way and blared the horn. Peter looked intently through his rearview mirror as a large man with white clothes ran down the road after them.

"Peter! Don't do that, you almost got us in a wreck." Martha quickly accelerated and turned the corner.

"No, slow down mom! He won't be able to catch

James Andrew Wilson

up!"

"Who won't be able to catch up? Peter are you sure you're okay?"

"The man with the—the sword and cape, and the bow and the white clothes." Peter searched the rearview mirror but he couldn't see the follower anywhere.

His mom said something else, but Peter just continued to watch the mirror all the way to school. He didn't spot the man again the entire ride. Martha pulled the van up to the front of the school. Nobody was outside playing in the yard so Peter knew that he was late, again.

* * * * *

The first class of the day was math, and Peter couldn't care less about it. He slumped into his desk and fiddled with a pencil when Mr. Wiggy, the ancient teacher with glasses too big for a giant, stood and spoke. "Today, class," his voice whistled when he sounded an 's', "we will be practicing long division." The kids groaned. "Now we won't be having any of that. When I was your age I couldn't even spell much less divide. You're lucky that you have all this schoolin." He trailed off about something utterly uninteresting, then turned and started scribbling on the board.

After a long hour of boredom, a couple stray paper airplanes, and numerous note passing, a noise sounded behind Peter. "Psst…" A boy nudged Peter's shoulder. "Hey!" the kid whispered. "Give

Peter Crossings And The Gate Of Abaddon

this to Tom." A folded piece of paper flopped onto Peter's desk. It had strange drawings on it, and bled with heavy black ink. Peter looked to Tom. He was just kiddy-corner, but it would be a stretch to get the note there without being noticed. Peter didn't care about what the note said, he just wanted to get rid of it. He stretched over toward Tom until he was hanging half way out of his desk. Just then Mr. Wiggy turned from the board.

"Peter? What are you doing?" Peter froze and slinked back into his seat. "What have you got there?"

"Oh man! What should I do now?" Peter thought to himself. *"Drop it? No, too obvious. Hide it? Too risky."* Peter looked back to the boy who had handed it to him. It was Judas Fitzgerald: The bully of the school. The bully shook his head at Peter and clenched his fist. Peter gulped and turned back.

"Peter, please bring that up here," Mr. Wiggy said. Peter was terrified. He scooted out from his desk and stood slowly. Every eye in the room was glued on him.

He gripped the note in one hand, as sweat started to pour in the other. The floor creaked when he walked by Bartholomew Farthing. Bartholomew was the biggest kid Peter had ever seen. He would sprawl out in his desk and sneak candy and cookies into his vacuum mouth when the teacher wasn't looking. He looked up at Peter and grinned a toothy smile revealing his crooked yellow chompers.

Peter reached the front of the classroom and handed the note to Mr. Wiggy. Feeble hands reached out and snapped the paper from Peter. Old eyes glared at him through those giant glasses. The teacher unfolded the note and mumbled something as he looked it over. The kids in the room whispered and snickered loudly. Peter cautiously looked back over his shoulder to see some kids pointing at him and clutching their mouths to contain the giggling. Peter felt sick.

"Peter, I would like to see you after school today," Mr. Wiggy announced. Peter felt his stomach roll. He could hear the distinct chuckle of Judas behind him. "And Mr. Fitzgerald, I would like to see you also."

Judas' mouth dropped. "But what did I do? Come on man! You can't do this!" Judas was standing up and raising an arm into the air.

"Sit down young man! I will see you after school!" The bell rang and the kids eagerly left the room.

Judas swept by Peter bumping into his shoulder. "Now you're in for it buddy," the bully taunted shoving him aside. Peter grabbed his books and sighed. He had the feeling that things weren't about to get any better.

* * * * *

The next class of the day was theater. Peter disliked theater class the most. The old stage was always cold and hard, and the director was a mean old hag. Her name was Mrs. Frudie, and all the kids despised her—except for Sally Andrews, who was her niece *and* favorite student. Sally always had a main part in the play, and almost always got her way.

Peter Crossings And The Gate Of Abaddon

None of the kids liked her either. There was, of course, the group of girls who tried to be like her, but they secretly despised her as well. So there were many groans and complaints when the sixth grade class fumbled into the auditorium.

The play this year was a story about a lonely Pilgrim's journey and his encounter with the Indians. The Pilgrim, Thomas Finland, had feet too big for his shoes and he was too skinny for his clothes. He was awkward, but somehow managed to get the main part. Sally was supposed to be his sweetheart, but she disliked the idea very much and whined each time she had to say how handsome he was.

Practice started late, and Mrs. Frudie was in a bad mood, which was no surprise to Peter. Peter had the joy of being the turkey. He had to wear a very hot and scratchy costume that always made him sneeze.

"Alright people, let's get going. We have approximately two months until we have to have this thing perfect! Finland!" Mrs. Frudie addressed each of the kids by their last name as if she were an Army Sergeant. "FINLAND!"

"Uh, yes sir, ma'am I mean." The lanky boy perked up and looked about with a confused look on his face.

"Finland, where is your hat?" Frudie snapped.

"Uh, I didn't, that is, I don't know. I didn't know I had a hat." Thomas was an expert at fumbling over his words.

"Of course you have a hat! You're a pilgrim! All pilgrims have hats!" Frudie's black curly hair bounced when she shouted. Her heavy eyes grew large and mean and her lips curled down creating little wrinkles on her cheeks. She looked like a teapot ready to burst.

"Excuse me Mrs. Frudie?" Sally spoke up with a tinny voice. "I believe that we left the hat in the prop room. I would go get it for you, but I think that I hurt my ankle yesterday, and those stairs would ruin it for sure. You should have someone else go and get it." Sally blinked with her long eyelashes and smiled, showing her perfect teeth.

"Thank you dear." Frudie smiled with her thin lips stretched across her not so perfect teeth. Then her expression changed and she shouted, "Crossings!"

Peter was busy trying to find the head hole in his turkey costume. He finally managed to pop his head up through the opening. "Crossings! Take off that terrible thing and go get Finland's hat from the prop room!"

Peter froze. The prop room was up the rickety old stairs and in the darkness above the stage. There was a rumor that an old crazy man lived there and would walk through the school at night howling and moaning. Peter swallowed hard.

"Don't just sit there Crossings! Get going!" Peter crawled out of the scratchy turkey and breathed a sigh of relief. He found the winding stairs at the back of the stage and looked them up and down. He closed his eyes and breathed deep. He then started up the stairs clutching the railing as he went. The last thing he heard from Frudie was something about Hatch missing again.

Each step up to the room squeaked under Peter's

Peter Crossings And The Gate Of Abaddon

trembling legs. The air smelled musty, and a slight breeze seemed to be coming from above. He soon reached the first landing of the stairs and gazed up at the aluminum vents winding their way through the walls and into the ceiling as though they were giant snakes. Peter continued up the stairs until he finally came to the small landing that was the entrance to the prop room. The stage was far below and Peter dared not look down. He could hear muffled shouts from Frudie and the rustling of feet on the stage. Sally was trying to sing her solo, but her screeching made Peter think that she was trying to break the windows more than trying to sing.

The door waited. Dark and tall, it loomed over him, staring him down and daring him to enter. Peter almost reached to open it, but suddenly heard a long deep moaning sound. The sound seemed to come from under the door.

"Oh no!" Peter thought. *"It's the crazy old man. He's probably waiting for me inside."*

Peter knew he couldn't return to the stage without the hat, but he was scared to venture into the room. He tried to tell himself that there was nothing in the old room except cardboard props, boxes, and the hat. But his mind kept telling him that there were spiders, and monsters, and crazy old men who locked kids in their lockers. He fought with himself for a few minutes and finally gained enough courage to reach out and grasp the door handle. It felt like ice as he turned it slowly, revealing the darkness of the room within. Peter gulped, and cautiously stepped in.

A dull and dusty light crept in from the opening

of the door. Peter's shadow lay long and taunting on the rustic floor. The only noise was that of his deep breathing as he entered one step at a time. His eyes scanned the expanse of the room. In the dimness he could make out the long string attached to a single bulb in the center of the room. He stepped forward and reached for the string. A sudden slam behind him cut the light and sealed off the room.

Peter searched franticly for the string and pulled on the light. It barely illuminated the room showing the many years of dust that floated about. He heard breathing—but it wasn't his. "Who...who's there?" he shuddered. Some boxes stirred in the corner and a light shot to the ceiling. Peter scooted back tripping over boxes until he was shivering with fear in the opposite corner. A head popped up from the boxes and scowled at him. A light flashing from its chin cast shadows on its eyes and nose.

"Boo!" the head exclaimed and then began to laugh. "I got you good didn't I?" A boy emerged from the opposite corner of the room and stood beneath the light. He was wearing a plaid shirt and faded jeans with a rip in the left knee. Wild red hair lay splattered over his freckled face. It was Andrew Hatch, the boy Frudie was looking for.

Peter was speechless. His heart was pounding through his chest, but he finally managed to stammer, "You...you scared me."

Andrew laughed. Peter had seen the redheaded boy before, but never paid much attention to him. He always seemed to be getting into trouble. "You should have seen your face! I heard someone coming up the stairs, so I turned off the light and hid in the corner. Did you hear me blow the horn?"

"The horn?" Peter asked.

"Yeah." Andrew dug in a nearby box and pulled out a small horn. He placed his lips on it and blew. The moaning sound echoed through the room. "It's the howling of the old man that lives here," Andrew smiled.

"You mean you're the old man?" Peter asked.

"No, but I'm the one who started the rumor, and made the howling noise. Great isn't it?" A wide grin spread across his freckled face.

"I uh, I need to get the pilgrim hat. Do you know where it is?" Peter asked standing to his feet.

"Pilgrim hat? Of course, but it's not easy to get to." Andrew pointed to a dark corner high in the room. "It's up there."

Peter looked up at a stack of boxes and saw a slight glimmer from a buckle on the hat. "Mrs. Frudie sent me up here to get it."

"Oh, Mrs. Frudie did, huh? Did she say anything about me?"

Peter cleared his throat, he wasn't used to all the dust. "I heard her say something about you. Why don't you ever stay for practice?"

"Are you kidding!? Where have you been? Mrs. Frudie would love to pounce on me and rip my ears off if I gave her the chance. Say, you're Peter right?"

"Yeah," Peter replied.

"You're the turkey! Ha ha!" Andrew laughed as Peter blushed. "No it's okay, better than poor Finland! He has to have Sally kiss him on the cheek! Yuck! Say

Peter, why don't you ever talk to anyone, I mean you usually just sit there?"

Peter fidgeted. He looked to the ground and mumbled, "I don't know…"

"Oh, I get it. You're shy? That's ok, I'm shy too," (Peter had a hard time believing this). "But not here, in here I can be whoever I want to be! Anyways, let's get that hat." Andrew started for the corner, but before he reached the first box, the room immediately fell into a cloud of darkness.

"Oh man, the light must have gone out," Andrew's voice echoed through the blackness. Suddenly the kids felt an overwhelming presence, as though someone, or *something* else was in the room with them. The sense that one gets before something terrible is about to happen. The feeling one has in a dream right before they fall into a bottomless pit—bone-chilling fear.

Then a raspy, high-shrilled voice scratched through the room, "Peter…Crossings." It became louder. "Peter…Crossingsss." Peter looked about in horror and saw two menacing, red eyes appear over him. The eyes of the shadow creature were watching him, staring at him, piercing through him. In the darkness Peter felt a cold touch on his hand and he jerked it back in fright. "You're…coming with me…Peter……Crossingsssss!" The voice, shrill and horrific, intensified. Coldness crept over him as he started rising from the ground. He felt a tight grip around his neck and suddenly couldn't breathe. Fowl breath emitted from the darkness and crept over him. Peter reached to his neck and tried to pry the icy hands

Peter Crossings And The Gate Of Abaddon

loose. The eyes continued to stare right through him.

Suddenly the door burst open allowing light to spill in. In a brief amount of seconds many things happened. There was a flash of white, and then there was a glimmer of what appeared to be a sword. The sword sliced through the shadow's arm and the creature wailed horribly. Peter fell to the floor with a thump, and Andrew would have screamed had he not been in shock.

There was a lot of scuffling and fighting as the shadow lashed out at the man. He stumbled back and tripped over some boxes, then stood again. In a flash he whipped out the bow from behind his back. The shadow drifted nearer screaming shrilly. In a single smooth action the man grabbed an arrow from the pouch on his back and placed it on the bowstring. Just as the shadow was about to jump at him, an arrow of light pierced its chest sending it to the ground where it disappeared with a shrill scream.

Peter looked in awe as the man dressed in white slung the bow across his back, picked up his sword and slid it into its sheath. This was the same man who he had seen on his deck, the same man who had been running down the road. He had to be the same man who had saved him from the shadow creature before.

"Wow, who are you?" Andrew asked, suddenly coming out from behind a pile of boxes.

The man looked surprised and started fidgeting with his cape. At first he tried to hide behind it, then he made sure it was strapped tightly to his shoulders. All this time he stared at the boys as if to see if he might suddenly disappear before them. Finally he gave up and spoke, "Well that is rather odd...I can't understand why..." he mumbled something else and checked his cape once more. The boys just gazed at him not knowing what to say. "Oh well, I guess it can't be helped now. To answer your question lad, my name is Gaberilin, and I come from the land of Eden."

Chapter Two

Bullies, Shells, Freckles, and Friends

"Eden? What are you talking about?" Andrew asked.

"Eden is where I live. It is the land that I came from," the man replied.

"You saved me from the shadow in my room, didn't you?" Peter asked.

The man looked down at Peter. "Yes, I did."

"You shot it with your bow, right?"

"Yes, I sure did."

"Now wait a second," Andrew said suddenly. "What's going on here? I just saw some pretty weird things, and now you two are talking like buddies or something. And you," Andrew pointed at the man, "why were you playing around with your cape just now? Were you trying to disappear or something? What are you anyways, a magician?"

James Andrew Wilson

The man laughed. "Perhaps we should all sit down." Everyone pulled up a box and sat. Gaberilin rubbed his hands together and then spoke, "As I said, I came from Eden. Eden is a long way from here; it is actually a different world! When we started to see a lot of shadows gathering near to the portal, we were very curious. We became worried when they started going through the portal. So we sent some scouts to follow them and see where they were going. It was apparent that they were looking for someone," Gaberilin paused and looked at Peter.

"We discovered that they were after you. So I was sent to protect you. We felt that it was our responsibility since they were our enemies, and since they came from our world," Gaberilin said. "Although, I'm not sure why the shadows are after you, I will do everything I can to keep you safe."

Peter sat motionless. He couldn't take his eyes off the muscular figure, and he certainly wasn't sure what to think about what he was hearing.

"Well this all sounds really weird to me, but you still haven't answered my question," Andrew said. "What's with the cape thing?"

"Oh yes! I haven't figured that out yet either. This is an invisible cape, that is to say, it makes the person who wears it invisible."

"Well it must be broken because I can see you plain as day," Andrew said bluntly.

"Yes, apparently so," Gaberilin chuckled at Andrew. "I just realized lads, I haven't received your names yet."

"Well I'm Andrew, Andrew Hatch." Andrew

Peter Crossings And The Gate Of Abaddon

extended a hand. Gaberilin shook it as lightly as he could, but Andrew still thought he was going to have his arm ripped off.

"And you?" Gaberilin asked looking at Peter.

"My name is Peter Crossings," Peter replied. His mind was still racing with questions so he didn't even think to extend his hand.

"Well it is very nice to meet you Peter," Gaberilin said.

And then Peter noticed something about Gaberilin that he hadn't seen yet. Tied around his neck by a thin strand of golden brown leather, was a shell. It looked a lot like the seashells Peter had picked up at the beach on his family's last vacation. "What's that for?" Peter asked pointing to the shell.

"Oh this?" Gaberilin grabbed the shell. "This is a Trans-Portal Shell, but we usually just call it a T.P.S. This is the only way that we can communicate through the portal."

"Cool!" Andrew exclaimed. "It's a cell phone."

Gaberilin seemed confused. Peter noticed and tried to clear things up, "We use cell phones here to talk to each other when we are in different places."

"I see," Gaberilin replied. "Well in that case, I guess you could say that this is my cell phone." The boys smiled.

"So, Gaberilin," Andrew said, "you keep on talking about a portal. Well, where is this thing?"

But before Gaberilin could answer, the door burst open. "I knew it!" Mrs. Frudie bellowed. "Andrew Hatch! I found you!" The boys spun around to see Frudie standing like a horrible statue in the doorway.

She glared down at Peter. "Crossings, why haven't you gotten that hat?" Peter looked frantically to Gaberilin, and then he realized that Frudie couldn't see the big man.

"Well I came—" Peter tried to speak but he was quickly interrupted.

"I suppose it's your fault isn't it Mr. Hatch?"

"No ma'am," Andrew said. "We were about to get the hat, but then that shadow monster came in, and Mr. G. here," he motioned to what Frudie saw as a lonely box, "he came in and saved Peter. He was just telling us—"

"That is quite enough young man!" Frudie burst. "I've had enough of your games! Both of you! Now get up, and get that hat!"

The boys sat still. "NOW!" screamed Frudie.

Andrew leapt up and darted for the pile of boxes. He quickly climbed up them and dug around for the hat. Peter looked at Gaberilin. The two just stared at each other, both of them deep in thought. Andrew suddenly came flying through the air grasping the hat in one hand. A dust cloud exploded when he landed, covering Frudie in dust. She staggered back for a second. Then she reached forward and grasped the doorframe, sneezing so loudly that Peter was afraid the room might cave in.

"AHCHOOOO!!!"

Before the dust settled, Andrew squeezed past Frudie and darted down the stairs with the hat atop his head. Frudie whirled around and started after him screaming all sorts of threats about detention and the like.

Peter Crossings And The Gate Of Abaddon

Gaberilin chuckled. "Your friend seems to be quite the troublemaker."

"Oh, he's not my friend," Peter quickly replied.

"Really? My mistake, you look like friends." Gaberilin stepped forward and put a hand on Peter's shoulder. "Peter, I'm not sure why the shadows are after you, and I am very sorry that you are in this terrible danger, but I will do all that I can to make sure you're safe, and to get you back to your normal life as soon as possible."

Peter thanked Gaberilin, but as he thought about it, he wasn't so sure that he wanted things to return to normal. In fact, he secretly hoped that they wouldn't.

* * * * *

Lunch finally came and the cafeteria filled with excited, and very hungry boys and girls. Peter took his tray, grabbed a miniature carton of milk, and found his usual table. Gaberilin was no longer following him, but Peter had the feeling he was somewhere near.

As Peter slowly began eating he pondered deeply about Gaberilin and the shadows. As his thoughts wound down a long winding road, he had a strange memory.

It was raining; he was cold and wet. He stood on an unfamiliar sidewalk, in an unfamiliar part of town, in front of an unfamiliar building. An arched word over the door to the building read "Library." Peter didn't remember ever seeing this library before. Lightning lit up the sky and Peter quickly ran to the front door. The door handles were shiny gold, and the doors were solid wood. He pulled open the door and scooted in. For a second he stood dripping water all over the entryway, but then he crept further into the library.

It was a very large building with rows and rows of bookshelves and green tiles covered the floor. The building appeared empty. "Hello? Is there anybody here?" Peter's voice echoed through the building.

A very strangely dressed person suddenly appeared from behind a bookshelf and scooted over to him. The person was wearing a maroon cloak that reached all the way to the ground. For some reason Peter couldn't see the face. And then everything went blurry.

"Can I sit here?" Peter blinked and found himself back in the cafeteria. He looked up to see the freckled face of Andrew. His hair, a bright red with hints of blond, lay uncombed about his eyes. His eyes were a sharp blue filled with wonder and a curious glimmer.

"Sure," Peter said, still trying to figure out what he was remembering. Was this something that had happened to him?

Suddenly Andrew's face was very close to his. "So, Peter, where's Mr. G.?" Andrew whispered.

"I don't know," Peter replied.

Andrew pulled his face away and started eating. "That was really weird Peter," Andrew said with a mouth full of food. "I mean, I saw those eyes, and that shadow thing. And then Gaberilin came in and sliced it like butter with his big sword." Andrew shook his head and swallowed. "Weird stuff man."

Peter Crossings And The Gate Of Abaddon

Peter didn't respond.

"You know, if you would talk more, maybe open up a bit, you might have some more friends," Andrew suggested.

"I don't really want any friends," Peter mumbled.

"Why not, man?"

"I just don't I guess."

"Well, okay…" Andrew grabbed his milk carton and popped it open. He put it to his lips and raised his eyebrows at Peter. Then he closed his eyes and bent his head back guzzling the whole carton. He slammed the container on the table and arched his back. Then he let out a loud belch. Some girls nearby cringed and left the table. Andrew smiled a wide toothy grin at Peter, creamy milk still dripping from his lips.

Peter was not amused. He took a sip of his own milk, astonished at Andrew's lack of manners.

"Say Peter, have you ever had goulash?" Andrew asked placing a bit of mashed potato neatly on his tongue, then quickly devouring it.

"Uh, no," Peter replied.

"Oh man, it is so good! My mom makes it once a week and she puts a lot of peppers in it. It's really spicy, but I usually put a lot of hot sauce on it anyways. Do you like spicy food?"

"Not really." Peter was beginning to feel rather uncomfortable.

"Oh, so I bet you like ice cream. I love ice cream! My favorite flavor is cookie dough. Ohhh, it's so good!" Andrew rubbed his stomach and rolled his eyes.

James Andrew Wilson

Some other kids were staring at Peter and Andrew and whispering. Peter was feeling very embarrassed and he was half tempted to move to another table, but a sudden tap on his shoulder caused him to turn and discover the face of Judas Fitzgerald. The army camouflage of his shirt matched his hard brown eyes. His hair was short, black, and spiked. A gold chain hung about his neck and glimmered in the cafeteria light. His lips, bent low and mean, moved only slightly when he spoke. "Crossings, we need to talk."

Judas addressed the other kids just like his aunt, Mrs. Frudie always did. He gripped Peter's shirt and pulled him from the table. Judas was at least five inches taller than Peter, and his arms seemed bigger than Peter's legs. "You got me in trouble Crossings! No one gets Judas Fitzgerald in trouble and gets away with it!" Judas raised a clenched fist back into the air and smiled a villainous grin.

Peter closed his eyes, expecting to wake up on a hospital bed, unaware and unable to recall the event that was about to take place. A dull *thud* sounded and caused him to open his eyes. He uncovered them to discover another hand holding back the fist of Judas. "I wouldn't do that if I were you, buddy." It was Andrew. He stood on the table smiling through his freckles at Judas. "If you hurt him the shadows will get you."

"What are you talking about Hatch? Let go of me!" Judas pulled his fist back.

"The shadows man! All the dark and scary things that hide under your bed at night, and creep through your house. They'll get you good if you lay a finger

Peter Crossings And The Gate Of Abaddon

on him."

"Shut up Hatch! This is between me and Crossings!" Judas lifted his fist back again.

"Don't say I didn't warn you Judas! They'll get you, they know where you sleep at night," Andrew said with an eerie echo hinting from his voice.

Judas looked at Andrew, then turned and glared at Peter. By this time a crowd of kids had started to gather. Judas looked about the expectant faces, then he saw a teacher coming his way. He tightened his grip at Peter's collar. "I'll get you later, Crossings." He pushed Peter back to the floor and stormed off.

Peter exhaled a long breath. The crowd dispersed and he stood to brush himself off and adjust his stretched collar. Andrew leapt from the table and stood before him.

"Good thing your *friend* was here huh?" Andrew smiled wide.

Peter looked at the boy before him. *"Friend?"* He tossed the word around in his head. "Uh, thanks..."

"No problem bud!" Andrew took Peter's hand and shook it violently. The two sat down, finished their lunch, then left for recess.

* * * * *

Gaberilin rested outside underneath a large maple tree. The covering of the leaves shielded him from the bright sun. He picked up his Trans-Portal Shell and put it to his mouth.

"Hello? Edesha, are you there?" he spoke into the shell, and then he placed it to his ear.

A comforting, yet strong voice echoed from the other side, "Yes! Hello Gaberilin!"

"Edesha! It's good to talk to you, how are things going back home?"

He heard some background noises, and then Edesha responded again, "Oh, things are going normal, and you know what that means. Have you found the boy?"

"Yes, actually, I have found two boys."

"Two? What do you mean?"

And then Gaberilin's voice softened as if he were about to tell a great secret, "Edesha, they were able to see me. I was still wearing the cape."

There was silence at first and then the reply came, "I've never heard of such a thing from someone from Beyond. Very peculiar..."

"Yes, I thought so too. And both of them were able to see me. Anyway, there's no hiding from them now."

"I suppose not. Gaberilin, what is the shadow activity like?"

"I've already killed two. If I hadn't been there, they would certainly have killed the boy, or whatever they were planning to do with him."

There was a silence again on the other side. Then Gaberilin heard the muffled sound of another voice. Edesha's voice suddenly came back through, "Gaberilin, some of our tower watchmen have just informed me that they have spotted more shadows entering the portal. Somewhere in the number around twenty."

"Edesha, why are the shadows after this poor

boy, I just can't understand."

"I'm not sure either Gaberilin…." Silence again. "Gaberilin, you know what to do if things get out of hand.

"Yes, I am prepared for that, should I need to."

"Good, I will keep my T.P.S. close. Oh and Gaberilin, may Tehus guide you."

"Thank you, you as well."

Gaberilin dropped the shell and let it dangle around his neck once more. He pulled his sword from its sheath, and then reached into his pocket and pulled out a small stone. He carefully sharpened the blade. With each stroke of the stone the sword shone with a bright light. He feared that he would have to use it again, very soon.

* * * * *

"Come on Peter! Let's go play soccer," Andrew said running ahead.

"Ah, no thanks. I'll just watch," Peter replied.

"No way. You have to play! Come on, I'll make sure you're on my team." Andrew thumped his chest with his thumb. "You can be the goalie. All you have to do is stand there and make sure they don't score a goal."

"Easy for you to say," Peter thought as he followed Andrew to the field. A group of kids were chatting loudly and kicking a ball around when the two came up to the crowd. Andrew was picked as a captain, along with Chad Roberts, a black boy who always wore white basketball shoes.

After a round of rock, paper, scissors, Andrew picked first. "Peter," he said without hesitation. It was the first time Peter was not the last to be picked. He had attempted to play soccer only a few times before, but tried to forget those scarring memories.

The captains continued to pick until the teams were completely assembled. Peter stood between the two bright orange cones, shielding his eyes from the sun. He spotted Bartholomew in goalie position across the field. Sweat was dripping down into his eyes making it nearly impossible to see the game.

Andrew was speeding down the field, winding his way through the kids. He kicked the ball between his feet with ease until he had a clear shot for a goal. He took a step and kicked the ball sending it with great speed toward the opening between Bartholomew and the cone. The big kid ran and dove through the air. The ball bounced off him and the two hit the ground at the same time, no point scored.

The game continued on for a short time without Peter seeing much action. But suddenly things changed. Chad stole the ball from Andrew and made his way quickly toward Peter. Peter panicked and tried to stand in a goalie position the best that he could. Chad kicked the ball sending it sailing through the air. It looked like a rocket speeding straight at him. Peter dashed for it and dove. The ball flew under him and between the cones. Peter smashed to the ground and rammed into the cone knocking it over, and nearly knocking himself out.

Chad cheered and ran back to his team to be welcomed by high fives. Peter stood up and brushed

Peter Crossings And The Gate Of Abaddon

himself off.

"You missed it Peter," Andrew said running up to him. And then he noticed that Peter had grass stains up and down his legs, and a nice scrape along his elbow. "Are you alright man?"

"No, I'm not. I didn't want to play this stupid game and you made me. I quit," Peter said turning on his heels and walking away from the field.

"But Peter, ah come on man!" Andrew didn't follow, but returned to the game.

Peter went to a spot on the playground where many large maple trees provided cool shade. He sat against the edge of the brick school, crunching into a little ball and clutching his knees. He watched the soccer game in between the row of trees.

"I knew I shouldn't have played," he thought to himself. *"What's the use? I'm a lot better off without friends anyways."*

Recess finally ended, much to Peter's relief. He waited for the other kids to make their way back to the doors before he stood. He trudged slowly to the corner of the building, which he would have to round before he could see the doors. But something stopped him before he had the chance.

Peter rounded the corner just in time to meet the rock hard body of Judas Fitzgerald. He slammed into him and then fell back to the ground. Specks of sunlight spotted his body in the shade of the trees. He lay helplessly on the dirt as Judas came closer.

"We have something to settle Crossings." Judas took another step closer. "You've done nothing today but get me into trouble!" He stepped forward again.

"Now I can't let you get away with something like that." Judas reached down and grabbed Peter by the already stretched collar and thrust him into the air. Peter squirmed in his grip.

Judas laughed. "What's the matter Crossings? No Hatch to save you this time? Oh, no, you're all mine now!"

The bully reached back his fist, smiled cruelly, and then shot his knuckles at Peter's teeth. Peter flinched, and closed his eyes. Nothing happened. He opened his eyes and saw a gigantic hand grasping Judas' fist. Judas looked oddly at his fist and pulled it back. Gaberilin stepped out from behind Peter to his side. He looked down at the boy and winked.

Judas swung another punch, but it stopped three inches from Peter's face. "What in the world?" Judas said as he cocked his fist again, this time looking desperate. He fired again only to be stopped again. "Crossings! What are you doing?" Judas was furious.

Peter just shrugged and then smiled. The veins in Judas' neck were bulging. His head looked like a big tomato as he stormed around Peter, punching and kicking, but none of his strikes ever landed.

Judas looked so angry that Peter thought he just might explode. And then the bully thrust a hand into his pocket and brought forth a small black item. He pulled a blade out of the handle and started twirling the knife around in his fingers. "Alright Crossings, I don't know what's going on here, but nobody gets away with getting me into trouble!" Judas grabbed Peter's hand and lifted the knife back into the air.

But just before he thrust the knife at Peter, he

Peter Crossings And The Gate Of Abaddon

froze in terror. The bright, long blade of a sword rested between the knife and Peter. Judas looked up the blade horrified. His eyes followed the massive arm grasping the sword until he saw the glaring face of Gaberilin. Peter thought that Judas Fitzgerald swallowed his tonsils right then and there.

"I wouldn't do that if I were you Mr. Fitzgerald," Gaberilin's voice boomed from behind Peter. The knife fell from Judas' quivering fingers to the soft dirt. He backed away and then tripped over an exposed tree root.

He stood and pointed at Gaberilin, eyes wide with fear. "Who— wh— wh— what— how…." He tripped again. Peter watched joyfully as Gaberilin stepped out from behind him and inched closer to Judas. Peter noticed that one shoulder tie of the cape was undone. "Stay away from me man!" Judas shouted standing again and scooting back.

"If I ever see you hurting, trying to hurt, or even thinking about hurting this boy again…" Gaberilin raised his sword into the air.

Judas cowered down and covered his head. "I'm sorry! I'll leave him alone. Please don't hurt me! I promise, I'll leave him alone. I promise!" Judas waited for a second and then peeked out from beneath his hands.

Gaberilin sheathed his sword and stepped back. "Alright, I'll hold you to that Judas." And then the massive figure disappeared right before Judas' very tear stained eyes.

Peter was nearly sure he heard Judas scream like a girl and then stand and run away around the building, arms flailing. Gaberilin laughed a great hearty laugh as he crossed his arms and watched Judas run off. Peter was beginning to like having his own personal bodyguard around. Especially when it came to dealing with Judas Fitzgerald, who he figured would never bother picking on him ever again, much to Peter's delight.

Chapter Three

The Hall of Faces

As Peter turned around to look at Gaberilin, Andrew jumped out from behind a tree, laughing hysterically. "You got him good Gaberilin!" Andrew leaped into the air and slapped hands with the grinning bodyguard. Then he turned and smiled at Peter, his eyes filled with delight.

"Wait a minute, were you there all the time?" Peter asked.

Andrew looked up at Gaberilin smiling. "Yep, I sure was."

"Andrew was the one who told me that Judas was causing you trouble," Gaberilin said.

"I've never seen Judas run like that before!" Andrew ran around the tree sobbing and waving his hands in the air. Everyone laughed at his impersonation of the bully. Finally, when Peter's sides were aching, Andrew stopped his antics.

Gaberilin let out a long sigh and then spoke in a

deep voice, "Boys, I have something to tell you."

"Alright, what's up?" Andrew asked.

"I have received news from Eden that many more shadows have gone through the portal. I am not sure how much longer I will be able to hold them all off, especially if the numbers continue to increase." He stopped as if to let that sink in.

"What do you mean?" Peter asked fearfully.

"Well," Gaberilin hesitated, "it could mean a couple of things. I can continue to protect you, at least *try* to protect you. Where I come from I am a mighty warrior, but I can only protect you from so many shadows, and I can't fight forever."

"What else can we do?" Peter asked. "That doesn't give me much hope."

"Well, the other option is for me to take you to a safe place. I would have to take you to Eden."

Peter suddenly lost his breath. His mind twirled at the thought of it. A different world...

"Gaberilin..." The boys heard a voice come from the shell around Gaberilin's neck. It sounded like a tiny speaker. "Gaberilin!"

"Yes? I'm here," Gaberilin said into the shell.

The boys waited anxiously as Gaberilin listened to the Trans-Portal Shell. "How many?" he responded franticly.

"Yes, I'm on my way!" Gaberilin let the shell drop to his chest. He looked at the boys quickly; his eyes were wild. "There has been an attack on one of the towns in Eden. Now you must listen to me carefully." In that moment, Gaberilin had both of the boys' complete attention. "We have no choice now.

Peter, I must take you with me to Eden."

Peter immediately turned and looked at Andrew. He had never really cared about having a friend before, but now he was afraid to be without one. "What about Andrew?" he asked.

"Yeah! You can't just leave me here. Why, I'm a part of this thing now!" Andrew chimed in.

"Fine, Andrew you are free to join us. Now listen, I must tell you this now in case I don't have the chance to later. As soon as we pass through the portal, I will have Atris take you to Castle Edeneth. You should be safe there, unless, Tehus forbid, the castle has been attacked as well. When you get there, seek out Solomon, he will make sure you are taken care of. I'm not sure how long it will be until I will come and meet you, but you must not leave the castle. Don't even go outside. Do you understand?"

Both of the boys nodded. "Gotcha, stay in the castle, find Solomon, no prob," Andrew replied.

"Now we must be quick, follow me!" Gaberilin started around the corner toward the doors to the school, with the boys quickly behind him. They came up to the glass doors and Gaberilin opened them for the boys. Sally Andrews happened to be walking by just then to see the strangest sight. The doors opened all by themselves for the boys to come in. Andrew couldn't help but laugh at the look of confusion on her face.

They followed Gaberilin through the hallways, weaving in and out of the kids until Gaberilin stopped at the door to the auditorium. "Wait here," he told the boys, and then cracked open the door and slid in. A moment later his head poked out. "Alright, come on."

Peter reached forward to pull the door open further, but a rather chubby hand with long purple fingernails slammed the door shut smacking Gaberilin's nose. "Mr. Crossings! Just where do you imagine that you are off to?" Peter didn't have to turn around to know that Mrs. Frudie stood behind him.

Now Peter was never the type of boy to lie. But as he turned around to see the wrinkled face of Frudie, a million things sped through his mind that he could tell her. Peter sighed inwardly, he knew that lies would get him nowhere. "I was following somebody Mrs. Frudie, and he went in here." Peter pointed back to the door.

Andrew looked at Peter with an expression like stretched silly putty. Andrew was the type of boy that always seemed to get into trouble, and always seemed to lie his way out of it. He was very confused by Peter's actions.

"And just *who* were you following?" Frudie asked standing up straight and slapping her hands to her wide hips.

"Somebody that I met today at school," Peter replied.

Frudie eyed him suspiciously. She looked at Andrew with a deathly glare, then looked back to Peter. "Well... I suppose it's okay if you study in there." She glanced at her watch. "But you've only got twenty more minutes of study hall, and then I expect you to scram!"

"Thank you Mrs. Frudie." Peter felt like someone had just lifted a house off of his stomach. He thought for sure that Frudie was going to send him straight to the principal's office.

"Yeah…now don't go getting into trouble…" She mumbled something, turned, and wandered down the hall.

Peter wiped the beads of sweat from his forehead. "Phew, that was close."

Andrew looked like he had swallowed a frog. "Close? Man I thought she was going to cook us, or something. I can't believe you got away with telling her the truth."

"My parents taught me to always tell the truth, sometimes you get punished, but it's the right thing to do."

Andrew continued digesting the frog. "I'm gonna have to get used to this."

The door cracked open again and Gaberilin poked his head out. His nose was still intact, but it was beginning to turn red. "Boys, come on."

Peter and Andrew scooted into the auditorium. Most of the enormous room was shrouded in darkness, yet a single blue light was reflecting off the stage floor from the rack of lights connected to the ceiling. Nobody else was in the room, unless there were unseen watchers dwelling in the rows of chairs that stood lined like a graveyard. The room was colder than normal and Peter's footsteps echoed louder than usual. The entire room seemed very eerie.

The boys carefully followed Gaberilin's enormous figure toward the stage. Peter noticed that Gaberilin had his sword drawn, and that he was watching every corner very carefully. They came to the stage, and Gaberilin slightly bent his knees, then leapt all the way up onto the platform landing softly. The boys reached up, grabbed the trim of the stage, and pulled themselves up.

"Peter?" Andrew tried to whisper, "What are we doing?"

"I'm not sure."

"Shhh!" Gaberilin turned and hushed the boys. He crept across the stage, his footsteps barely making a noise, but the boys' footsteps sounded like a heard of elephants, especially Andrew's. They walked into the ghostly blue light shining on the stage and then Gaberilin stopped. He knelt down and ran his large hand across the black plywood.

A rusty creak scratched through the auditorium as Gaberilin pulled open a small trapdoor from the stage's surface. He opened it all the way revealing a hauntingly dark hole that led underneath the platform. Gaberilin reached into a pocket and pulled out a stone that was connected to a strand of leather. He placed it around his neck where it rested on his chest just beside his Trans-Portal Shell.

"Alright, follow me, and be very careful." With his sword drawn, Gaberilin hung his legs down into the opening, slid forward, and disappeared into the darkness. The boys looked down into the hole to see the small stone around Gaberilin's neck gleaming in the dimness. It looked like he had a small blue flame resting on his chest. He looked up and motioned for them to come down.

Andrew scooted to the edge and fell down into

Peter Crossings And The Gate Of Abaddon

the hole landing a few feet later. Peter followed. He didn't land as well as Andrew, but he still managed to keep his feet. Gaberilin reached up and closed the trapdoor.

The boys looked around the dust covered storage room. From the small light around Gaberilin's neck they could see a few old boxes, and some strangely carved cardboard props that appeared as though they were huge lizards in the dim light.

But one box looked different from all the others. It was very tall, and had considerably less dust than those around it. It wasn't tan like all the others, rather it was a shiny green color, and it had gold tape holding it together. Gaberilin, with his sword still drawn, went over to the green box. He made sure the boys were right beside him; then he scooted the box slightly to the right.

The boys were shocked to see an archway carved into the cement wall. Through the opening they could see a line of steps that wound down into the darkness and curved out of sight. Excitement was rising within Peter's heart, but a terrible fear was rising right behind. Gaberilin seemed to be taking so much caution that Peter couldn't help but feel like there were hundreds of shadows waiting around the corners.

"Come on," Gaberilin whispered as he lifted the glowing stone over his head, and held it in front of himself almost like a torch. It illuminated the stairs with a soft blue glow. The boys scooted forward, and Gaberilin moved the box back over the opening. With Gaberilin in the lead, they started down the winding corridor. The walls and ceiling surrounding them were made of stones, which were all the same rectangular shape. They were very large, and looked awfully heavy. Peter wondered how somebody could build such a thing.

Not long after they had begun their descent, Peter could see some flickers of light coming from below. They soon came to a torch with a snapping flame, that rested in a gold ring secured to the wall. Gaberilin placed the stone back around his neck, and removed the torch from the ring.

They continued down the stairs until stopping suddenly at the foot of the winding staircase. The path before them stretched out now like a long hall-way. The walls were many different colors, and as they traveled through the hall, Peter noticed some-thing quite astonishing about the walls. Upon their stone surface many things were painted, such as strong looking men wearing shimmering gold armor, and enormous birds which appeared to have other men riding atop them; and even people who looked like giants. But what was most amazing is that the people, and clouds, and rivers that were painted upon the walls seemed to move. As they ventured down the hall, Peter watched in awe as a painted man moved along the wall wielding a shining sword much like Gaberilin's. The man on the wall ran across a flowing stream of blue paint and disappeared behind some paint strokes of trees.

Peter was most amazed at this, and found that he had stopped to gaze at the TV-like mural that moved. Andrew had stopped as well and stood with mouth agape, watching the mural. It was a great battle with hundreds, even thousands of men in gold armor with long blue feathers protruding from their helmets. They were all running along an enormous field toward the opposing force. A black-cloaked army of ghostly shapes met the warriors at the middle of the wall. The miniature painted figures slashed their swords, and the cloaked ones wielded crude looking knives and other deadly weapons. Bright red paint spilled from some of the dying figures, while brilliant white paint exploded from the warriors swords, slicing through the cloaks and destroying the ghosts.

"Amazing isn't it?" Peter jumped and turned to see Gaberilin shining his torch upon the wall. "Ethral, the master painter of ages past, knew of a way to make his paintings come alive. He painted this mural many ages ago, and it still lives on. I am amazed every time I see it…"

Peter looked back at the mural. The battle was still raging as more and more warriors appeared from the edges of the painting. It was truly amazing.

"Come, we must continue," Gaberilin said turning and casting the light of the torch elsewhere. The boys reluctantly followed, forcing their eyes away from the moving mural.

The hallway was very long, and the boys soon found that they were walking upon a very lush maroon carpet with veins of gold running throughout it. Portraits of very unfamiliar faces were positioned upon the walls, and they all seemed to stare down at the boys. Peter was almost sure he saw the eyes of one certain portrait of a man move, and he stopped suddenly when the picture spoke.

"Well blues and reds, it's a new pair of strapping brushes!" Peter had never been quite as shocked in his entire life. The man in the picture had shiny green eyes, very fair skin, and a few curls of blond that poked out from his beneath his purple artist's hat.

Gaberilin turned quickly around to explain, "This is a self portrait Ethral did of himself. He's the same painter who did the moving mural. Don't worry, he won't bite."

The painting chuckled. "Well of course I won't bite, I'm a painting. I don't even eat. Although, I do sometimes wish that I had painted a nice bowl of grapes, or maybe a glass of water, throat gets a little dry after two hundred years."

Peter and Andrew were speechless. Neither one of them had ever talked to a picture before, especially one that talked back.

"But I suppose that's the way it goes, I can't go back and repaint my life. You remember that young brushes; you can't go back and change the strokes, but you can always make new ones. You only get one canvas, better make sure it's a good one!" Ethral yawned loudly, the paint at his cheeks cracking.

"Always a pleasure Ethral, but we had best be moving on," Gaberilin said.

"Right, right, right. It was nice meeting you young brushes. Now don't be useless colors, and make sure to stop by again sometime."

The boys only nodded and then continued down the hall after Gaberilin. They could hear painted Ethral snoring nearly ten seconds after they had

Peter Crossings And The Gate Of Abaddon

continued on.

Peter gazed at all the portraits as they continued quickly down the hall. The light from the torch danced on all the strange faces. There was a portrait of a woman with straight brown hair playing a harp, and another of a man with very blue eyes who was holding a tall staff and a sword with a golden blade, and many others lined the walls. But then Peter halted at the sight of another portrait. Between the cherry wood frame was painted a withered old man in a long maroon cloak, and he held a very large book in the cleft of his left arm. His small eyes peered through a set of gold-rimmed bifocals resting on his large nose. Silver streaks swam through his snow-white hair. Peter looked intently at the picture, and as he did, he couldn't help but feel as though he had seen this man somewhere before.

"Can I help you young man?"

Peter blinked and found himself back in the strange library. The old man from the painting was staring down at him oddly. "Young man? Can I help you?"

Peter stared through the bifocals to the curious brown eyes. This man was the same as the man in the painting, only he seemed younger. Yet his hair was still white, and his face still had many little wrinkles.

"Well, I say, can't you understand me lad?"

"Oh, I was just outside, when I, uh...?" *When what?* What was Peter supposed to say? He had no idea where he was, or how he had even gotten there. He looked about at the enormous library. Except for all the lines of bookshelves, and the millions of books resting in them, the library was empty. The only living beings were himself and the curious man, as far as he could tell.

"Well, I'm not very sure that I can help you," the man said.

Peter suddenly felt that he did not want to leave the library. Like there was a large bulldog waiting for him outside, or some other sort of vicious thing which he did not want to meet. "Um, I'm here for a book."

The man looked very surprised, and he strolled quickly around Peter looking him up and down. "Mmmm....... Very strange. What book are you looking for my lad?"

Peter looked at the rows of bookshelves, it seemed as thought even more had materialized. "I'm uh, well I'm not sure. Which would you suggest?"

"Come right this way…"

"Peter, you alright?" Gaberilin asked snapping him back to the long hallway lined with portraits.

The old man in the picture was still there: nothing but paint and canvas. "Uh, yeah." Peter looked to Gaberilin. "Yes, I'm fine."

Gaberilin eyed him suspiciously. "Alright. Come on."

They walked a few more feet when Peter suddenly halted at the sight of yet another portrait. This one was very dark, and in fact the face of the person in the painting was scratched out by three long scrapes in the canvas. The rest of the picture was faded and smeared. Chipped pieces of wood lay on the ground from the frame that resembled a termite house. Peter looked intently at the strange outline of

Peter Crossings And The Gate Of Abaddon

the face, mesmerized by its oddity. It seemed as though something were inside the canvas, something very dark, something like a......

Peter gasped and leapt back as two red eyes opened in the face, and then a ghostly black shape floated out from the picture and screamed. Gaberilin whirled around and sliced at the shadow. The bright sword swiped cleanly through the creature causing it to dissolve into nothingness.

A black hand reached from the cracks in the wall and smothered out the torch. The hall echoed with horrifying screams, and many sets of crimson eyes appeared. "Run!" Gaberilin grabbed Peter's hand, and yanked him forward. The stone around Gaberilin's neck was very dim now, and barely let off any light as they dashed forward in the darkness. Andrew followed quickly behind and watched as Gaberilin sliced and cut at the eyes, some of them disappearing, others shifting out of the way.

Peter could feel hands grabbing at him, and pulling on him. He had the sensation like thousands of hairy spiders were crawling all over him. He yelled, and tried to push them away. Finally they dragged him down, and Gaberilin lost his grip. Darkness overwhelmed him, and he felt his breath being pulled from his lungs.

Suddenly, Peter saw many shafts of light flying overhead, some of them striking the shadow creatures. He managed to stand and discover that he was in a large room with pillars lining the walls. There were hundreds of eyes flying about the room. At the other end there were at least twenty men in brilliant gold armor, all armed with bows. Behind the archers was a large, framed, oval object that looked much like a mirror, only the glass seemed to move like water. It let out a brilliant light that lit the entire expanse of the room. Another archer suddenly appeared from the wall of water, strung his bow, and shot an arrow that sped past Peter's head and struck a screaming shadow behind.

"Peter, come on!" Gaberilin shouted from somewhere near the small army of archers. Peter pushed his way through, most of the shadows falling around him. He took another step, and then a mighty hand grabbed him and placed him behind the armor-clad men. Before he could take another breath, Andrew was plopped down beside him. The archers scooted back in closer, forcing the boys toward the strange mirror.

"Go!" Peter heard Gaberilin, and looked up to see him drawing an arrow from the quiver at his back. "Both of you; go through the portal!" He shot the light arrow into the horde of oncoming shadows.

The boys turned and looked at the moving wall of water: The Portal. Andrew stepped forward, and then without hesitation leapt through the water disappearing to the other side. Peter glanced back at the archers, took a deep breath, turned back around, and dove through the portal.

Chapter Four

The Flight to Edeneth

The portal felt like a whirlpool as it sucked Peter in, and then forced him sharply out. He landed on something incredibly soft that seemed like cotton. Peter found that he had closed his eyes, so he opened them slowly to a very shocking sight. Miles and miles beneath him the peak of a tall mountain poked upwards toward the sky, toward him! He immediately thought that he was falling, but then realized that he was suspended in midair. After further investigation, he discovered that he was on a very large, and very fluffy cloud.

"Whoa, watch your step." Peter turned to see Gaberilin coming through the portal. The portal from this side was much different. It was a solid white circle in the sky, which was surrounded by a purple and red haze that looked much like a sunset. "The Yafna placed this cloud here many ages ago, and it has developed some holes."

"What are Yafna?" Andrew asked.

"Cloud people," Gaberilin explained. "Now we must hurry, the archers are going to hold off the shadows as long as they can, but I must get you out of here."

Just then, one of the archers came through the portal looking very worried. "Gaberilin, get them out of here. We're losing warriors fast!"

Gaberilin nodded and then ran to the edge of the cloud and looked down over the rim. "Where is she?" Peter heard him ask frantically.

He ran to the other edge of the cloud and searched below. Gaberilin leapt back as a very high, and almost shrill call sounded through the air. A giant bird with fluffy white feathers, a silver beak, and golden eyes shot up beside the cloud. It circled around, descended, and landed softly on the cloud causing it to lean and shake like a boat in the water. Peter noticed that the enormous bird was a lot like the ones he had seen in the moving mural, which men were riding. Upon this bird there was a shiny leather saddle, with green carvings etched into the surface of it.

Gaberilin went over to the bird and placed a hand on its neck. "Atris, I need you to take these boys as quickly as you can to Castle Edeneth. Make sure they find Solomon." The bird nodded.

Gaberilin turned to the boys, who stood motionless like shocked statutes. "Peter, Andrew, this is Atris. She is what we call a bajet, and she is going to take you to the castle. Remember, do not leave the castle until I come to meet you."

And then the mighty bajet turned and looked at

Peter. "Don't worry Peter, I will make sure you and your friend are safe," she assured them.

Peter was so surprised to hear this strange animal speak, that he nearly fainted. He managed to nod a 'thanks', and then to follow Andrew, who was very excited, and already climbing up into the saddle. By the time both of the boys sat snuggly in the saddle, many more bajets had gathered around the cloud. Gaberilin mounted a black-feathered one, as archers came through the portal and mounted the others.

"Go Atris! Fly!" Gaberilin said. Then the bajet flapped its mighty wings, and thrust from the cloud stirring it slightly.

The boys grasped the silky feathers as the bajet soared high into the air. Peter glanced down at the landscape far below. Directly beneath them he could see a long range of silver peaked mountains crawling along the landscape. Dark green trees speckled the mountainsides, and continued down into the valleys. Past the mountains, in the direction they were flying, there was a long field with a wide river slithering through it. Just beyond the field Peter spotted some clumps of burning fires. The fires shot billowing smoke high into the air, concealing Peter's view of what lay beyond.

Atris sped through the sky like a bullet, pulling her wings to her sides and slicing through the air. "Hold on tightly little ones!" the bajet commanded as she suddenly dipped her beak down and fell straight toward the ground. Peter closed his eyes in shear terror, Andrew screamed wildly with delight, and Atris called loudly. Just as they were about to crash into a tall pine-like tree, Atris flushed out her wings, and the boys' shoes scrapped through the green needles as they leveled out and shot across a wide field. Little blue and white flowers covered the field like millions of raindrops. Here and there, bright yellow leaved bushes poked out like large eyes watching the flyers.

Peter dared to open his eyes and saw that they were speeding quickly toward the walls of smoke. He was able to catch a glimpse of what lay beyond. There were many tall buildings, which looked like houses. He also spotted a figure in gold who grasped a large spear in his right hand, and in his left, a long golden whip. And then he saw at least fifty more of the gold-clad warriors, some with the whips, some with the spears, some with bright swords and shields, some with maces, and even more with bows. The archers were positioned atop the houses that weren't burning, and other warriors were either atop the houses, or making their way through the tight dirt streets.

Atris suddenly lifted her wings, and then thrust them down sending them up further. They flew up above the burning walls of fire and smoke surrounding the town, and Peter was able to look down at the scene within. There were even more warriors than he had first spotted, sprawling through the town. They were advancing toward a dark swarm of shapes that shifted strangely through the streets. Peter knew exactly what the dark shapes were. The shadows were wielding swords, and many strange spiked weapons that glowed bright orange and red like they were actually flames. When one of the dark warriors

Peter Crossings And The Gate Of Abaddon

sliced through a barrel causing it to explode and shoot down the street toward a warrior in gold, Peter concluded that the weapons were actually fire.

Both of the boys whirled around at the sound of bajet calls echoing behind them. They spotted Gaberilin riding upon his black bajet with twenty or more other warriors riding upon bajets behind his lead. And behind them, to Peter's horror, a very large creature with one dull grey blue wing, and one fiery red wing, chased madly. Two hideous heads that matched the color of the wing upon their side bobbed up and down connected to long scaly necks. Jagged horns were at the furthest reach of the wings. The monster roared loudly.

"What's that?" Andrew asked, his teeth chattering.

Peter gulped. He knew what it was, and yet he never imagined, even in his deepest dreams, that he would ever actually see one. "It's a dragon….a two headed, fire and ice breathing dragon."

"Watch out!" Gaberilin shouted. All the warriors' bajets shot down as the dragon spewed a long flame from the fire head. It caught one of the warriors and immediately engulfed him in yellow flames. His body convulsed as it fell from the bajet. Nothing but black ashes landed upon the ground.

"Atris, get the boys out of here!" Gaberilin shouted, as his bajet quickly turned back around and darted for the dragon. In a flash, Gaberilin withdrew his bow, notched an arrow, and let it fly toward the beast. The razor edge of the arrow tip slid in between the scales piercing blue flesh. The ice head screeched, then bent its jagged neck and spewed blue flame from its throat upon the wound, which then turned to a shield of ice. It still appeared to be in pain but flashed its angry eyes at Gaberilin and let its voice wail.

Atris shot up into the air; her wings pounded and hurled them higher and higher. Far below, like pieces on a game board, hundreds of figures in gold armor advanced through the town, meeting the dark opposition. Suddenly Peter's vision was engulfed in a white haze.

Mere seconds later they rose above the cloud cover and leveled out above the white sea. It was harder to breathe at the high altitude, but whether it had been easy or not, the boys' breath would still have been taken. The clouds covered as far as their eyes could gaze. Here and there, large pillars, almost like buildings, rose higher above the cloud sea. Atris wound her way through the pillars, as more and more came into view. At first they were smaller pillars, with only a few taller ones in between, but soon hundreds of towers surfaced all around, many of them miles high. And though the site of the cloud city was astounding, what roamed among the pillars far surpassed the landscape.

"What are they?" Peter asked breathlessly.

"They are Yafna," Atris answered. "Cloud people."

The Yafna were all very tall, the smallest ones being nearly ten feet in height, Peter guessed. They moved with such graceful motions as though they were floating, or perhaps like they were gliding through water. Their garments, all of which were cloud white with gold lines, floated continuously around their bodies. They were devoid of any hair, and yet their eyes were very large and shaped like tall ovals in their heads, which seemed too small for their bodies. Their necks were longer than Peter would have imagined, and their arms long as well. The hands of the Yafna were enormously large, and upon each hand were ten fingers, including the two thumbs upon each side. The overall tint of their skin, if that is what it could be called, was a pale grey, and some of them bore darker spots almost like freckles.

"The Yafna are very peaceful creatures, but lately they have been moving closer toward Abaddon. I have heard them say that the clouds have grown dark and foul over that land. Although I do not know what they intend to do, they continue to drift upon the wind, always carrying Yafnaleen with them. That is the name of this city. Within the tallest tower there," the boys looked at the tower in the center of the city that shot up higher than all the others, "dwells the father of Yafna, Tafar. Some say that Tafar is seeking war with whatever dark thing has polluted his clouds. Although, I don't know with what fashion that Yafna would fight. They have always been known as peaceful, but perhaps the time has come when they are to change. I suppose we shall see, many strange things seem to be happening lately."

Atris glided quicker than the boys would have liked through the rest of the passing Yafnaleen without another word. The boys watched behind them as the cloud city started to disappear from sight until it appeared no more than a tall white mountain far away. And then Atris fell again down through the white sea and into the sky beneath.

A roaring line of fire scratched across the sky nearly close enough to singe Andrew's baggy shirt. Atris whirled her wings to the side, and then fell for a second as another stream of flame shot overhead. The boys glanced back to see the bobbing heads of the dragon reaching for them. The bajet was barely able to keep ahead of the mighty wings with which the dragon thrust. Atris continually weaved back and forth, falling, pulling up, and calling loudly.

Ahead no more than a mile, Peter and Andrew both spotted a gleaming tower. And then, for the first time, the boys beheld the glory of Edeneth, the great castle of all that is right and true in Eden, and it took their breath away. They nearly forgot about the monster looming behind them as they looked upon, perhaps like one who is able to peer into a dream world, the many tall spikes of towers and rooftops that sprouted from the white walls high into the reaches of the sky. There was, as far as they were able to see, two very large roofs that appeared as the top half of enormous globes protruding from the castle, one near to the center, the other closer to the side of the walls. For the most part, the towering outer walls leaned upon the very edge of sickening drops of cliffs, which surrounded the castle; except for a very large field, which was fenced in, that had a few tents upon its width. The only other flat portions atop the cliffs that the boys could see from their distance was a long road, that wound all the way from the gate to the bottom of the cliff. And there was a small landing with a

Peter Crossings And The Gate Of Abaddon

wooden building that appeared very small next to the castle. This is what the boys were able to see of Edeneth and its enormity. Although their short glance was a very small part of the castle's glory, it made them feel almost like warriors of a strange land and place in which they had been enveloped. It gave Peter a very strange feeling…and though he knew it impossible, he could not deny that somehow this was all familiar to him, and that familiarity scared him.

"Hold on!" Peter was snatched back to the present situation. He grabbed the silky feathers of the bajet as she curled her wings into the air-cutting position, and fell toward the castle. The dragon roared behind her and followed with great speed. Peter could hear the beast making deep guttural noises, and he supposed it was speaking some horrible dragon language. Searing fire, and shards of ice shot beside them as they dove nearer and nearer to Edeneth.

Soon there were wisps of light coming from the castle towers. Peter dared to look and spotted a few archers pulling back their bows and letting loose blue feathered shafts. Although many of them hit their target, the diamond-like scales of the dragon's breast could not be easily penetrated. Only a few of the razors managed to pierce flesh, but none bore enough potency to kill the beast.

Atris dashed down toward the castle and wound amongst its towers. The dragon followed closely behind, still spewing its fire and ice. A hot flame missed the dashing bajet and engulfed the roof of a tower. An archer fell from its height with a yell while the flames crawled among the shingles. The fire was quickly put out though, by buckets of water splashing from inside its burning timbers.

Atris determined that she would not be able to out-fly the beast, and so a plan formed quickly in her head, and she acted upon it. She thrust her wings out, and then shot back into the sky. She found what she was looking for, and dove into the white cloud. It took the dragon a second to figure out where she had gone, which was all the time she needed.

"Boys, listen to me," she spoke quickly. "I need you to trust me. When I say so, I want you to let go of my back and let yourself fall."

"What?" Andrew blurted out. "But we'll die!"

"Andrew! I need you to trust me." She waited for a second and then said, "Now! Let go!"

Although they had very little faith in the bajet's command, the boys loosened their grip, and let themselves fall. What happened next took place so quickly that all Peter remembered was landing again upon the back of Atris with Andrew already upon her, and the dragon nowhere in sight.

In fact it was the cunning of Atris who caused the dragon to find its death. The head of fire had spotted the boys first, and flapped its wing toward their falling bodies. The bajet's high call sounded half a second later, and this is what drew the attention of the ice head. Both heads drew their fowl breath from their stomachs into their throats and let loose their fury. A flame barely smoked out the nostrils before the fire head was suddenly frozen in a bulging blue statue. The ice head had aimed its coldness at the bajet but not taken notice of it's brother and therefore

Peter Crossings And The Gate Of Abaddon

exploded ice all over it. The fireside of the dragon quickly froze solid and shattered. Fire from its stomach spilled onto the remaining side of the dragon, and soon there was no more of the beast as both sides destroyed the other. Thus was the end of the dragon.

So with the boys upon her back once again, Atris didn't waste any time in descending to the castle. She landed beside the wooden building. Peter could see now that it had a straw roof, and was much larger than he had first thought it to be. Behind them, the cliff fell suddenly to sharp rocks below.

Atris lifted her great talloned feet and walked toward the foot of a tall tower. There was a small door there, made of dark wooden planks, which opened suddenly. From its interior there came a man of some age. His frail body was draped in a maroon cloak. Upon his nose rested gold-rimmed bifocals. His hair, which was mostly white, reached just below his shoulders and it was combed very straight.

He came up to the bajet, and Peter suddenly recognized him. He was the same man that he had seen in the portrait in the hall of faces: the one holding the book in his arm, although he appeared much older now.

"Atris, thank Tehus. I beheld the dragon and I feared that I may not see you come." Although his body was weak, his voice seemed strong.

"I managed to outwit the dragon at his own game," Atris replied.

The man smiled. "Well, that is a tale I would dearly love to hear, but another time perhaps." He then looked up at the boys, who were still atop the bajet. "Welcome dear boys, to Edeneth. Under such strange times you have come, though you need not fear while in the strength of this castle." And then his eyes met Peter's, and the two stared for a silent time. The silence lingered until Andrew finally broke it.

"Um... Mr. G. told us that we need to find Solomon. Do you know where he is?" Andrew asked feeling a bit awkward.

The man motioned for the boys to come down from the saddle as he smiled. "I do know where he is." Then he bent slightly as if to bow. When he rose, the smile was still upon his face. "I am Solomon."

Chapter Five

An Un-welcome Welcoming

Away down the hill, past the first steps of the road, and into the valley, the battle raged. The name of the town was Edren. It was a well-known establishment in Eden, and was the dwelling place of many fair people. Nearly half of it lay now in ruin, and the entire circle of its border was burning inward with a great wall of fire. There was a vast stronghold of warriors still holding ground against the opposing force. The count of shadows was unknown, but those that had already been vanquished numbered past two hundred. Along with these, three dragons had been felled, not including the one that Atris had destroyed.

Many of the warriors had been called forth, except for those of a small number that remained in Edeneth and some of distant lands. The mighty Gaberilin led his bajet riders into the fray. They were a fearsome charge, and vanquished many shadows in their attacks. The flaming weapons of the dark swarms, however, had already licked many of the warriors.

Now there remained just over five hundred of the warriors. At their lead though, was the mightiest warrior of all Eden, except for those in ages long past. His name was Edesha, and he was a High Servant of the Light, one of Seven in the land. Along with his shining sword, he held aloft a tall staff. This was the Master of the castle of Edeneth, and the head of the Seven. He was known, and feared abroad.

On the opposing force, a leader was also established. His name was Macthon, and a horrible beast he was. Although his rank among the darkness did not compare with that of Edesha. He bore the same height as a man, but his face and body was more that of a gnarled monster. He had incredible strength, which was mostly given to him because of his loyalty to the darkness. And in his back, tucked behind, were two black wings that had been sewn into his leathery skin. Macthon extended his weapon forward, an enormous double headed axe of fire, and commanded his forces to continue the charge.

The beastly shadows screamed like hundreds of rats as they shifted through the smolders of Edren into the heart of the battle. They chanted, "Flames of blood! Kill Light, eat Light, shadow the Light. Flames of blood! Flames of blood!"

On the opposite side, Edesha commanded his forces forward. It was evident to both sides, that unless Edesha bore some secret plan, or force, the darkness would surly win. It was at this moment that

Peter Crossings And The Gate Of Abaddon

Edesha paused, sheathed his blade, and looked toward the sky. Those around him saw that he closed his eyelids. His lips moved forming words they could not describe. After a moment, he opened his eyes and looked with determination toward the oncoming shadows. Lifting his unsheathed sword toward the sky, he proclaimed, "Rise warriors! March with the strength of the Light! Tehus has given us this victory! Now is the time to show His Power. Go forth with His strength in your blades!"

As the warriors marched forward wielding their blades, a wind rushed up from the town. It swept up the road to the top of the tall cliff upon which Edeneth rested. The wind dashed around the tall white walls of the castle and toward the bajet stable. Andrew and Peter were just sliding off of Atris' back when the wind gusted through her feathers. She turned her head suddenly and looked intently toward the cloud of smoke in the short distance away. In very bird-like fashion she tilted her head as if listening intently to the voice of the wind.

Solomon had just risen from his bow. "I am Solomon."

"Solomon!" Atris proclaimed. "Do you feel it?"

Solomon's expression changed, he closed his eyes and listened. Then Solomon popped open his eyes, and the man and the bajet both said the same name, "Jubal!"

Solomon turned quickly without a word and shuffled toward the tower. He threw open the door and quickly shut it behind him.

"What's going on?" Peter asked Atris.

The bajet looked at the boys. "Oh my dears, you have really been caught up in this thing haven't you? Solomon is going for Jubal, she is desperately needed in the battle."

The bajet didn't say more, and this hardly answered the boy's curiosity. They both imagined that this Jubal was some type of mighty warrior. They were both shocked and amazed though, when the door to the castle tower opened and Solomon came forth with a woman following him, clutching his hand. She was dressed in a full-length emerald green dress, with a long shawl of a lighter green. She seemed to be a young woman, one of much beauty. In her left arm she held a golden harp. Her hair was very long, and it reached nearly past her waist. Her eyes almost seemed like gold, but they were of a brown tint that matched her hair. Her eyes never wavered, and they seemed to be gazing continually off into the distance.

Neither Peter nor Andrew could understand what this fair lady was needed for in war. She didn't even bear a weapon as far as they could tell. She never turned to look at them, but walked at the lead of Solomon to Atris. The bajet knelt down and the lady sat carefully upon the saddle with her legs both hanging over the same edge. Atris rose quickly into the air, and descended down the cliff toward the cloud of ever-rising smoke.

Solomon stood on the edge of the cliff waving until the bajet disappeared into the smoke wall. Then he turned to the boys and placed a hand on each of their shoulders. "Come, it is not in our hands any longer."

Peter Crossings And The Gate Of Abaddon

* * * * *

As her golden brown hair blew in the wind, the graceful hands of Jubal rested on the harp's tightly drawn strings. The bajet flapped its wings, and they dashed through the wall of smoke. Beneath, there was a great battle raging, which nearly ceased when the flyer and rider were overhead. Indeed, it seemed as though time itself paused and watched the event. Her hands began to glide over the strings, and though she barley plucked them, the sound of her song filled the entire battle plain. And then her voice lifted itself in glory and praise to the one she called Tehus.

Atris flew boldly, directly over the heart of the battle. As Jubal continued to play, a hole cleared in the smoke sky and a strong ray of light burst through. It caught the wings of the bajet and followed the animal as Atris wound her way over the town. All the screams, and shrill clashes of weapons, everything, every sound ceased, except for a clear song that rang from Jubal's lips and golden harp. Together the two sounds seemed to blend and then an echo followed the song. Every warrior dropped his guard and looked toward the gleaming ray of light. The shadows cowered and covered their faces in fear. Even Macthon turned his gaze downward.

Edesha closed his eyes and whispered his mysterious words toward the sky. Then he opened them, and there was a fierceness and boldness there that was of another Power. Raising his staff skyward, his voice rang out across the field of battle blending with the song of Jubal.

James Andrew Wilson

"Take now the sword of the Light, and grasp tightly in your hand the shield of Steadfastness, with which you will defeat the flames. Rise and march for Tehus, the One of Light in the shadows of darkness! In the name of Tehus, claim victory!"

This proclamation rang out through the battered town as the clouds of smoke continued to clear. The shadows screamed and wailed and fled like ants back from the warriors. Every warrior tightened the grip on their swords and marched after the fleeing ones. Many of the shadows fell in their flight, until finally the army of dark ones had left. Before their final departure, Macthon gazed across the ruins and his black eyes met those of Edesha. Edesha stared unwavering until the dark figure grunted, spilled out his wings, and flew off back toward the evil land of Abaddon.

* * * * *

"Come young ones, follow me now through these many halls," Solomon's voice echoed. They had entered the castle and watched as Solomon pulled a softly glowing torch from its ring upon the wall, and then started up a series of winding stairs. The concrete steps wound around a golden pole that shot up through the tower as far as the boys could see. They followed the old man who stumbled up the steps much slower than they were used to.

Every now and then he would mumble something, or make a strange grunting noise, but neither Andrew nor Peter asked him to speak up. Finally they came to a landing with a closed door.

"Ahh, here we are," Solomon said as he adjusted his bifocals and then reached for the handle, but not before he placed the torch in the ring at the side of the door.

The three went through the great doorway and found themselves in a long hallway lined with windows and paintings. It reminded Peter of the secret hallway beneath the stage back in his world. Peter paused, *in his world...* It was no surprise to him, of course he knew that he was in a different world, what caused him to halt was the thought that his world was behind him. He began to wonder all the things that go through a child's mind when they enter a different world. Things such as: *"Will I make it home again? What about my parents? Why am I here?"*

Andrew was having somewhat similar thoughts, but they consisted of things more like: *"I wonder what type of food they have here. Maybe I'll never have to go to school again. Wow, this guy looks older than my grandma!"*

And so Solomon led them through that hall, and into another much like it, and after five others, Peter stopped counting. Most of them looked the same, like something out of a museum.

There were many paintings, and he guessed that they were all painted by Ethral; although none of these paintings seemed to be alive. Most of them were portraits, yet every now and then there would be a landscape. Peter liked these the most. There was one such landscape that especially caught his attention. It was a mighty waterfall that seemed to be spilling over the enormous cliffs within the paint.

Clustered together on the cliffs were hundreds, no, more like thousands of small huts. They had round holes for doors, and straw roofs. Wherever there wasn't a hut, there was a clump of some type of green bush clinging to the cliff. The painting was very large, taller than Peter, and its colors were so vivid, he almost thought it was a window.

"Ahh, I see you have found Bajet Falls," Solomon said, suddenly at Peter's side.

The boy looked up at the strangely familiar man. "What are all of the little houses for?" Peter asked.

"They are bajet houses. I know they look small compared to the mighty waterfall, but many of them are actually quite large."

Andrew stepped over and looked closely at one of the bajet houses. "So you've been there?" he asked.

Solomon chuckled. "Well, yes. Actually this old man has!"

"Wow, I wish I lived there. I would live in that one." Andrew pointed to the largest house right near the top of the waterfall.

"Ahh, that is where Airoth lives. He is the king of the bajets."

"Does Atris live in one of these?" Peter asked.

"Yes, and…now which one was it?" Solomon scratched his head. "I can't remember which one. Ha! I am getting very old." He chuckled. "Come now, let us continue."

"Where are we going?" Andrew asked. "I'm hungry!"

Solomon laughed, and then contained a following cough. "Well, I was going to show you the Library, but perhaps we should take care of those tummies first."

"Yeah! That sounds more like it!" Andrew proclaimed.

"Alright, then. Come, to the kitchen!" Solomon put a frail finger forward like a Captain leading his army, and then they headed off.

* * * * *

"This battle has been won," said Edesha solemnly as he watched the remaining battle worn warriors ascend the tall road to the castle. Gaberilin was at his side. He had acquired a long cut across his left cheek during the battle, but the blood was mostly dried now.

"Master, the warriors are tired. And the people..." he sighed, "not only have many of them lost their homes, but they are losing trust in Tehus as well. I am fearful."

Edesha turned his gaze and looked at the strong hazel eyes of Gaberilin. He searched them for a moment, but only sighed and turned his eyes back toward the walking warriors.

"Master, have you nothing to say? I know you see it as well."

Edesha dropped his gaze. "Yes Gaberilin. I have noticed for some time the lack of trust. And yet, I have a strange hope now in this strange time. I am not sure from what source I am receiving this hope, but it is stronger now than it has been in some time." He placed a hand on the warrior beside him. "And I am at peace my dear Gaberilin. Somehow, within this time of war, I have found peace, and hope."

Gaberilin let out a long sigh. Then he drew forth his sword and gazed at it. "Forgive me Edesha... Sometimes I forget that we do not battle with weapons alone."

There was a call in the setting sky, and the two looked up to see Atris returning to the castle with Jubal still atop her back. "No Gaberilin, we do not battle with weapons alone. And yet..." he looked back to the hazel eyes, "neither do our enemies."

There was a short silence before Gaberilin spoke again. "Why is it that the two boys have come to this war-torn land?"

"That is something that has been on my mind and heart continually ever since they have arrived." Edesha looked to the castle with the last light of the setting sun gleaming on its white walls. "I think Gaberilin, that it is for a reason that neither you nor I could have ever imagined..."

* * * * *

"Ah, here we are," Solomon said as he scooted through the doorway. "I welcome you to the kitchen of the greatest cooker in all of Eden!"

There was a hearty laugh to be heard as Andrew, then Peter, came into the kitchen. They were nearly knocked over with an attack of smells that had never entered their nostrils before. It couldn't be described, what they smelled, but it had the sensation of a Thanksgiving Day meal, which has been simmering for hours on end.

Near the wall, and in front of an enormous oven, there stood a very brawny man with a white baker's hat atop his head. He was partially covered from sight because the boys couldn't see over the towering table right in their way. But they heard his laugh, and his funny singing very clearly.

"Jatod! How are things here today?" Solomon asked.

"Well, well, well...can't really say! I'm doin fine, maybe even a bit more than fine. Ha! I guess I can't really complain! Just a cookin'! Cook—cook—cook away!" He let out a loud laugh and turned from his business with the oven. "Why I was ju—" Then he spotted Andrew and Peter. "Great tators of gardenia! What have we here?" The cook stomped over to the table, placed two enormous hands atop it (shaking all the plates and cups) and bent over it to examine the boys.

"Andrew, Peter, this is Jatod. He is the finest cook you'll ever eat from!" Solomon said.

"Well now, don't listen to the crazy old fool!" Jatod laughed. "He's just makin' it all up. But my, my, my, I am pleased to meet ya!" And then Jatod did something that surprised both the boys very much. From underneath the table there extended two brawny hands. And when Andrew looked beneath the table, he discovered that the hands were connected to arms. And the arms were connected to the side of Jatod.

"Four arms!" Andrew exclaimed. "You have four arms!" He took one of the hands and shook it, so did Peter.

"Ha, what make you think that?" Jatod placed his

James Andrew Wilson

bottom left hand on his round stomach and bellowed another laugh. "Oh my, oh me! You'll have to excuse me! I think I put a bit to much sugar in me breakfast!" He laughed again.

Peter and Andrew looked at each other, a bit amused, very much confused. Solomon noticed and tried to help things. "Jatod, you wouldn't happen to have something the boys could eat would you? They are rather hungry."

"Somthin' to eat? What you think this is, a kitchen?" He laughed aloud again, and wiped a tear from his eye. "Oh, oh…to much laughin' and it goes to one's gut." He clenched his stomach then sighed. "Of course I got somethin' for em to eat. First of all they need to have a seat!" Jatod reached to either end of the table and spun two chairs around for the boys to sit in.

Soon Peter and Andrew found themselves propped up at the table with a feast before their eyes. "Alright, while you two eat, this old man is going to go and see if I can't get you a room set up. I'll be back shortly."

"Later Solomon!" Andrew said right before he dove into the food like an animal. Solomon left and the boys ate happily for a short while. Jatod made a few more jokes before going back to his cooking, and obnoxious singing.

Soon, both Peter and Andrew were stuffed. Andrew leaned back in his chair and sighed. He looked around at the kitchen while twiddling his thumbs. Then he bent forward across the table. "Hey Peter. Let's go explore," he whispered.

Peter Crossings And The Gate Of Abaddon

"But Solomon said he was coming back," Peter protested.

"Yeah, but we'll be back before he gets here. Come on, I'm dying of boredom, and I'm sure this place is filled with cool stuff!"

Peter looked over to Jatod. "But what about him?" He pointed to the four-armed cook.

"He'll never notice, and he won't hear us because he sings too loudly."

"A tator, and a mator! But em together, you get a matortator!" Jatod bellowed out.

"Come on!" Andrew slid from his chair, but not before grabbing another piece of bread, and then tip-toed toward the door. Peter hesitated then followed cautiously and they found themselves out in the hall.

At first they just followed the long hallways, looking at pictures and tapestries, but that soon lost their curiosity. They ventured to open a few doors, and after finding mostly storage rooms, Andrew had an idea. "Hey Peter, let's try and find a way to get outside!"

"But Gaberilin said not to leave the castle, remember?"

"Yeah, but he was just telling us that because he thought we wouldn't be careful. We'll make sure and be careful. Besides, we'll come right back, I just want to see what it's like!"

"I don't know Andrew, I think we should stay in here…"

"Come on! How many times in your life do you think you'll get the chance to explore a different world! Where is your sense of adventure?"

"Well…ok. But we have to come right back in."

"We will! I promise."

It wasn't much longer before Andrew had found a door that led outside. He was a very curious boy, and a great explorer, so it is not surprising that he came upon the door so quickly. Andrew grasped the handle and pulled. Just as the boys stepped outside and shut the door behind them, Jatod came bounding around the hall franticly searching for them a second too late.

"Ah, feel that fresh air!" Andrew closed his eyes and inhaled. "Reminds me of home."

The sky was dark for the sun was nearly set, and the stars were out in extreme abundance. In Eden the stars are much different than ours, and there are many more. Although the boys were unaware of this—above them there was an entirely different sky, with different constellations, and different winds.

The boys had exited onto a small landing of rock that was mostly overgrown with bushes. There was a bench there, and on it sat a rather fat little man. His head was upon his round stomach and he was snoring lightly. A brown beard reached down between his stout black boots, and just brushed the ground. Andrew thought the man to be very funny, and had to cover his mouth to keep from laughing.

There wasn't much of a view here, because the bushes had overgrown so much. Andrew wanted to see more, so he looked for a way to climb for a better vantage point. Off to their right, the cliff climbed up to the side of the white castle wall. Various vines ran along it, and the cliff and wall appeared to have sufficient hand holds for climbing. Andrew tiptoed over to the protruding rock. There was an opening in the bushes big enough for him to crawl through. He did, and grabbed a handhold on the face of the cliff. His foot scraped a pebble and he looked back to see it fall off into the darkness, but he didn't hear it land.

The face of the rock was a blue shade from the evening sky as Andrew crawled up it. Peter stood below, watching the red haired climber ascend. "Andrew," Peter tried to whisper so he wouldn't wake the sleeping man on the bench, "can you see anything?"

"Hold on, I'm gonna try and get to the top." The "top" that he was referring to was the wide width of the castle wall. He was no more than six feet from it.

SCRAPE! Peter jumped and for some reason ducked. The man on the bench rustled, but didn't wake. Andrew turned and looked back. "What was that?" he asked.

And then Peter saw it. A small black shape three feet from his face was climbing up the cliff. It looked like an overgrown beetle. He caught a glimpse of its yellow eyes, and smelled its fowl breath, but what it really was, he did not know. The shape scurried up the rock, apparently it hadn't noticed him, but it had noticed Andrew, and it was coming up on him quick.

Peter stood. "Andrew! It's coming!"

"What's coming?" Andrew replied.

And then a lot of things happened. The sleeping man burst from his dreams and sputtered something. Andrew slipped and nearly fell, but managed to grab a small lip of the rock. And then the black creature turned its gaze on Peter, made a terrifying noise, and leapt from the rock landing atop Peter's body, sending him to the ground. Peter yelled franticly and flailed his arms at the attacker. The shape scurried over his body. It must have had claws, for Peter felt many pricks in his skin. The bearded man leapt up and shouted at the creature. Andrew made his way quickly down the cliff, but it was the person who suddenly burst from the door of the castle that saved Peter. There was a flash of a blue cape, and then the singing of a sword being drawn. A slash, and then the black shape fell in two. Everything for Peter went dark.

* * * * *

"Why did you go outside? I told you two not to leave the castle!"

"But…we were just going to *look* outside."

"That was very dangerous! You could ha—"

"Gaberilin, let him be. Look, he's awake."

Peter opened his eyes to see five faces come into focus. The light in the room was very dim, and shadows lay restless on everyone's faces. Three of them he recognized. Andrew was there, and his eyes looked red from tears. Gaberilin was there as well, a very stern look on his face. And there was also the bearded man that had been on the bench. There were two others, but he didn't recognize them.

"How do you feel boy?" one of the unfamiliar faces asked. The person looked a lot like Solomon, but his hair had more color in it and not as many wrinkles were on his face.

"I feel...dizzy..." Peter replied.

"Come now, lets have him sit up," the man said. Peter felt the big hands of Gaberilin pull him to a sitting position.

"There, now take a drink of this." A vial was placed to Peter's lips. He took a sip and felt the warm liquid flow down his throat and into his stomach. It made him feel warm inside like on Christmas day after drinking hot cider.

"How do you feel now?" the man asked.

"Much better," Peter replied.

"Yes, well my name is Aramil A. Allamar. I am the doctor for Edeneth. You're lucky that Tehus was watching out for you."

Peter tried to take in all of the strange new names. "Who is Tehus?" he asked.

The other unfamiliar face spoke. "Tehus is the Father of all that is good in Eden, and He was indeed watching out for you. My name is Edesha."

Edesha extended a hand and Peter shook it. "I am the Master of this castle. I am very excited to talk with you and Andrew, but I need a good rest before that, and so do you." Peter noticed that Edesha appeared worn from battle, but his features were hard to see clearly in the dim light. Then Gaberilin, who could hardly contain himself any longer, burst out. "Peter, you could have been killed by that devourer! A single bite has enough fear-poison to destroy even a warrior's heart. Why did you go outside? I told you not to leave!"

Edesha put a firm hand on Gaberilin's shoulder

and the big man calmed down. Peter noticed that Edesha was not quite as tall as Gaberilin, and not nearly as muscular. But there was a certain power to his presence.

"So if you are feeling well, and everything is fine?" Edesha looked to Doctor Allamar.

"Uh, yes, as far as I can tell the boy is fine. I don't see any bites, although it would be hard to tell until later. But he seems fine, and those few scratches should heal up in time," Aramil said.

"Good." Edesha turned once more to Peter. "Very well then, Philophos will lead you to your room." Edesha turned around and opened the door.

Philophos scooted into the already crowded space. He was a very tall and thin man. He wore bifocals on his skinny nose. His hair was blond, straight, and it reached slightly past his shoulders. He did not seem very muscular, but he did appear to have a sword at his belt. He was a very odd looking character, and Peter wasn't sure if he was a warrior, or a professor, or both.

"Philophos, this is Peter, and Andrew. They will be staying with us for a short time. Take them to the third tower guest room please. Solomon has already had it prepared."

Philophos looked over his bifocals at Peter, and then down at Andrew. "And how did you two stumble into Eden?" he asked.

"Gaberilin brought us!" Andrew replied.

Philophos eyed Gaberilin and arched an assuming eyebrow. "Uh huh, well…now that you're here I suppose I shall do everything in my power to make

Peter Crossings And The Gate Of Abaddon

your stay one of comfort." Philophos gave a slight bow. Peter couldn't help but feel like this strange man was mocking him.

Gaberilin gave a grunt of disgust and stepped out of the room. Edesha put his face close to Philophos and whispered, "Make sure nothing happens to these boys, do you understand me."

Philophos tilted his head up, and then nodded slowly. Edesha released him and then followed Gaberilin out of the room. Dr. Allamar rubbed his hands together and then said, "Okay, well I best be off. It was nice meeting you boys." And he left.

The short bearded man (who was so quiet, Peter almost forgot he was there) just grunted, pulled up his belt and left the room. So the boys were left alone with Philophos, and they did not like that very well.

"Alright you two, come on, I'll show you to your room." They followed Philophos out the doorway.

* * * * *

"Gaberilin, come here." Edesha pulled him off to the side of the hallway.

"Yes, what is it?"

Edesha looked up and down the hall and then whispered, "There is something about that boy, Gaberilin. He is here for a reason. That devourer was intent on getting him…but I'm not sure why."

"What do you think it could be?" Gaberilin asked.

"I'm not sure right now, but I want you to keep an eye on him, and the other boy as well. I need to go talk to Solomon."

Gaberilin nodded. "I will watch out for him."

"Good, thank you."

* * * * *

"And here is you room." Philophos opened the wooden door and showed them in.

Inside they found a room with two beds, and a large window at the far end. A lush green rug covered the hard ground. The ceiling arched to the center and from it a stone pillar ran through the middle of the room. Candle stands were in all four corners, and their small flickering flames revealed the room. Each bed had a stand beside it with a candle. The covers on each bed were a deep blue color, with silver and gold designs embroidered into them. There were two wardrobes, both exactly the same, on either side of the room. They were made of a dark wood with green etchings on their doors. Another smaller room could be entered at the immediate right of the door. It held a tub, and a sink. A large candle glowed in the small room, and rested upon a tall candle stand. It was lit, revealing steaming hot water in the tub.

"Whoa, is this where we get to stay?" Andrew asked excitedly.

"Yes, as long as you are here at Edeneth you will stay in this room."

"Wait a second," Andrew replied. "Don't we get to explore the castle, or something? We have to stay in this room the whole time?"

"Well, that would be preferable. Things are not

Peter Crossings And The Gate Of Abaddon

quite as jolly here as you may think. We are in the middle of a war if you haven't already noticed. Now the last thing we need is two troublemakers running around the castle. Edesha has a lot to think about, and he doesn't need to be watching out for two bothersome children. So stay quiet, and stay out of everybody's way." And then Philophos went to the door and was about to leave but then turned. "Good night." The door slammed behind him.

Chapter Six

A Meeting with the Master

"Come right this way," the old man said as he turned and walked toward the bookshelves.

Peter followed his slow footsteps. Every step made an eerie echo that climbed to the top of the tall ceiling and echoed back down, resounding off the floor. They walked between two of the towering bookshelves that seemed to curve over their heads.

"What is your name lad?" the man asked without turning his head.

"Peter...Peter Crossings."

The man halted for a moment and placed a finger to his lips in thought. He grunted and then continued on.

Lighting cracked outside and flashed through a row of high windows surrounding the building. The library lit up with a blue light. Peter then saw how big the building really was. Endless rows of book-shelves spanned across countless green tiles.

Then Peter found that he had come to a four-way hall with the option to go forward, to the right, to the left, or turn back around. He looked down each of the halls for the man, but he was gone. Peter turned back around toward the door, but it was nowhere to be seen. All that was left were rows of bookshelves. In every direction he looked the shelves spanned on forever. Fear quickly enveloped him.

He started to run. Rows of book-spines flashed past his vision. Every time he came to a four-way hall, he took a different direction. Peter felt trapped. It was like he was in some type of never ending labyrinth. He continued to run. His heart was beating madly. His footsteps echoed loudly.

"Help! Somebody! Help me!!!!"

Finally, entirely out of breath, he collapsed. Tears fell from Peter's eyes as he looked up at the shelf in front of him. All the books were blurry—everything was blurry. Except that. *What was it?* There was something golden on the shelf. Peter stood and walked toward the object. It was like swimming through fog as his vision continued to blur. The gold thing glowed brighter. When finally he reached out and touched it, everything else in his vision faded to dust, and he found himself standing in utter darkness, except for what he held now in his trembling hands. It was a book. Gold covered, gold edged pages, and a golden ribbon was tucked into it. The book felt heavy, yet at the same time it seemed to float in his hands. Peter took a breath, grasped the thick cover, and turned it open to the marked page.

It fell suddenly from his grasp. In slow motion the book plummeted down toward his feet, but when it should have stopped, it kept on falling. It fell through the darkness that surrounded him and twirled in circles until finally disappearing out of view. Peter took in a slow breath and felt the darkness thicken around him. He looked up. There in the distance stood a shape. A cloak of dark red covered it, and its hair was white. It stepped toward him. Then it turned its head upward and Peter could see its eyes. They appeared hollow like vast pools of emptiness.

Peter tried to turn and run, but he couldn't move! The figure came closer. Another step. Another. It reached out its hands. Peter tried to scream, but he couldn't. The shape came right up to him, and then it knelt and grasped something in its bony hands. It stood back up and handed the object to Peter.

"What is your name boy?" a voice echoed through his head.

"Peter Crossings."

Suddenly the darkness fled and the library reappeared. The book was back in Peter's hands. There was nobody around him. He looked down to the opened page and began to read.

"Peter! Snap out of it man!"

"Andrew?" Peter opened his eyes. It was hot, and he was drenched in sweat. For some reason his shoulder hurt.

"You okay man?" Andrew asked as he held Peter up from his pillow. "You were having a dream or something."

"A dream?" The library flashed through his mind. "Yeah. I'm okay."

"Okay." Andrew let go of Peter and stood. "Next time you have a dream, keep it down, you woke me up." Andrew went to the other side of the room and flopped back his covers.

A sudden *rat-tat-tat* on the door made Andrew jump.

"Hello? Peter? Andrew?" a voice came from behind the closed door. "Are you two ready for breakfast?"

"Is that guy crazy?" Andrew looked at Peter. "It must be seven in the morning! I never get up this early on Saturday."

"Who is it?" Peter asked, not recognizing the voice.

"I think it's that guy that we met last night. What was his name, Phillyofopos?"

"Philophos." Peter was not very excited to see him.

"Yeah, him."

"Hello? Anyone in there?" the voice came again.

"Yeah, hold on a sec!" Andrew said, scooting to the door and opening it. Philophos stood with hands on his hips. He glared down at the boy.

"Good morning sir Andrew," he said sarcastically.

"Morning," Andrew said rubbing his eyes at the fake gleefulness of Philophos. "I'm going back to bed. Peter's over there if you want him." Andrew turned and walked for his bed.

"I'm afraid that breakfast is waiting, and Edesha

as well young sir. We must get going." Philophos ducked into the room. He looked to the bed that Peter was crawling out of.

"Come on Philophos," Andrew said crawling back under the covers. "Give us another hour."

Philophos walked over to the bed where Andrew lay, and ripped the covers off. "I hate to be stern young Andrew, but the Master *is* waiting. Get up now!"

Andrew was curled up, looking with wide eyes now at the towering figure of Philophos. "Okay, okay." He crawled out of bed.

"Very good." Philophos went to the wardrobe and opened it. "Now get cleaned up and then put these on." He pulled out a dark blue cloak. Holding it up by the hood, he stomped to the opposite wardrobe and pulled out another. He also brought forth two pairs of matching tan pants and shirts. The boys washed their faces, and put on the strange new clothes and cloaks, then went to slide on their shoes.

"No, no," Philophos said. "Here, put these on." He held up two pairs of leather boots with blue rims around the tops. The boys took them and stuffed their feet into them.

"They feel like moccasins," Andrew said hopping to his feet. "I like 'em!"

"Alright then, let us be on our way!" Philophos led them out of the room and down the long climb of stairs. Windows lined the staircase and let in a golden sun that spilled all over the white stone surrounding them. They came finally to the bottom of the stairs and followed Philophos through halls and passageways.

Soon they came to a hallway with pillars lining one side, and a windowed wall on the other. The windows looked out on a rolling landscape of hills and a great sea far beyond. In between each of the pillars on the other side of the walkway was a court-yard. Tall maples and weeping willow trees were growing there. Philophos turned suddenly and walked through the courtyard following a stone path. At the other side of the yard was a tall, wide gazebo. It was white with golden designs, and lush green vines crawling up it. Brilliant purple flowers bloomed from the vines, the whites of the honey guides glistening in the sun. The three came to the gazebo and stepped up the stairs into its shelter.

Inside, there was a round table piled with food, and two chairs plump with cushions at either end. They were greeted, "Welcome young ones! This is the breakfast gazebo, and your breakfast is waiting!" The big figure of Jatod stood behind the table. He waved his top right arm, as his bottom right hand held a glass and the top left poured a white liquid into it. "Come Andrew! Come Peter! Sit and eat!"

"Alright!" Andrew said running and sliding into a chair. Peter walked and sat down in the other.

"I will return when you have finished eating, and then I will take you to the Master." Philophos turned and walked away quickly.

"This is good Jatod!" Andrew said with a full mouth. "What is it?"

"That my dear boy is a grape, haven't you ever eaten a grape before?"

"Well yeah, but this is a *huge* grape!" Andrew

Peter Crossings And The Gate Of Abaddon

held up another grape. It was easily the size of an orange, and a dark red color. He looked deviously at Peter. Then he aimed and bit the top of the grape. A hole burst in the bottom and juice shot across the table smacking Peter in the nose.

"Ha ha! Got you good didn't I?" Andrew laughed.

Peter wiped his nose of the grape juice and gave Andrew a disgusted look.

"Come on Peter! I was just having some fun." Andrew went back to investigating the table. Peter looked at the bowl before him, then he scanned the array of food. There were many different colors of grapes, some white cakes, hot sausages, and many of other strange foods. Peter began to eat and discovered that the food was very good. Andrew and Peter talked about the castle, about Eden, and anything else that came to mind. Jatod stood quietly by, merrily watching the boys.

"Peter, how do you like the food?" he asked.

Peter stopped chewing and looked at Jatod's big smile. "It's good," he replied. "Where do you get all of this?"

"Some of it, like the cakes and rolls, I bake here at the castle. We purchase the supplies from Edren. The grapes and other fruits, we either grow ourselves, or pick them from Galatian Wood."

"What is Galatian Wood like?" Peter asked. He imagined it to be a wonderful place since the fruit tasted as good as it did.

"It is a place where every type of fruit grows. There are miles of trees that bear all sorts of luscious

James Andrew Wilson

fruit. A great host travels there every season to pick. The fruit is ripe at all times. It is a wonderful place."

"Wow, that sounds awesome!" Andrew said biting into another giant piece of fruit and splattering his face with juice.

They continued to talk for a short time until diving back into breakfast. Peter thought he would try one of the white cakes. He picked it up and took a bite. "Mmm…" he said. "These taste like strawberry short cakes."

"Ooo! Let me try!" Andrew reached across the table and grabbed a cake, then stuffed it into his mouth. "Yeah they do! Mmm!"

They ate sausages, cakes, fruits, breads, and drank many cups of the white drink until they were full to the brim.

"I'm stuffed!" Andrew said leaning back and patting his stomach. Peter did the same.

Jatod laughed. "Good, good!" Just then Philophos appeared in the entryway.

"I didn't even hear you come!" Andrew said.

Philophos didn't answer, but spoke in a rather unfriendly tone, "If you have finished, I have just returned from speaking with the Master and he will see you now."

"Great! Lets go! I have a lot of questions." Andrew stood to his feet as Jatod, laughing to himself, began to clear the table.

Peter stood and the two boys followed Philophos back through the courtyard and into the pillared hallway. They took a left and followed the hall back into the castle. The three came to a large room with a flight

Peter Crossings And The Gate Of Abaddon

of steps at the end. The steps were gold with a maroon carpet running up the center. At the foot of the steps was a large desk with a withered old man behind it. The man held up a leather bound book, and through his bifocals was studying its contents intently. He looked up when the three entered the room.

"Ahh Philophos, you have come back I see," he said.

"Yes Herbert, I have come, and with me are the boys. We have come to see the Master."

"I see." Herbert put the book down that he had been reading and reached under his desk. He withdrew a very large, black bound book and plopped it down in front of himself. He spoke casually while flipping through the pages.

"Let's see, I will need names of the boys, Philophos, signatures..." he continued to mumble to himself. "Ah!" he exclaimed, "here we are." He brushed the page down with his hand and picked up the long silky feather from its bath of ink. Applying the tip of the feather to the page, a black series of words were inscribed. When he had finished, he turned the book to face the three and handed the feather to Philophos. "You know the procedure, any new visitors must be recorded, please have the two boys sign their names, and sign yours as their escort here." Herbert pointed to a scribbled line with his frail finger.

Philophos etched his name onto the line and then handed the feather to Peter. "Just sign your name here Peter," Philophos said as he pointed to a scraggly 'X'. Peter held the feather like a pencil and wrote

107

James Andrew Wilson

---

in his name. He was surprised to find that it was most difficult to write with the feather point. Andrew did the same and the book was handed back to Herbert.

The old man quickly re-adjusted his bifocals, then cleaned, and fitted them back on his old nose again. "Okay. So we have Philophos…yes, okay…and oh my! Some writing from the Land Beyond. I shall have to remember how to read it. Let's see here… a Peter Crossings," he giggled to himself here, but Peter couldn't figure out why, "and a Mr.—oh that is funny, he put a Mr. in front of his little name." Here, he giggled again. "A Mr. Andrew Hatch. Yes very well. This is very good."

"I hate to rush you, but can we please get on with it?" Philophos asked sternly. Peter thought he was a very impatient man.

"Well, there is no need now to get upset. I was just checking to make sure we had it all." He scribbled something else on the page then shut the big book. He then adjusted, and cleaned his bifocals once more before saying, "Alright, you may go up now."

Philophos grumbled something under his breath. He walked to the side of Herbert's desk and started up the stairs. The two boys followed him.

There were more steps than they had first thought, but it was not long before they reached the top.

"We have reached the landing," Philophos said stepping up the last stair. Peter stood beside him and took in the awe-inspiring entryway. Two mighty pillars were before them. They were a brilliant white with golden etched vines climbing them. They

Peter Crossings And The Gate Of Abaddon

reached high until the etched vines crawled across the ceiling giving it a brilliant golden glow. Tall torches were on either side of each of the pillars, and in the center were two green doors with golden handles.

Two guards stood on either side. They wore gold armor with long green feathers coming from the top of their helmets. Each one held a mace in one hand and a shield in the other. They stood so still, that Peter almost thought they were statues—until one of them blinked.

"Wow…" Andrew said looking at the surroundings. "Do we get to go in?"

"Well yes, of course you do. Now remember, the Master has much to attend to. Don't ask him a bunch of meaningless questions. We simply don't have time." Then he cleared his throat and with a mighty voice said, "Welcome to the hall of the Master." With that, Philophos opened one of the tall doors and showed them in.

Brilliant light was the first thing that met their eyes when they stepped in. Then the room opened into a wonderful and overwhelming dwelling. The room was round, and very large. A window covered the entire far wall with a view of the great ocean far away. Pillars lined the entire walls of the room, and were all white with gold vines like those of the entryway. The ceiling was shaped like a bowl and held a majestic mural. The mural showed many things that Peter did not understand, and some that he thought would fit into the books he loved to read. There were dragons and knights, giants, hills, mountains, trees, streams: an entire world seemed to be painted upon the ceiling. Peter looked to the far end of the room. There, raised upon three steps that stretched the width of the room rested a throne. On a platform a step down from the throne were two chairs facing it. Edesha was there at the far end. He stood from his throne and raised a hand as the three entered.

A soothing, yet powerful voice came from him, "Welcome Peter and Andrew to my hall. Please come and sit, we have much to talk of."

The boys followed Philophos to the end of the room. They stepped up onto lush maroon carpet and stood before the Master. Peter looked at him with wonder. He was dressed in a white robe that glistened in the sun from the window. He looked like a strong leader.

"Thank you Philophos, I will take the boys now."

Philophos bowed, and quietly left the hall, closing the door behind him.

Peter Crossings, and Andrew Hatch stood before one who was a stranger to their eyes, yet one they felt as though they had always known. The Master sat down and leaned on one fist as the boys sat. For a strange and uneasy moment, the boys looked around the room silently. Edesha, all along sat watching them, especially Peter. Finally, after it seemed that the silence could no longer be held, he spoke.

"What do you think?" he kindly asked.

Peter looked at Andrew, Andrew looked at Peter. Andrew spoke, "It's uh, it's big."

The Master chuckled. "Yes, it is quite large, but that is of no importance." He sat upright now. "I am aware of the fact that you two are full of questions,

Peter Crossings And The Gate Of Abaddon

and very anxious to have them answered. So, please, ask and I in turn will answer."

"Alright, lets get right to it then," Andrew said. "First of all, that Phillyofpos guy is really rude. You should talk to him about treating guests better. And second of all, why are we here. I mean, Gaberilin told us we would be safe here because those creeping shadow things are after Peter. But that weird crawling thing last night nearly ripped him apart. So what's going on here, and why are we here?" Andrew took a breath. "There, I'm done," he said slouching into his chair.

Edesha smiled. He was rather amused by Andrew. "Well, I suppose you are correct about Philophos. He does have some things to work on, but you needn't worry about that. As far as Peter being attacked last night…you two *were* told not to leave the castle."

"Yeah, I know. We shouldn't have done that," Andrew said apologetically.

"Now to deal with your next question." He sighed and then looked at Peter. The boy sat still, gazing into Edesha's eyes. They looked at each other for a moment in silence. "Peter, I honestly do not know why the shadows are after you."

"Well this is just great!" Andrew said standing. "So now we're stuck here, and nobody even knows why!"

"Please Andrew, sit down and let me explain. I do not know why Peter is here, but maybe after I tell you something else, things will be more clear."

Andrew eyed Edesha and then slumped into his chair again.

"I am going to tell you a story about Eden, please listen. Long ago in this land there was a great battle of forces. An army of evil had arisen and declared war on the dwelling citizens. Evil had even come from distant lands, and a great war was upon Eden. An evil so great was this, that the people began to fear defeat and lost their strength to survive. The inhabitants began to fall, and soon it appeared as though evil would rule. Though evil is very cunning, it can always be overcome. The remaining strength gathered and began a journey to the heart of the evil to seal it. The journey across the land was not without attack, and some fell. Finally they stood at the edge of darkness and evil. There in the depths was where it could be sealed, the only cage powerful enough to hold the evil until final destruction. Beneath the sealing of The Gate of Abaddon."

Peter winced at the final word. The sound of the name echoed through his head piercing his thoughts with darkness. This name seemed familiar. He groaned and rubbed his temples. His shoulder hurt again.

"Are you okay Peter?" Edesha asked.

"Yes, it's just that," it left. "Yeah, I'm fine.

The Master began again. "The evil was sealed and the remaining returned to their homes, and life once again flourished in Eden."

"So everything is fine now?" Andrew asked.

"No, dear Andrew. Evil has once again corrupted the mind of one, and the gate has been opened. Evil has begun to spread under the command of a new General. Nefarious grows ever stronger as his evil

Peter Crossings And The Gate Of Abaddon

ruler twists and pollutes his mind. Under the command of Sheol, Nefarious has taken the key and let loose the chained. We are at war with the shadows, and others that you have not yet seen. We must find a way to seal them once again under the strength of the gate."

"So why don't you?" Andrew asked.

Edesha sighed once more. "The gate holds a power like nothing we could ever imagine. It is a good power, a true power, but it cannot be released without the proper knowledge. It lies somewhere in the dark land, but we are not sure exactly where it is. The gate is locked, and only one key may open it."

"So where is this key?" asked Andrew.

"Somewhere in the dark land. We are not sure where it is, but we think that Nefarious has it. That is not the only problem. The gate holds a secret to opening it. There is a legend of a book that contains the answer to opening the gate."

"Let me guess," Andrew said, "you don't have that either."

"No Andrew, we do not."

"So what does all of this have to do with Peter?"

"Maybe nothing. Although, both of you were able to see Gaberilin. He was wearing an invisible cloak. The cloaks are very rare, and they only make the wearer invisible when they are in your world. All people from our land are able to see those who wear the cloaks, but I have never heard of any from your world being able to."

"So what are you trying to say?" Andrew asked.

"I believe that Tehus has revealed something to

James Andrew Wilson

---

you Peter. He showed you Gaberilin for a reason, and I believe that he showed you something more. I can't imagine any other reason why Nefarious would want you. But it would make sense if you had some type of knowledge of the gate. Is there something that you know?" Edesha asked.

Edesha looked intently at Peter and Andrew did as well. They both waited for his answer.

Images of the dream came to Peter. He remembered the book, but what was in it? Was it only a dream? *"Come on Peter, think!"* What was there…?

"Anything Peter? Is there anything you can think of?"

Peter looked past Edesha's throne to the sea far beyond the windows. Then something came. "A map…" Peter said.

"You remember a map?" Edesha asked.

"I think so." Peter sighed. "I had a dream, I think it was a dream anyways. I was in a huge library and I found a book there."

"What did the book look like?" Edesha asked.

"It was gold. All of it was gold. It was very big, and heavy."

Edesha looked surprised and excited. "Go on."

"I looked in the book, but I can't remember everything that I saw. I think I remember a map though."

"A map? What good does that do us?" Andrew asked.

"It may do us a lot of good." Edesha stood quickly. "We are going to see if you can remember more of this map. Both of you follow me," he said as

Peter Crossings And The Gate Of Abaddon

he walked quickly toward the door.

Peter and Andrew looked at each other. Andrew shrugged, then they got up and followed Edesha out of the room.

They quickly descended the steps and passed by Herbert, who looked up in time to see the three already down the hallway and nearly out of sight. The boys could barely keep up with Edesha. They went through hallways passing by strange people who watched them intently.

Finally they arrived at the map room of the castle, which was a very impressive sight. Upon first entering the room, one would assume it to be rather small. This is because the architecture of the room fools the eye into minimizing the great expanse of the map observatory. After rounding the pillars that reached to the ceiling, they took in the large room.

"Ah, welcome to the map room!" A very interesting character came out from behind a pillar. An extremely short man he was, with withered skin and a scraggly old cane. He had a long nose, and yet, the brightest and keenest green eyes Peter had ever seen. His long, silky white hair lay thin on his balding head. He spoke again, "My name is Miyo. I am the map master of this castle, and very delighted to see you two. It has been long since I remember someone of my height in the map room. And what may be the reason you come to visit an old man today?"

"Miyo," Edesha said, "Peter here needs to look at one of your maps. Can you show him to the charting chair?"

"Well, yes! Yes of course." Miyo looked to Peter.

115

James Andrew Wilson

"Peter eh? Well it is wonderful to meet you."

"Thank you," Peter said, and for some reason he wasn't sure of, he bowed before Miyo, feeling very welcomed and comfortable with the kind old man.

Andrew looked oddly at him. Edesha smiled and Miyo spoke, "A true gentleman you have brought sir."

"That he is. This is his friend, Andrew."

Andrew looked at Peter now coming up from his bow. Feeling very much uneasy and awkward, Andrew took a bow best he could. "Nice to meet you Meeow."

Peter chuckled at Andrew's attempt to pronounce the name. Miyo just smiled. "Well, now that we have that out of the way, let me show you my room."

The three followed Miyo across the marble floor. Peter gazed about at the large pieces of parchment skins tacked to the walls. They had sketches of maps, trees, mountains, rivers, and many other things that had to do with geography upon their surfaces. Nothing looked familiar. There were a few desks here and there, but all of them were vacant. They came then to an area where the floor sunk down into a large bowl. Everyone followed Miyo down a small set of stairs. There was a single chair in the center of the bowl. It had a padded back and seat, and two arms that had a series of levers and buttons installed into them.

"This is the charting chair," Miyo said walking to the chair. "Come my boy, have a seat." He motioned for Peter to sit down.

Peter cautiously went to the chair and crawled up

Peter Crossings And The Gate Of Abaddon

into it. "This lever here," Miyo pointed to a lever with a brass ball at its top, "rotates the map, and this button zooms in closer." He continued to show him the controls, Peter trying all along to make a mental note of each of them.

"And now," Miyo leaned on his cane and walked around the chair to the opposite side, "take a look." He rotated a lever and the chair began to tilt back.

"Whoa!" Peter held tighter to the chair.

"Cool!" Andrew exclaimed.

When the chair was fully rotated back, Peter gazed up at a gigantic map covering the domed ceiling. He moved one of the levers, and to his amazement, the map rotated. Everyone arched their necks back and gazed up at the map.

"How does it do that?" Peter asked as the map moved across the ceiling with no sign of any type of projector. It really seemed as though the map etched into the ceiling was crawling at his command.

Miyo suddenly rattled off a bunch of words that neither Peter nor Andrew could make much sense of. "…and that's how it works, in a nut shell anyways." Miyo winked at Edesha. "So what are we looking for?" Miyo asked anybody that would answer.

"Peter said he remembers something about a map. It may help us in the war if my hunch is correct," said Edesha.

Miyo raised his eyebrows excitedly. "Ah, I see. Well take your time lad. See if anything comes back to you."

Peter moved the levers exploring the strange landscape. "So this is Eden?"

James Andrew Wilson

"Yes, well, the northern part of it anyway. There are some areas that we have not charted as much as others. But this is most of what we have discovered. We have yet to chart much of the southern regions into this map, but other than that, yes, this is Eden."

"I can't read any of the names," Peter said feeling rather confused.

"Oh my!" Miyo exclaimed. "I forgot to put it into Land Beyond writing." Then Miyo pushed a little silver button on the chair and all of the names changed to English lettering.

"It's so detailed..." Peter zoomed into a cluster of trees. He could see the outline of them, and a few paths leading through them. The names of the areas were now readable. He read some of them until discovering one he knew. "Edeneth, that's where we are," he said zooming into the castle. It was entirely surrounded by cliffs, except for a long road leading down from it.

"Yes, Castle Edeneth. You're right Peter," said Miyo very pleased. "Is there anything else that looks familiar?"

Peter moved across the map some more. "Oh, that's Galatian Wood. Jatod was telling us about it."

"Good good. But is there something else?" Miyo asked with baited breath.

"What's this area?" Peter asked zooming into a canyon etched into the map.

"Oh! That is the Unknown Canyon, at least, that is its name at this point. We have yet to explore it extensively. Don't worry about that area. Is there anything else that seems familiar?"

Peter continued to search. "Wait a minute..." He paused over a dark area of the map. Miyo and the Master looked hesitantly to each other. Peter zoomed into the terrain. It wasn't extremely detailed like the other areas. He could see many dark, jagged mountains surrounding a smoky, black part of the land.

"This seems familiar..." He zoomed in a little closer and sounded out the name inscribed "Abaddon..."

The world suddenly darkened. His vision faded for a second. He could see eyes...red eyes...shadows. *"Peter Crossings!"* a shrill voice screamed. It seemed then like a steaming hot nail pierced into his shoulder. Pain pulsed through his veins.

"Peter, Peter!"

Peter opened his eyes. He was lying down on the ground. Edesha was clutching his shoulders and kneeling over him.

"Wha...what happened?" Peter asked as he sat up. Andrew looked scared.

"Peter, I want you to try something for me," the Master said.

"Um, okay," Peter replied breathlessly.

The Master helped him to his feet. "I want you to try and walk in a circle around the chair for me."

Peter slowly started to walk around the chair. His shoulder was searing with pain. Both the Master and Miyo watched intently. Suddenly Edesha shouted, "Abaddon!"

Peter clenched his shoulder and fell to the ground. His entire body ignited into a sharp pain. The Master rushed to his side and grabbed him into his arms.

"It appeared as so," he said. Edesha pulled Peter's shirt aside enough to see his shoulder. Two little holes were punctured through his skin. "It is as I feared. He was indeed bitten."

"Bitten, by—by what?" Miyo asked.

"A devourer. Last night. I had Aramil look him over, but he seemed fine then, and the bite marks hadn't appeared yet."

"If he was bitten last night, then the poison is well on its way to his heart. He might not have much time."

Edesha scooped him up into his arms. "I am taking him to Aramil. Miyo, take Andrew and go get Solomon for me. Tell him to come to Doctor Allamar's room. Quickly!"

* * * * *

"The poison is indeed very strong. There is nothing though, that I can do for him here," Doctor Allamar said.

Edesha let out a shout of anger. Just then Solomon crashed through the door followed by Miyo and Andrew.

"What is it?" Solomon asked.

"The boy has been bitten by a devourer. Solomon, he seems to remember something about a map. He said he had a dream about the Golden Book."

Solomon seemed shocked by a sudden thought.

"What?" Edesha asked.

But Solomon didn't respond. "Doctor Allamar, how much time do we have?" Solomon asked.

The doctor put a finger to his lips in thought. "I would say…he might survive the day, and maybe one more."

"Edesha, may I talk with you?" Solomon and Edesha stepped out of the room.

Everything for Peter was blurry. He was laying on the table he had been on last night. He could hear bits and pieces of the conversations around him. He heard Solomon and Edesha speaking quickly but couldn't catch any of the words. They came back in abruptly.

Edesha scooped Peter up into his arms again. "What are you planning to do?" Doctor Allamar asked.

"We are going to take him to Patmos," Edesha said, and then hurried out of the room.

"Patmos!" exclaimed Miyo, following him. "That island has not been visited or even seen since the war of long ago. Are you sure that it is even still there?" Miyo asked intently.

"We have no choice in the matter. The poison will kill him if we do not hurry. He must be cleansed there. Miyo, I want you to go with us. We will need your maps as well."

"Really? I would be honored to. I have desired to see the hidden shores of Patmos for many a year." Then he went away toward the map room to gather his things.

"I shall go and summon Gaberilin," Solomon said, and then hurried off.

James Andrew Wilson

Andrew felt very confused and scared at the events. He looked at Peter stretched out in the Master's arms. He was covered in sweat and his eyes would not open. "How long does it take to get to Patmos?" Andrew asked.

"Longer than we have," Edesha said, "but it is said that those seeking healing who are traveling for Patmos will grow stronger as their journey passes. This is the only chance we have."

Andrew bit his lower lip as Miyo quickly returned clutching a bag and some maps under his arms. "Okay, I'm ready."

For only a moment Peter raised his head and heard the voice of Edesha, "To Patmos we travel, and may Tehus guide our way." Then all went black.

Chapter Seven

The Hidden Shores of Patmos

"Patmos?" Philophos exclaimed. "But that island is just a myth!"

"History would suggest otherwise," Miyo defended. "Besides, what other choice do we have?"

"Please Philophos, I need you to take care of some things while I am gone," Edesha pleaded.

"You are going as well? But Master, I insist that you absolutely must stay in the castle! We are in the middle of war. Who knows when Abaddon will attack again?"

"If they do, hold the castle. Philophos, there are no other options right now."

"But why must you go? Can not Gaberilin take the boy?"

"I must go with the boy and Gaberilin as well. He knows something very special that Nefarious doesn't want us to know. He must be protected."

"There is no time for this bickering!" Miyo said waving his cane at Philophos. "We have no choice! The devourer's poison is on its way to the boy's heart, we must act quickly or he will be lost to darkness!"

"Philophos, stay here at the castle. We will all return within eight days time," the Master said.

Philophos sighed. "Very well, as you will." He bowed.

Edesha set Peter down on a nearby bench and went quickly with Philophos to another room. Andrew, biting his lip, looked at Peter lying helplessly on the bench. Miyo came up to them. "Andrew," he put a hand on the boy's shoulder, "Peter's a strong lad, he'll be okay. Show him that you have strength as well."

Andrew looked up to Miyo. "Yeah, it's just kinda scary. I mean it's not every day that your friend is wanted by some evil thing from another world."

Miyo chuckled. "You know what I do whenever I get scared? I think of the sunshine."

"The sunshine?" Andrew asked.

"Yes, the sunshine. I think of big wide hills gleaming under the sunshine. And I know that even though I am scared, somewhere the sun is shining on those hills. And then that fear goes away, for a moment anyways." Miyo looked off into the distance like he was gazing at those hills.

Andrew closed his eyes and tried to imagine the scene. He could see them for a moment: hills being licked by a gleaming sun. He could almost feel the warmth on his face, but then it all faded away.

Peter Crossings And The Gate Of Abaddon

Andrew opened his eyes again to see Edesha return.

In his right hand he held a tall wooden staff, with the other he came and scooped up Peter over his shoulder. The four walked quickly through the hall and came soon to the outside. They exited onto the tall landing Peter and Andrew had first set foot on in Eden. A brilliant white bajet waited gracefully there, and perked up its head when the four came to it.

"Atris!" Andrew exclaimed.

"Hello Andrew, it is nice to see you again," Atris replied.

"You too."

"Thank you Atris," Edesha said as he set Peter upon her back, "for coming so quickly in our time of need. I would trust this mission to no other."

"I am honored to be of service. I was given wings and the ability to fly so I could be a help to others. I am only doing what I was created for."

"And so much more. You were always so humble," Miyo said stepping out from behind the Master.

"Miyo!" Atris exclaimed. "I never thought we would meet again."

"Well, I have some surprises up my sleeves yet. I remember those grand days upon your back. I was desperately trying to chart the landscape without dropping my page. Ah those were good days, but don't think me so old too soon." Miyo let a weathered smile creep across his face. "I see that you have indeed become an even grander site. I can not wait to see those wings in action again."

"Then are you to come with us to the Acco?" Atris asked.

James Andrew Wilson

"Yes, I am to come. Someone needs to find this hidden island!" Miyo replied.

Edesha chuckled. "Very well then, I can see that you two have some more catching up to do. I will ride Frenwar along with Andrew. Miyo, you take Atris along with Peter."

Just then, Gaberilin came running out from the castle. A short plump man was following him. Andrew recognized the little man as the one that had been sleeping on the bench the night before. "Master," Gaberilin said, "Mr. Timf here says that he won't let me leave unless he comes." Gaberilin winked at Edesha and then turned to the little man.

The little man bowed and Andrew noticed that he had a small, thick sword and a big backpack. His beard had been tucked up and tied into a knot so it didn't scrape the ground. "If you don't mind me saying so sir, it really is my fault that the poor boy is in this bit of trouble. I shouldn't a been sleepin' like I was. And Mr. Timf here, that being me (he sniffed loudly here) sees it as his duty to see the boy along to being healed. So I shan't let your Gaberilin go unless I am to come along as well." Then he crossed his thick arms and sniffed again.

Edesha raised his voice to a mighty tone, "Many dangers may lie in our path. It would be wise to have one such as you with us, please come."

Mr. Timf smiled widely. "Alright then! Forgive me Gaberilin. I wouldn't have really hurt you, but what could I do?"

Gaberilin patted Mr. Timf on the shoulder. "Nothing to forgive, I'm glad to have you along."

Peter Crossings And The Gate Of Abaddon

And then Gaberilin turned toward the stable and whistled. His mighty black bajet came forth with a saddle already atop his back. Gaberilin helped Mr. Timf up onto Aroh, and then he followed. The Master swung himself up onto Frenwar, a grey bajet, and then pulled Andrew up behind him. Peter was secured onto a saddle in front of Miyo. The three sets of two were then ready for departure.

"Wait," a soft voice came from the door to the castle. Everyone turned to see Jubal standing in an emerald dress clutching her golden harp. She stepped forward and Solomon came out from behind her. Andrew watched as Solomon led Jubal to the bajet he sat upon. It was then that Andrew realized that Jubal was blind, for she wouldn't take a step until Solomon led her, and her eyes continually stared off into the distance.

She reached her free hand upward and Edesha took it. "I shall not rest until you have returned," she said gracefully to Edesha.

Edesha rubbed her tiny hand with this thumb. "Tehus will watch out for us, do not worry my dear Jubal." Then he bent his head down and lightly kissed the lady's hand.

Small tears glistened from Jubal's unseeing eyes. Then she released Edesha's hand and began to pluck her harp. She started to sing as the tears continued to fall. Her song made Andrew feel like he was part of a grand quest and that he could take on the world.

Atris, Frenwar, and Aroh began to flap their mighty wings and rise from the ground. Andrew watched as Jubal continued to play her song, and

James Andrew Wilson

Solomon waved them off. Soon they were soaring up into the afternoon sky with ease. The castle was far below, and the beautiful landscape of Eden beneath and beyond.

"Where are we heading?" Andrew asked the Master after a short while of flying.

"We are heading to the sea town of Acco to board one of the ships. Then we will set out into the waters in search of Patmos."

"Why don't we just fly to Patmos?" Andrew asked.

"Patmos is said to be veiled by a strange fog that can only be passed through by ship. Even though the bajets have very keen eyes, Patmos still remains hidden."

"It sounds spooky to me," Andrew said. "Have you ever been there?"

"No, but I have read and heard many tales of the island. At one time, it was a wonderful and peaceful place, but I fear much has changed since then. We shall see what comes our way."

"Well whatever happens, I just hope Peter makes it."

By this time Peter had actually awoken and spoken briefly with Miyo. He felt very tired and dizzy, and nothing really made any sense to him that Miyo tried to explain. He soon shut his eyes again and drifted off back to dreams.

The group flew north for some time, and it was becoming evening when they finally began to descend. Andrew could see the lights of Acco illuminated and flickering off still, dark waters beyond.

Peter Crossings And The Gate Of Abaddon

Some lights were glowing from tall ships floating in the docking yards. As they descended closer, a steady lapping of water could be heard splashing up against the docks. They came finally, and landed on a street with many shops of sorts on one side, and a never ending black sea on the other. The sea breeze blew Andrew's hair along with a wet smell of salt. Some people wandered about the road, some ducking into buildings, others murmuring strange things to themselves as they staggered along the dock. Many peculiar faces and characters roamed this town. Acco was a well-known trading spot, and many shapes and sizes of people came through it.

"Gaberilin, will you go and see when one of my ships can be ready for the transport of six to Patmos?" the Master asked.

Gaberilin nodded and ducked away into the road and off to some unknown cubbyhole building. Andrew hopped off Frenwar and went over to Peter now being lifted from Atris. Peter was set down with the saddle as a chair onto the dusty ground. His eyes lifted slowly and looked at Andrew approaching.

"Andrew, where are we?" he managed.

"Peter! You're awake!" Andrew grabbed his hand and shook it.

"Yeah, where are we?" Peter tried again.

"We're at some sea town called Acco. We are going to get a ship and try and find Patmos. I guess it's an island hidden in the fog somewhere, and Edesha said it is the only chance we have of healing you. It sounds kind of spooky."

Peter looked about. He could hear the easy

splashing of water, and a muffled sound of passing voices. He looked at some of the people passing by, when one caught his eye. A darkly cloaked figure walked close by him. It turned its head and gazed down at him. Every thing seemed so blurry, but Peter was sure of what he saw. Two crimson red eyes looked from the cloaked darkness at him. A hissing voice echoed into his ears. "Abaddon... we're waiting Peter..."

Peter moaned and fell back into a dark sleep. Andrew tried to wake him but with no luck. The figure turned back and continued on its way.

Gaberilin returned suddenly and spoke with the Master. He told him that a ship was waiting and ready for their voyage at any time. Everyone grabbed their packs from the bajets. The Master untied his staff and lifted Peter up onto his shoulder again. Edesha instructed everyone to cover themselves with hoods so as not to draw attention. They all thanked the bajets and said farewell, then began to walk down the street following Gaberilin's lead.

As Gaberilin walked quickly through the streets, he bumped into a tall creature entirely cloaked. It spoke harshly to him with a scratchy voice.

"I'd watch were I was going if I were you pretty boy." The figure seemed to grow taller, and stood in their way towering over them. "You never know what you might run into," the thing hissed. Then it threw aside its cloak to reveal a very scaly and spider-like sort of creature with many long arms and spikes implanted at their ends.

Gaberilin stood up to the creature and looked it

directly in the face. "We wish not to deal with you. Move aside or I will have to squish you like the bug you are!" His voice seemed so powerful and strong. At first the creature backed away and cowered down crouching like a tiger. Then it leapt full force over the group and stared down into the frightened eyes of Mr. Timf.

"What tasty treat have we here?" it said licking its lips with a snake-forked tongue. The arms moved about in a mesmerizing pattern, spikes swinging closer and closer to Mr. Timf's head. Slimy green drool dribbled off the thin black lips. The creature opened its mouth wide to reveal hundreds of tiny spiked teeth, and a foul decaying breath. Mr. Timf quivered and pulled forth his sword to face the monster. It laughed harshly and struck with amazing speed at Mr. Timf. There was suddenly a bright flash of light. A fire shot forth from an outstretched staff, and a light arrow from Gaberilin's bow. The arrow pierced into the open mouth, and fire engulfed the creature as it emitted hideous screams and cries. It jumped about flailing its arms until falling into the water with a sizzling splash.

Gaberilin placed his bow again upon his back. The Master lowered his staff and flopped the hood back over his head. "Come, we have drawn too much attention." The others stood for a moment in wonder, then quickly followed

Andrew ran up to the side of Miyo. "What was that thing?" he asked.

"That was an Aracite. There is a dark history behind the Aracites. They come from deadly spiders found near the Catacomb Mountains. But hush now, we must be careful, for I fear there are many eyes watching, and many ears listening in the dark corners of this terrible place."

"An Aracite," Andrew said to himself. He decided that he wanted to have nothing ever again to do with the creatures.

After a short, quick walk they came to a moored ship glowing with lights. Figures of men walked about it hauling various things and preparing the ship for its journey. Following the Master, who had Peter in his arms, everyone crossed over a single placed board from the dock to the deck of the ship. The Master went up to one of the men and spoke with him. The man nodded then went away quickly to speak to some others. The group trailed Edesha underneath the deck and into the wide hull beneath.

Within the ship were many rooms, all crafted with extreme delicacy. They went through a hall until the Master entered one of the many doors on either side. The creaking of the door was not the only sound when they entered. There were some shouts above, and what felt like a nudging from the dock, then drifting out into the waters.

Inside the room everyone sat down on the circular couch rounding the circumference of the area. The Master lay Peter down on the plump cushions and then went and closed the door when all were seated.

He turned to them and spoke, "Welcome to my ship, this is the Toreth. We will be sailing for three days, and by the end of that time we hope to reach

Peter Crossings And The Gate Of Abaddon

Patmos. All chance of Peter's survival now depends upon Tehus. But He has placed the boy in our hands and we must do our part to ensure his safety. It may require sacrifice, and without a question, bravery." Then Edesha paused and seemed to be in thought. "Peter told me that he had a dream. A dream of the Golden Book."

Gaberilin looked surprised. "When I took him to the map room he remembered something, but then the poison took affect." Edesha sighed. "His survival may be vital to ours. We must all make sure that our senses are sharp, and the boy, Peter, must be protected at all costs."

Andrew listened intently to all these things. He could begin to see the real importance of Peter to Eden. He felt honored to have him as a friend, where as before, it never really mattered. But in that room, aboard that ship, on the journey to a hidden island, he knew that Peter would be a friend for a very long time.

"I will protect him the best that I can." Andrew stood and held his hands behind his back.

"That is very noble of you Andrew," Edesha said standing and leaning upon his staff. Andrew looked at the strong hands of the Master gripping the staff. The image of the Aracite burning came into his mind, and he remembered how the fire had come from the same staff. He wondered what sort of power it was, and where it had come from.

At that moment, Peter sat up and breathed deep holding his stomach. Everyone looked to him and Andrew rushed over to his side.

James Andrew Wilson

"Are you okay Peter?" he asked kneeling down.

"I don't know." Peter sat up straighter. "I feel like there is something inside my stomach. It feels like it's slowly eating me." He moaned and rolled over.

The Master came to his side and looked down on him. "What can we do?" Andrew asked looking up into his eyes.

Edesha knelt down beside Peter and rested a hand on his forehead. He uttered some words under his breath, and then reached into his cloak and pulled forth a small pouch. "He will sleep after a drink of this, and it will help with the pain." He popped out a cork and placed the pouch to Peter's mouth. The liquid entered his throat and ran down into his stomach. Peter could feel it's cool flavor and then fell into a sleep.

Not much more was said and everyone was showed to their rooms. Gaberilin and Mr. Timf shared a room, Andrew and Peter shared another, and Miyo and Edesha each had rooms of their own. The Master took Peter and placed him in a bed as Andrew watched. Edesha comforted Andrew and then left the room.

Sitting on the edge of his bed, Andrew looked across at Peter, who was quietly sleeping on the bed opposite of him. He thought for a while, then slipped off his boots and slid under his covers. It was then that he realized for the first time, the swaying of the ship. His bed seemed to rock him back and forth to sleep. The gentle running of the water along the ship came as a lullaby. Andrew pulled the covers up higher and rolled over onto his side. After some time, he finally fell asleep.

* * * * *

"The last known location of Patmos was here," said Miyo pointing to a location on the map. Everyone had awoken and gathered into the same round room after breakfast. Miyo was explaining their destination, "We will travel northwest, and after approximately two and a half days we *should* reach the island, or sooner if things go well."

"What about the fog?" asked Gaberilin. "How will we conduct a true northwest in the fog?"

"By use of a compass. It will not be an easy task, if we stray off course by any measure, we may miss the island. If my measurements are correct, we should be here." Miyo pointed to a spot in the large bay. Two fingers of land stretched out into the ocean leaving only a small exit. Within the bay the small island rested. According to Miyo, they were about three quarters of the way to their destination.

"If we can stay on course, we'll make it," Miyo said.

Edesha was sitting alone resting his chin upon his hand in deep thought. There had been something alarming him ever since they boarded, but he had spoken of it to no one. Miyo noticed him and inquired, "Master, is there something bothering you?"

Everyone looked to him as he looked up with worried eyes. "There may be more troubles ahead than merely keeping on course," he spoke quietly.

"What do you mean?" asked Gaberilin.

James Andrew Wilson

"There is a very old tale of a ship eater within this bay."

"You are referring to Leviathan?" Miyo asked.

"Yes, the breather of fire from the depths of water."

"Yes of course," said Miyo. "It is a very old tale."

"What is this Leviathan?" asked Gaberilin.

The Master and Miyo looked at each other. "Leviathan: The beast, the breather, the beater. Scales as stone, fire as sun, fierceness as death. Within the waters he comes forth to devour any he desires. His home is well hidden and none may enter unless he allows. Death will come if Leviathan desires. The beast, the breather, the beater." The Master finished the tale and the room fell to silence.

"But it is only a tale. How can we be sure that there is such a creature?" asked Gaberilin.

Miyo rubbed his temples in thought, "Leviathan has not been seen for over three hundred years."

"Yes, and neither has Patmos—" the Master paused all of a sudden. "I believe this is more than a coincidence."

"What do you mean?" Miyo asked.

"The tale speaks of his home being well hidden, and that none may enter unless he allows."

"Yes, yes! Of course! Patmos is his home!" Miyo said very excitedly.

"Wait a moment," said Gaberilin. "Are you saying that Leviathan has not allowed anyone to find Patmos for over three hundred years? But why?"

"Greed," Edesha said. "Patmos is a place of many jewels and wealth. Many have sought with greedy hearts in hopes of finding wealth for themselves, but none have returned. Leviathan has destroyed all that have sought Patmos because of their greed."

"But how could a sea monster know the hearts of men?" Miyo asked.

"Maybe he asked." Andrew had not spoken a word for the entire time, but stood now. Everyone looked at him curiously.

"Go on Andrew," the Master said.

Andrew cleared his throat. "When Peter and I first met Atris, we were really shocked that she was an animal and that she could talk. Animals can't talk where we come from, but I wish they could. Anyways, maybe this monster thing asked the sailors why they wanted to go to his home. From the sounds of it, I don't think that anybody could lie to something like that, especially not me. I mean, I don't think it's a good idea to lie anyways, then things get all messed up and you usually get in more trouble than if you just told your mom that you *did* take two cookies. That's what I learned from Peter anyways. He told the truth back in school, when I would have lied. And things worked out a lot better because of it."

Andrew finally finished and everyone stared at him in jaw dropped confusion. "So, you think that Leviathan just asks the sailors why they want to go to Patmos?" Gaberilin asked.

"Yeah, it makes sense to me," Andrew replied shrugging his shoulders.

"Well, perhaps the boy is correct," said Miyo. "There was a time long ago when Solomon and I had a conversation about Leviathan. I remember now

James Andrew Wilson

that Solomon had said something about the piercing eyes of Leviathan: the eyes that could look inside you and bring out the truth. I never thought much of it before, but now it does seem to make sense."

Edesha stood from his seat and walked over to Andrew. He knelt down and rested a hand on his shoulder. "You have much insight young Andrew."

"Thanks!" Andrew smiled wide.

The ship suddenly rocked to the side sending Andrew to the floor. There were shouts from above. "What is it?"

"I don't know! It hit us from the starboard side!"

"Arm the harpoons!"

"Leviathan… quickly!" Edesha said rushing out of the room.

Gaberilin grabbed Peter into his arms and everyone ran up onto the deck. There was much chaos as the men ran from side to side of the ship watching for Leviathan. The ship lurched forward and some fell to the deck.

"It's behind! Fire the harpoons."

"No!" said the Master raising his hands. All the men stopped and looked to him. "Let me deal with this." Edesha walked quickly to the bow of the ship and raised his voice. "Leviathan, show yourself that we may speak." There was a deep moving of the waters and a long dark shape appeared in front of the ship. The waters exploded as a gleaming head burst from them. A long creature with spikes upon it's back came forth and stared down at the Master. The face was dark and hideous. The head alone was the size of the entire ship, and the eyes twice the size of the tall figure of Edesha. Drops of water fell from the green scales as it breathed deep from its nostrils.

All the men shrank back in fear, Andrew ducked behind Gaberilin, and Mr. Timf shrank to a ball on the deck. Edesha stood tall before the monster and spoke boldly, "Leviathan, the great monster of the sea, I am the Master from the castle of Edeneth."

A deep rumble sounded from Leviathan. "What is your destination and reason for, bold speaker?"

The deep red eyes looked luminously at the Master. "We have come in search of the hidden shores of Patmos, and the pool of healing within."

Leviathan tilted his enormous head as if alarmed at the reply. "What need have you of the pool?"

"The boy, Peter Crossings, has been punctured by a devourer of darkness, and the poison will soon kill him if he is not healed."

"Where is this boy?" Leviathan asked.

"He is here." The Master motioned for Gaberilin to come forward. He placed Peter's limp body into the hands of Edesha. "Here is the boy." The Master held him up before Leviathan. Andrew gasped. He was sure that Peter was about to be eaten before his very eyes, but he was mistaken.

"Your heart and reason is true, Patmos you will see, and on this night. Bring me a rope."

Everyone felt relief. Gaberilin ran quickly and found a rope. "Tie it quickly to the mast," commanded Leviathan. Gaberilin did so. "Now make a loop at the other end." Gaberilin tied it quickly. "When I turn, secure the loop to the spike atop my head, then hold on," Leviathan said, then he turned around in the water shaking the ship, and a large spike upon his head glistened in the sun. Everyone held tight to the ship as Gaberilin swung the rope and landed it on the spike. After a second, the ship lurched forward very fast as Leviathan swam hurriedly through the waters.

* * * * *

He had fallen from his corner at the lurch of the ship. He spoke to himself harshly in the darkness. "Leviathan? They have appeased the eyes?"

His black robes surrounded him as he sat up and scooted back into the shadows. "Three hundred years of mystery unraveled in a moment. This boy is making things difficult. The poison would have killed him before they reached the island, and then Sheol would have won. Now things are more complicated…"

His dark intentions swam through his mind. "There may still be a way." He put his long dark finger to his pursed lips. "Will he believe me? He is not as strong as Peter. Yes, that is how. I will deceive him and use him."

He stood and looked about his dark hiding spot with evil eyes. "Abaddon is calling him, but he may need a little persuasion. After all, who wouldn't trust their friend? Come out, come out wherever you are…Andrew Hatch."

* * * * *

Peter Crossings And The Gate Of Abaddon

Leviathan's enormous body pierced through the waters. Everyone had finally settled down after the horrifying encounter. As they sped through the waters, a blinding fog neared. Soon they were enveloped in a thick white haze. Nobody could see anything further than their nose, so they all stayed very still for fear of falling off the ship. Miyo was very excited about everything, and wouldn't stop talking. Andrew thought that he couldn't bear it any longer when the ship began to slow and the fog began to fade. Gaberilin quickly scurried up a ladder to the crow's nest and arched his hand over his eyes peering into the clearing haze. All of a sudden, an island appeared before them. Jagged rocks sprouted from a dense thicket that covered the island like a blanket, yet in the center it seemed to glow.

"Land Ho!" shouted Gaberilin.

A convoy ship was prepared. Edesha, Mr. Timf, Gaberilin, Miyo, Peter, and Andrew all boarded the ship and were set down into the black waters. The shining stars were reflected perfectly on the glassy ocean. Leviathan had disappeared as soon as they reached the island, but everyone silently thanked him in their hearts. After a short row, they bumped into a beach of silky sand.

Miyo knelt down and scooped some of the sand into his hands. "The hidden shores of Patmos have once again been found," he said quietly to himself.

Chapter Eight

A Vision From Beyond

Camp was set up on the beach. Gaberilin and Mr. Timf unloaded supplies from the convoy ship. Some men had come with them to the shore, and they returned when the convoy was empty. The men said the island was haunted, and that none of them would stay on its shores. Supplies were unpacked and plans were put into action about building a fire. Mr. Timf found some wood in a nearby thicket, and a crackling flame was soon licking the night sky. The air seemed rather cold, so everyone gathered together blankets and sat around the glowing fire. Andrew curled himself up in the blue cloak he had been given the day before. He reached back and found the hood, then flopped it over his head. Like the faces of all the others around the circle, shadows danced across his countenance. They sat for a while, watching the limbs of

James Andrew Wilson

---

wood slowly crumble into ash.

"Where are we?" To everybody's surprise, Peter suddenly sat up and began to talk.

"Peter!" Andrew said gladly.

"Peter, my dear lad, we are on the shores of the island of Patmos," Edesha replied. He was sitting next to Peter on a piece of driftwood.

"Patmos?" Peter asked.

"Within the shores of this island is a pool of healing in which we hope to cleanse the poison from your body," the Master explained.

"Yes, how do you feel dear lad." Miyo was wrapped in a heavy wool blanket with his cane resting at the side of the driftwood he sat upon.

"I feel... well, hungry."

Everyone laughed and Mr. Timf rummaged around in his backpack and brought forth a large pan. "Let me fill up that poor stomach young lad!" exclaimed Mr. Timf as he gathered many cooking spices and utensils into his hands.

Peter looked hesitantly up to Edesha. He didn't remember Mr. Timf. "Oh yes, Peter this is Mr. Timf. He came along to aid us."

"Well, now he's a not quite getting' it all. I came along cause none a'this woulda' appened if I hadn't been asleep on that bench. Please accept my dear apology." Then Mr. Timf put a hand to his plump belly and bowed dropping some spices in the process.

Peter accepted the apology gladly as his stomach growled from hunger. They had taken food supplies from the ship. Out of these Mr. Timf chose five

Peter Crossings And The Gate Of Abaddon

choice pieces of meat and slapped them into the pan. He put many different sorts of spices on the meat, and patiently tended to his cooking while the others talked.

Peter was informed of all that he had missed, and Andrew made sure that not a single detail about the Aracite was left out, for it had scared him very much.

After a short while, the food was ready. Everyone that felt hungry ate, and were very satisfied with the tasty cooking. Soon the fire began to die down, and they all started dozing off to sleep. Andrew was the last to finally drift off.

Ever since they had left the ship, Andrew had felt very strange, like he was being watched. He looked to make sure that Peter was safe. His friend was snuggled down into a big wool blanket and softly snoring. Andrew wrapped his own blanket around himself and closed his eyes.

* * * * *

It couldn't have been any easier. No one had noticed him. Now all that remained was the boy. He had to be careful. The hood that draped over his face hid him well in the thicket. "That overgrown little hairy man almost saw me when he came to get that wood. But now everyone is asleep," he whispered hoarsely to himself. "Yes, now is the time." He rose from his hiding spot and began to make his move.

* * * * *

James Andrew Wilson

Noise. A strange presence. Calling. Calling me. Andrew wake up! Andrew sat up from his blanket wide eyed and looked about the camp. Everyone was still silently slumbering. The fire had completely died down, and now an eerie glow from the covering moon cast a blue haze on the beach. He stood. His feet began to walk ever so quietly, the leather boots almost gliding across the sandy floor. *The thicket.* He entered, confused by his own actions. *"Andrew."* Someone called his name.

"Yes, I'm here," he spoke, or at least his thoughts spoke.

"Further, come in further," the twisted branches called.

He ventured in through a small space in the choking, winding thicket. A strange animal cooed into the night, his heart began to race as he neared the beckoning voice. A clearing emerged from the branches. A puddle reflected the circumference of the moon within its perfectly rippling waters. At the edge of the reflection was a darkly colored bird that sat and carefully sipped the water. It looked up to see Andrew appear.

"Sit down." He heard a voice, though it seemed no one spoke it. A nearby rock suddenly came into view and he sat. The bird hopped to the other side of the puddle nearer to Andrew and bent down to the water again.

"You know its foolishness," said the voice. "They are lying to you. You are in terrible danger if you remain with them. So is Peter."

"No, not Peter," Andrew thought.

Peter Crossings And The Gate Of Abaddon

The bird rose from the water and cocked its head to one side. "Peter is in the most danger of all. If you don't warn him, they will surely kill him."

"No! How can I save him?"

The bird came and hopped up onto the rock beside Andrew. "Tomorrow, when you set out to find the pool, be sure to stay close to Peter. Make sure they don't put him in the waters."

"But how can I stop them?"

Something rustled nearby and the bird quickly turned its head in the direction of the noise. It waited for a second. "Distract them the best that you can until I can help, now go!"

Andrew stood quickly to his feet and turned toward the thicket. When he turned back to see the bird again, it was gone, and the puddle had dried to a cracked pit of mud. Andrew wound his way through the maze and made it back to the camp. Everyone was still sleeping as he crawled back under his blanket.

* * * * *

Mr. Timf yawned loudly stretching back into the morning air. He was the first one to rise, and liked it that way. After rolling his blanket and tying it with a strand of leather, Mr. Timf set about quickly and quietly to prepare breakfast. His first course of action was to gather wood. After a trample through the thicket, and a couple hacks with the hatchet he had brought along, he brought forth a hearty pile of wood. No one had awoken yet, so he tiptoed to the pack of food and ravaged through it.

Miyo heard the ravaging and mumbling of Mr. Timf. He rose from his blanket and went about fighting the sleep that tried to keep him in the early morning hours. All the others finally woke up, except for the boys. Mr. Timf had made a fine breakfast that finally tantalized the boys' noses causing them to sit up and rub their eyes. When everyone had gathered around the fire, Miyo noticed that Edesha was nowhere in sight.

"I do say, Mr. Timf, have you seen the Master this morning?" he asked.

"Huh? The Master?" Mr. Timf looked about the circle. "Why no, I don't think I have."

Gaberilin stood suddenly and withdrew his sword. "Quickly! Everyone spread out and find him!"

Andrew remembered what he had seen in the night and became fearful. Maybe that voice that had been talking to him had done something to the Master. But maybe Edesha *was* actually bad. Maybe all of them were actually bad.

Just then Edesha came from around the bend of the beach and sat down at the circle without a word.

"Master! Where have you been?" Gaberilin asked with his mighty sword still drawn.

"I have been scouting out the easiest course through the thicket. It seems as though there is a path around the bend that we can take."

"You had us a bit worried," Gaberilin said sheathing his sword and taking a seat.

"I appreciate your concern, but I do believe I can fend for myself," the Master said with a glimmer in his eye.

"Yes, well, I'm glad you are safe."

Everyone ate and packed up their things. Peter hadn't said much of anything; he was feeling sick to his stomach and ate very little. He sensed an unknown danger was lurking around the corner. At his request, Gaberilin carried him as they set out to find the pool of healing.

Everyone walked with their packs slouched over their backs along the beach, following the Master. He led them around a bend and to an opening in the thicket. Edesha ducked into the choking branches, wielding his staff tightly in front of him. Gaberilin took up the rear, carefully carrying Peter. It was very difficult to climb through the smothering brush. An eerie blackness seemed to reside within the branches. The thorns poked out scraping against the trespassers as though they were white, scaly fingers reaching for someone to suffocate. They trudged on for some time.

Mr. Timf could no longer stand it. He unbuckled the hatchet from his pack and began whacking wildly at the "whole mess of weeds," as he called it. The Master halted all of a sudden commanding Mr. Timf to stop the chaos. Mr. Timf stood almost dumbfounded and shyly put the hatchet away. Edesha did not take another step further but motioned for Gaberilin to come to the front of the line. Peter was handed into the arms of Mr. Timf and they sat down upon a rock in the small clearing the wild hatchet had created. Gaberilin pushed his way to where the Master leaned on his tall staff, staring intently ahead of them.

Gaberilin came up to his side and asked, "What is—" His question was cut off when he saw what had stopped them. "Oh no," he whispered pulling forth his sword.

* * * * *

Andrew's thoughts kept flying back to the strange encounter he had in the night. At first when he woke up, it seemed like it had all been a dream, but as the day grew, he was sure that it was no vision of sleep. Still it seemed so odd to him that no one had heard him get up, or return for that matter. And besides that, the whole business of the bird seemed rather strange. Was it true that Edesha was only setting out to *kill* Peter? But why?

He looked over at Peter who sat bent over on the stone with Mr. Timf at his side, patting him on the back. What was so special about his friend in this strange world that all these people were willing to risk their very lives for him? Or maybe try to destroy him? What did he know, and how…how did he know it? He pulled the silvery blue hood over his head and thought all these things over.

* * * * *

"I do say, what seems to be the hold up?" Miyo asked, finally reaching the side of the Master. "Oh my!" he exclaimed putting his hand to his mouth. "How many are there?"

"At least twenty," Gaberilin said leaning over one

Peter Crossings And The Gate Of Abaddon

of the piles of bones.

Within the clearing of the thicket lay many piles of broken and chipped bones. They looked almost as though they had been chewed on like a play toy by a dog. A large rock protruded from the ground like a tall monument, and Gaberilin climbed quickly up it. From his vantage point he could see that the thicket spanned for at least half a mile until it stopped abruptly at a wall of rocks much like the one he stood upon. He could not see over them to the inside of the circle they created, but noticed that they seemed to glow with a blue shade of color. As he scanned the terrain of Patmos, something caught his attention from the corner of his eye.

He looked to see a series of small wakes forming in the thicket not more than five hundred feet to his right. They were forming their way very quickly in the direction of the rock. More began to stream through the thicket until it seemed the whole island was rushing at him.

"Edesha, Miyo! Everyone get up here now!" He leapt off the rock, landing amongst the bones and dashed back into the thicket where Andrew and Mr. Timf were waiting. Gaberilin scooped Peter into his arms and rushed out of the thicket with the other two following. Edesha and Miyo had begun to climb up the rock when Gaberilin sped up behind them.

"What is it? What's going on?" Mr. Timf asked struggling up the rock.

"Mr. Timf, hurry!" Gaberilin shouted setting Peter down and rushing back to help the struggling little man. By this time Edesha could see the wakes that Gaberilin had spotted, rushing toward them from all corners of the island.

"Hurry you two!" Edesha yelled.

Gaberilin grabbed Mr. Timf and hoisted him further up the rock. They scrambled to the top just in time.

"What's happening?" Andrew asked, clutching to the side of Edesha.

"The island does not like us here," Miyo cried out. "It is coming to eat us."

Something grabbed Mr. Timf by the leg and pulled him to his back. "Arrgh!" he shouted. A green root had grabbed him and began winding up his leg pulling him toward the ground. The floor of the island swam like snakes as millions of green vines crawled over themselves.

Gaberilin leapt down by Mr. Timf, and with his sword cut cleanly through the vine freeing him. The vine curled and fell back into the swarm.

"Master, we are going to be eaten alive!" Miyo proclaimed.

Edesha said nothing, but walked further up the rock raising his staff to the air. Gaberilin and Mr. Timf busily hacked at the snake-like vines crawling up the rock. Andrew watched in horror as the safe space of the rock slowly became covered in the vines. They all backed closer together, surrounding Peter.

"You can not have him!" Gaberilin shouted at the vines climbing about them.

The Master stood upon the edge of the rock with his staff raised high. He stretched his other hand out and spoke in a thundering voice. "I am a Servant of the Light, and follower of The Way. In the name of The Righteous Ruler, I command you. Be still!" With that, a brilliant glowing light shot from the sky into his staff and spread across the entire island like a fire. The vines shrank away from the rock and weaved back into the island. As everyone watched, the vines began to come together and climb high into the air shooting out in all directions and becoming hard like trees. Leaves began to sprout from them, glowing in the light of the sky. The entire island, save the circle of rocks in the center, sprouted forth vegetation and all sorts of green plants, shrubs, and trees. Everything settled into its rightful place as Edesha lowered his staff to his side and bowed his head.

Edesha turned and walked past everyone solemnly. The group stood bewildered. Peter had seen the transformation, but was most interested to discover what Edesha meant by "the Light."

* * * * *

Everyone descended from the rock to a soft ground covered in lush moss. "The island has become fertile," Gaberilin said walking a little further and investigating the growth.

Mr. Timf came up to his side. "Well, I'll be. This sure does beat that nasty thicket, and those horrible thorns, and those vines gave me quite the scare. I would like to thank you Gaberilin, for helping me up there," he thanked the muscular figure.

"We all need to look out for each other, I am just thankful that we all made it alive."

Peter came and stood near to the two looking about at the freshly grown forest.

"Peter my dear lad! You seem to be well!" Mr. Timf said slapping him on the back.

"Actually, yes, I do feel a lot better," Peter replied.

"The poison reacts on fear, when evil is near it begins to leak into your body quicker," Edesha explained coming up to the group.

"Is it still inside of me then?" Peter asked.

"Yes, but soon we will reach the pool and its pure waters will cleanse you. So come quickly, let us continue on our way."

* * * * *

He had perched himself upon the high rock and peered down through the trees. His keen eyes spotted the small group making its way toward the towering stone wall he watched from.

"Not even Patmos could stop them. Time is running out, and soon Peter will be cleansed and strengthened. This is my only chance."

He lifted himself from the rock and flew quickly down into the trees making his way very swiftly toward his target.

* * * * *

They all trudged on through the foliage with Edesha in the lead, and Gaberilin taking up the rear. Soon they came to a small stream that bubbled up and down across a scatter of golden rocks. Everyone

Peter Crossings And The Gate Of Abaddon

was feeling very thirsty and rather tired, so they sat down for a few brief minutes. Miyo went to the stream, dipped his hand into the water and sipped the liquid.

"This stream flows from the pool within Patmos. Merely sipping the water brings overwhelming refreshment." He sipped the water again. Everyone took part of the cool water for themselves and felt very refreshed. Mr. Timf filled the water pouches and placed them back in his bag. With renewed strength, everyone got up and continued forward.

Having only gone on a little bit further, Andrew thought he heard something behind him. Still walking, he turned to see Gaberilin, sword still drawn, watching carefully each step of the group and scouting about for anything out of place. He heard it again. It sounded like a rustling noise, maybe someone walking. Then he saw a black shape flash out of the corner of his eye.

"Stop!" Gaberilin shouted. Everyone halted as Gaberilin ran to the front of the line and spoke quietly with the Master. Andrew looked about. He saw the black shape flash behind a tree and then peer out at him. It ducked away again and dashed to a bush.

"Peter, there's something out there," Andrew whispered scooting closer to Peter.

"What is it?" Peter asked.

"I don't know, but it's small and black."

"Peter, Andrew come up here," Edesha said. The boys came up to his side.

"There is an evil creature following us. I want you to stay beside Gaberilin and I."

"What is it?" Peter asked.

"A deceiver."

"Shh, I see it." Gaberilin held up a hand and gripped his sword tighter.

Out from the corner of a small boulder peered two relentless yellow eyes that were sunken into a slimy black head. Two jagged horns stabbed through its uppermost scalp. The mouth opened and scowled at the group, glaring its teeth that looked like the points of blood stained swords. A hollow emptiness was revealed in the gaping hole of its mouth. Then the creature sprang onto the boulder like a cat pouncing a bird. Peter could see then that the backbone of the monster was the only thing that connected the sprawling legs to the chest. Long claws clung to the rock, scraping it like nails on a blackboard. The creature hissed and spoke, "By order of darkness, I am commanded not to let you take the boy any further." Its voice reminded Peter most terribly of the shadows.

The Master stepped closer. The creature growled and scurried about on the boulder. "This child *will* go further, and neither you, nor any other slave of darkness is going to stop him," the Master said walking directly toward the creature.

"Back away Servant or you will fall where you stand!"

The Master came straight up to the creature and stared into its hideous face. "Be careful of your words slave, they may return to yourself."

"Arghh!" The monster leapt over Edesha, darted to Andrew, and grabbed him by the throat.

"No, let him go!" Peter shouted.

The slimy head turned and stared straight at Peter. "You are such a friend aren't you? What if I told you that Andrew here was planning on abandoning you?"

"What are you talking about?" Peter asked clutching his shoulder.

Gaberilin sheathed his sword, drew his bow, and notched an arrow.

"Put down your bow or I will slice his little throat!" the beast warned as it ran a claw along Andrew's neck.

"No! Let go of him!" Peter shouted. The blood in his veins felt hot like steaming water. He grabbed his shoulder tightly and began to choke.

"Are you afraid Peter? Are you afraid of me?" it hissed.

"No, I—" Peter fell to the ground. Miyo and Mr. Timf rushed to his side.

"Ha ha!" it laughed a cruel chant.

"Let go of me!" Andrew shouted.

The creature tilted its head and glared at Andrew. "Let go of you? Why would I do that? I thought we were in this together." It laughed again and hissed at Gaberilin. "Drop your bow fool. Now!"

"No!!!" Out of nowhere Peter dashed for the creature and kicked it in the exposed backbone.

"Argh!" Andrew fell down to the ground and scurried quickly away. "You were of no help to me fool!" it shouted to Andrew. Then in a flash, Peter was in the creature's grasp.

"Leave him be!" the Master commanded as a beam of light illuminated his staff from the sky.

James Andrew Wilson

"The boy is mine!" The creature raised its claw into air and then flashed it down toward Peter's heart.

Andrew turned his face. Gaberilin let loose his arrow. There was a flash of light from Edesha's staff that blinded everybody for a moment. When the light died down there was no sign of the deceiver, but Peter lay face down in the moss.

Andrew ran to Peter and slid down beside him. "Peter! No! Peter wake up!" Tears streamed down his face. "Please Peter... please wake up. I'm so sorry..." The tears covered his cheeks. "No!!!!"

* * * * *

She stood on the high balcony from her room. The wind swept through her hair. The sun was setting out across the sea. Then words came on the wind to her ears.

"Jubal. Peter has fallen. We are near to the pool. Lift up your voice, we need you now."

Jubal's breath fell away. She turned back into her room and came back out with her harp. "Edesha..." she whispered.

As tears fell from her viewless eyes, she raised her voice. She beckoned for healing. She cried for help.

Her voice traveled on the wind. Across the sea and through timeless fogs until passing through newly sprouted trees and finding its way to a fallen boy. Andrew clutched Peter in his arms. His small tears fell upon his friend. Everyone bowed their heads and silence resided.

And then he stirred. "I...I'm okay." Peter rose

from the ground.

"Peter!" Andrew hugged him. "Oh, I was afraid you were dead!"

"I might be if you don't get off my throat," Peter choked.

Andrew stood to his feet and wiped the tears from his eyes. "Oh, sorry."

Everyone let out a sigh of relief. Then Peter stood and brushed himself off. There was a great slash in his shirt, but his skin underneath appeared untouched. Peter looked at Andrew. "Andrew, what was that thing talking about? He said something about you."

"I uh…" Andrew stumbled over his words. How could he tell Peter?

"Go ahead Andrew, what happened?" Edesha came up to the two.

Andrew took a deep breath. "Last night I had a dream, or maybe it wasn't a dream, it seemed like it, anyways, I woke up and thought I heard somebody calling my name. It was really weird…" Andrew went on to explain the meeting with the bird.

"I'm sorry Peter, I'm sorry all of you, I didn't know, I was just…well, deceived."

"Andrew," the Master began, "what you met last night was not a bird, but an evil minion known in Eden as a shadow deceiver. They are terrible beasts whose true form is this creature that you saw here. Deceivers are able to take on any image, human or animal, unless they are in the presence of a Servant of the Light."

"Are you a Servant of the Light?" Peter asked

James Andrew Wilson

quickly, intent on answering his curiosity.

"Yes, I am a High Servant, one of seven in this land."

"What about Gaberilin?" Peter asked. "Isn't he a Servant, because the shadows in my world didn't turn into their true forms?"

"Yes, I am a Servant of the Light," Gaberilin answered. "But the shadows always remain in their shadow form in your land."

"How do you become a Servant?" Andrew asked. "Do you have to take a test, I hate tests!"

Everyone laughed, and were glad to have Andrew with them. "It is something that would take more time than we have to explain, when we return to the castle, I will tell you, but come now, the pool is near!"

"But I feel much better!" Peter said.

"That is because you are so near to a place of healing. The poison is still in your body, if you were to leave this place you would surely die."

"Well, let's get going then! No use in just sittin' around here," Mr. Timf spoke up.

"Yes, on our way now!" The Master took to the lead again.

It was not long before they came to the end of the trees, and to the foot of the towering rock wall. A blue glow emitted from the wall casting a cool light on everyone's face as they stood before the soaring obstacle.

Edesha walked up to the wall and placed a hand upon it. Everyone watched with great anticipation. "Peter," he called.

Peter Crossings And The Gate Of Abaddon

Peter walked to his side. "Rest your hand on the rock," said the Master. Peter reached out and touched the cool surface. "The walls of the pool only open when the waters are stirred."

"How do we stir the waters?" Peter asked.

"Do you believe that you will be healed?" the Master questioned.

"Well, yes I do." Edesha smiled and then removed his hand from the rock.

Before Peter could blink, something very strange happened. As he looked about himself, he discovered that he was no longer standing on the outside of the wall, but was now in a brilliant glowing place. All around him was a wall of shimmering blue rock that looked like crystal. The ground was very fine sand. He knelt and scooped some into his hand. It looked like specks of gold as it flowed over his palm. There was no sound to be heard except for a gentle moving of water. He looked and saw seven pillars, tall and gold like the sand. Within their circle it appeared a large drop of water was continually falling and rippling across the metallic sand. He then realized that he was within the walls.

Peter thought he heard a soft voice calling his name, and he ventured toward the water. He felt almost as though he was floating when he found himself at the edge of the water. It was then, when he looked down, that he discovered that he was barefoot and that his boots had been removed. He heard the soft voice call again. Peter stepped into the waters.

The water gave him a feeling he had never experienced or imagined. It seemed to cover his entire

James Andrew Wilson

body. If peace, or joy, or love can be held and felt, then that was what the water felt like. He soon came to the center of the water, where the ripples continuously flowed. As he watched, a dark color swam out from his body toward the edge of the pool. He felt as if a weight of pain was flowing from his veins into the pure waters. The dark color moved toward the edge of the pool until it evaporated and was no more. And then he felt as though he was being lifted into the air and a powerful presence surrounded him.

The pool and the pillars faded from his view and he saw, as if in a dream, a boy standing in a brilliant white place. The boy was bowing before a great golden throne so Peter could not see his face. Then he saw the boy holding a shining silver sword high into the air. And then there was an image of two boys in a much darker place. He saw that there was another person with them. This person seemed very evil to Peter, and it seemed as though the evil person was saying something terrible to the boys. An image of the boy with the silver sword appeared. He was very dirty and seemed tired, but he wielded the sword high, and in a brilliant flash of light he swiped it through the dark shape. The dark shape collapsed to the ground and from the bundle fell a golden item. The boy went and picked up the object. Peter could then see that the object was a key with a long blue ribbon tied to it. The last thing that Peter saw astonished him more than anything he had yet seen in Eden. The boy in the image turned and faced Peter. To his amazement, the boy was himself. He felt as though he was peering into a mirror as the image of himself took the key and ran quickly away.

The pillars and the pool came back into view and he stood now among a still water. He waited there for an untold time, thinking about the visions. Then, when he thought he would never be able to move again, and never wanted to leave the glorious place, he heard a voice speak clearly to him.

"Now go and do as you must. Have strength and do not fear," the soft voice echoed through the inner walls.

Peter stepped from the waters and walked lightly to the crystal walls. He turned and looked back to the waters resting still, as though they had never been touched. He breathed a deep long breath, reached out, and touched the wall.

Chapter Nine

Many Things are Revealed

His dark robes flashed quickly down the curved stairs. Slamming open the two doors, he exited into the crimson red air. All the creatures cowered down as he passed their presence until he came to a growling, snarling dark shape. Coming up to the fowl creature he stared it in the eyes.

"Macthon, I need you to send a message to Queen Lebijez."

"Anything you desire master," Macthon hissed.

"Tell the queen that we are in need of her speed and that action must be taken immediately," Nefarious commanded.

"What action must be taken my lord?" Macthon asked

"We must prepare for a final battle."

"The final battle?" Macthon rose from the ground

James Andrew Wilson

and hovered over his dark lord. His spiked wings stirred the jet-black ash about the ground. "I will deliver the message as you wish."

"One more thing Macthon," Nefarious stopped him. "Tell her that the boys will be at the Festival of the Stars. She will understand."

"Yes my lord."

Nefarious turned as Macthon rose and flew quickly away. The fires of Abaddon burned hot as Nefarious went about preparing his evil minions for war.

* * * * *

Peter wasn't sure how long he had been within the walls, for when he appeared again on the outside, everyone was sitting as though they had been there for a long time. Andrew was the first one to notice when Peter appeared.

"Peter! You're back!" He ran up to his side.

Peter looked at him and smiled. Andrew could tell that there was something strangely different about his friend.

"I am beginning to remember. I have seen the Golden Book, and I have read what it contained. And now...now I am beginning to remember."

No one responded at first, they all just gazed quietly at Peter. He appeared to have a glow about his face, and a powerful presence resided about him.

"He has been with Tehus... Now things will be much different," Miyo said at last.

Peter looked at Edesha. "Take me back to

Peter Crossings And The Gate Of Abaddon

Edeneth. I have something to show you in the map room."

So they set out from the pool and made their way back through the forests of Patmos. Sometime in the night they reached the beach. A scout noticed them from the crow's nest of the ship, and a boat was sent out. Soon they found themselves back on the Toreth and sailing the blue waters again.

That night Peter and Andrew slept in the same room that they had before. Andrew asked Peter all about what happened in the pool, and Peter as well, asked Andrew many things that he had missed. After some time they fell into a deep peaceful sleep.

They sailed smoothly on the crystal waters for nearly three days then they arrived back at Acco on a starry evening. They all cloaked themselves and followed the Master to a small inn hidden away in an alley. They stayed the night in a cozy room. The Master told them that the bajets would be watching from the skies in the morning. Everyone slept somewhat peacefully considering the many noises coming from the streets outside.

In the morning, they rose early. They took their things and went out into the streets. Some men were out and about in the morning fog. They would pass through the white haze from time to time going their busy ways.

"Look, the bajets are coming." Gaberilin pointed up to the sky as the three bajets circled slowly and descended.

"Welcome back!" Atris said to everyone. "We have been watching every morning since your

James Andrew Wilson

departure for your return. My dear boy Peter!" Atris said lifting her great talon feet and walking over to the boy. "I am so glad to see you well again!" She leaned her head down and Peter hugged the great animal.

Miyo and Peter rode on Atris, Andrew and the Master sat upon Frenwar, and Gaberilin and Mr. Timf took again to Aroh. They all departed from Acco and flew into the sky.

"What an adventure this has been!" Miyo said to Peter as they glided through the soft, fluffy clouds. "I should like to return to Patmos someday and chart the strange island. At first, when the island was dead, it seemed like such a horrid place. But after the forest sprouted forth and the rivers ran through, it seemed like such a wonderful place."

"Miyo?" Peter asked.

"Yes Peter?"

"Edesha said something about The Way. What is The Way?" Peter asked.

"The Way is our life. It is what we breathe and live. It is what we believe and what we follow. It is what we live by, it is our code, or religion as some would say."

Peter thought this over and then fell silent. He watched the scenery far below and spotted some trees, and a few small rolling hills.

The afternoon had almost slipped into night when they began to descend down through the clouds. Then everyone could see the tall towers of Edeneth glimmering in the setting light.

After they landed, everyone dismounted from the

bajets and bid them farewell, then they entered the castle. No one had expected them to return for a few more days, so there wasn't a single person waiting when they entered the hall.

By this time Peter was extremely tired. He asked if he could go to his room and then to the map room in the morning.

"I think that would be just fine," Edesha said. "Rest well young Peter, and you too Andrew."

* * * * *

Macthon dove quickly through the billowing smoke. He looked down to see a monstrous volcano erupting and spilling red-hot lava all over the black land. It was nearly evening, although this wouldn't change much until he was over the Petra Mountains. Abaddon was always covered with a thick black cloud, shutting any sunlight off that would dare to venture in. He could see hundreds of dark little shapes moving about below. The shadows were taking the melting lava, slopping it into buckets, and carrying it back to the armory. He grimaced at the lower forms of evil. He really despised the shadows and their "immaturity." "Annoying little dogs," as he would often refer to them.

His mighty wings scooped through the black smoke. Soon he found that the haze began to clear, and he could make out the jagged, spiky Petra Mountains. Just beyond the range was the great globe city of the queen. It was nestled down between the Catacomb Mountains to the north, and the northernmost mountains of Petra.

The city was a massive globe of web and sticky glue like liquid. Many wide, tightly bound strands of web reached out from the metropolis and were wrapped around the peaks of the mountains. The only entrance to the city was through an opening at the top. The outer shell of the web was coated with a slick goop making it nearly impossible to climb to the entrance, except for those that dwelt within. It was Aracon, the city of the Aracites and home of Queen Lebijez.

Macthon could now see the twinkling stars set against the black sky. Behind him, a black cloud rested, erupting from time to time with a red burst of flame. He thrust his mighty wings into the wind that blew in from the western sea, and made his way down toward the city.

* * * * *

The next morning, after breakfast, Peter found himself back in the charting chair of the map room. Miyo, Edesha, Solomon, Philophos, and Andrew were there as well. The chair lowered back and Peter gazed up again at the great map. Before he started to move the levers he shut his eyes and thought. The image of the dream came back to him. He remembered opening the Golden Book and seeing the map. Only it was different. There was a very distinct marking that the map in the castle lacked.

He opened his eyes and moved the lever until it rested over the dark land of Abaddon. After zooming

Peter Crossings And The Gate Of Abaddon

in, he searched the landscape trying to recall the exact location. The images of the Golden Book flashed back, and then he found it. Miyo had shown him how to make the marker appear. He pushed the silver button and a small black cursor appeared on the ceiling. Peter moved it over the location.

"This is the location of the gate," Peter said turning to Edesha. "I remember seeing it in the book."

"Nonsense!" Philophos suddenly blurted out. "How can we be sure of such a thing?"

"I saw it I tell you!" Peter said. "I remember that marking on the map in the book."

"How can we trust you though?" Philophos questioned.

"What do you mean?" Peter asked.

"How do we know that *you* are not somebody sent by Nefarious to lead us into a trap?"

All this time Andrew had been intently watching Solomon. The old figure's eyes never strayed from Peter. He seemed very deep in thought. At last when a sparkle came to his eyes, he spoke. "The boy is telling the truth," he said.

All eyes turned to Solomon. "Peter is telling the truth."

Edesha put a hand on Solomon's shoulder. "What is it friend?" he asked.

"There is something I must explain. But first, Miyo, mark the spot on the map."

Peter was helped out of the chair and Miyo hopped up into it. His old fingers flew over the buttons and levers and soon the words "The Gate" were inscribed over the spot Peter had marked.

"Good. Now let us meet in the Master's hall. I shall be there shortly." Then Solomon turned and left the map room.

"What is this all about?" Philophos grumbled as he left the room as well.

Miyo was very excited about the new addition to his map, and hardly stopped chattering about it all the way to the Master's hall. Herbert made sure everybody signed in before they all ascended the steps. While they climbed, Andrew questioned Peter.

"What do you think Solomon is going to say?" he asked.

"I'm not quite sure Andrew." As Peter said this, Andrew noticed that there was some worry in his friend's eyes.

"What's wrong Peter?"

But before he could answer the doors to the Master's hall opened. Inside they found that there was now a circle of royal chairs. There was one chair for each of them, and as they sat, Peter noticed there was an extra chair (not counting Solomon's, who had not come yet).

As they waited, Philophos continued to grumble and watch Peter strangely. Edesha seemed deep in thought and anticipation. Miyo was still excited about the map, but Peter and Andrew both felt nervous.

Soon the doors were opened once more, and there stood Jubal. She was now wearing a flowing yellow dress. Edesha stood immediately at the sight of her, and the others followed. Solomon came out from behind her and led her to the chair. Then Solomon asked the guards to shut the door, after

Peter Crossings And The Gate Of Abaddon

which he sat.

Solomon started off with a long sigh. He bowed his head and closed his eyes and Peter saw his lips moving. Then he raised his head and opened his eyes. "Some time ago, before I came to live in Edeneth, I had a small house near Galatian Wood. There I lived with my wonderful wife and our lovely young daughter. I was at that time a gardener for much of the trees in the woods. I was a much younger man and not much involved in the wide world.

"One evening while we were having dinner, there came a knock on our door. I went to answer it. It was snowing then, and very cold outside. There at my door stood a man dressed entirely in white. In his arms he clutched a package covered with a blue cloth. I invited him in, but he refused. He handed me the package and gave me these instructions.

" 'You are to travel to the Land Beyond with this package. There you will meet a man who will take you to a building. Follow his instructions.' He then handed me the package and before I could ask another question, he was gone.

"I told nothing of this to my wife nor daughter for some time. I took the package and hid it under one of the trees in the orchard. Try as I might, I could not forget about it, and I had many restless nights. I'm not sure what I was afraid of, but I couldn't bring myself to take the journey. I had never ventured much further than the woods, so to go to the Land Beyond was far from my mind.

"So the years went by, and my daughter grew into a running and singing girl. I began to grow older, and

James Andrew Wilson

my wife stayed the love of my life. Then one day when I was tending to the orchard, I fell from the ladder. I landed on something hard and brushed away the leaves to find the package I had buried there. A great amount of guilt came over me and I felt compelled to do what that man had told me.

"My wife did not understand, but she supported my decision, only she asked that I take somebody with me. I had a good friend that I worked with in the orchard and I asked him to come. At that time the Yafna still visited the land, and one of them took us to the portal.

"There was much in the Land Beyond that I did not understand, but I was soon met by a man in a black suit. He told me he had only been waiting for a few minutes. This I did not understand until much later in my life when I discovered that our Eden time is much different than the Land Beyond. One second here may be ten years there, or it may be no time at all. Where as many years here, may only be a few minutes there.

"And so the man took me in what he called a car, and we traveled to a building. He then instructed me to take the package inside, unwrap it, and place it on a certain shelf. My friend and I left the car and went into the building. It was raining very hard, and lightning often lit up the sky.

"I unwrapped the package, which had much dirt on it from being buried so long, and inside I found the Golden Book. I had never heard of it before, so I did not find much interest in it. I placed it on the shelf the man in the suit had instructed me to. He had

Peter Crossings And The Gate Of Abaddon

also told me that somebody would come, and that I was to show them to the book."

At this point Peter began to realize what Solomon was talking about. "It was me, wasn't it?" Peter asked.

"Yes," Solomon replied. "You came Peter, and you were not too much younger than you are now. I was very surprised and I must say that I did not understand at all what was going on, but I took you to the book. At least, I tried to, but something went wrong. I lost you in the library. I could not find my friend for a long time either. Finally I found him, and we searched for you, but you were gone. The book was still on the shelf, and the library was empty.

"I had no other instructions, so we decided to leave. I left the Golden Book there and we left the library. The man in the suit was standing outside in the rain. He said nothing, but had us follow him and soon we were back in another car and heading toward the portal.

"My friend and I returned home. My wife and daughter were safe, and it appeared as though no time had passed at all. I went back to working in the orchard, and my friend did as well. Soon though, my friend told me that he was going on a trip and that he wouldn't be back for some time. He never told me where he was going; he just left the very next day.

"During that time that he was away, I had to work extra hard in the orchard and had less time to spend with my wife and daughter. Then one terrible, dark day, my life was forever changed. I was working out in the woods and it was very hot. And as I looked up through the trees I saw a billow of smoke rising into the air. And then I heard the scream of my daughter. I dropped what I was doing and ran as fast as I could back toward the house. But...I was too late.

"I never saw my wife again, but my daughter survived, although the impact of the fire stayed with her for the rest of her life. It blinded her." Solomon stood then, tears streaming down his withered old face. "Jubal is my daughter. The only surviving family I have."

Peter and Andrew were very surprised by this, but Edesha and the others were even more so. Edesha stood. "Solomon, Jubal...I am very sorry."

Solomon sat back down. "There is more that I must tell." He wiped away some of the tears. "I scooped Jubal into my arms and took her up the hill to my friend's house. I hoped that he had returned from his journey, and he had. He took us in for the night.

"I told him everything that had happened. He told me that he had seen some strange figures run from my house after it had been lit on fire. He told me that I wasn't safe here, that neither of us were. So the next day we left for Edeneth, and have lived here ever since.

"It was a longer time before I learned another startling truth. As my daughter grew into this beautiful woman, I had a fear growing within me. My friend seemed to become attached to her, and I felt as though I could not trust him."

Then Edesha stood. "Your friend. It was Riousafen, wasn't it?" he asked with horror in his eyes.

Solomon looked into Edesha's deep eyes. "Yes... Riousafen was the one."

Peter watched as Edesha sat back down and shut his eyes tightly. "Who is Riousafen?" Peter asked.

Solomon answered, "Riousafen no longer goes by that name. He now goes by his true and rightful title: Nefarious."

"Nefarious?" Andrew asked. "But isn't that the person who we're fighting against?"

"Yes," Edesha replied. "Riousafen was once a part of this castle. But he became corrupted and now he resides in Abaddon as the ruler of the shadows."

Solomon continued, "I couldn't figure out why on that awful day, Riousafen didn't come running down to my house. He said he saw some strange figures running from the house, but why didn't he come down to help? It was because he had set the house on fire, and the story of the strange figures was all a lie. The trip he had taken was to Abaddon. I never understood why, until now." Then he turned and looked at Peter. "You met him in the library, didn't you Peter?"

The image of the man with hollow eyes from Peter's dream flashed across his mind. "Yes..." Peter replied. "I did meet him in the library. He told me he was your friend. I had dropped the Golden Book and he came and picked it up. He looked at it with me and then went away quickly."

"That explains it," Edesha said. "Riousafen then went to Abaddon to make a deal with the sealed evil. He knew how to open the gate and where to find it. That is why he came to the castle, to get the key."

"Yes, but one thing still stood in his way," said

Solomon. "Perhaps he tried to kill me in the fire because he thought I had looked in the Golden Book, but I never had. And once he discovered that, his only other threat was Peter."

"And therefore," Edesha said, "he sent his shadows after you Peter, in hopes that he might kill you. Even that devourer was intent on killing you. The devourer's are not under his command, but it seems that all evil is intent on your destruction."

"Or his capture," said Miyo. "If the enemy were to capture Peter, they could use him as a sort of bait. I have studied the dark Petra Mountains that surround Abaddon. There are only two ways into the land. One is through the Petra Passage. It is a narrow canyon not more than a hundred strides in width."

"Why can't the bajets fly over the mountains?" Philophos asked.

"At one time they may have been able to. But the air is so fowl now that most bajets would suffocate. Atris is the only one that I know who may have the strength and speed needed to pass through that smoke. But nearer to the Aracite city, which is just on the other side of the northern Petra Mountains, the air is not quite as thick. Fresh air from the sea travels through there, and there may be a chance for some bajets to make it that way, but not many of them."

"Just what are you getting at Miyo?" Philophos questioned.

"Just this, if Peter were to be captured and we were to attempt to rescue him, our chances of winning a battle on the enemy's turf are near impossible."

"Then what is to be done?" Philophos asked.

Peter Crossings And The Gate Of Abaddon

"The boys cannot stay here in the castle for the rest of their lives. I assume they have families at home."

"No, they cannot stay here in Eden forever," Edesha agreed. "But, neither can they return home, for they would be in even more danger there, until Nefarious is defeated."

A silence came over the room. Andrew and Peter both felt rather frightened. All the others sat deep in thought. Finally Edesha stood. "These are matters of war. Let my hall not be the place in which we discuss these things. And let the lady and children be free from these words of gloom. Let us gather again in the meeting room after lunch. Peter, Andrew, feel free to explore the castle, only stay inside, and Jubal, you are free to do as you will."

* * * * *

Peter and Andrew didn't see much of Edesha, Solomon, Miyo, or Philophos for the next three days, except on rare occasion. They did much exploring and discovered many things. Andrew's favorite place quickly became the kitchen. Peter's though, was the library. They discovered while in the library that Mr. Timf was a type of person called a Widdle.

"A Widdle?" Andrew had said. "What a funny type of name."

Solomon told them that the Widdles rarely ever went by their first names, and that some of them didn't even have first names, only last.

They questioned Mr. Timf about this. "Oh yes, that be the truth. My great granddad didn't have a first name. Nor did my mother."

"Do you?" Andrew asked.

"Aye, but I couldn't tell it to ya." He winked and sniffed.

They also walked along the halls and looked at all of the paintings. Most of them were by Ethral, but they only found a few that were alive. Mostly the living ones were landscapes, in which the sun would rise and set, or a river would flow, or trees would sway. They didn't find any other living portraits.

They listened to Jubal play her harp, and talked with her often as well.

"So how did you get to be so good at playing the harp?" Andrew asked. "I mean, being blind and everything."

"I was gifted," she replied. "I was given the ability to sing and play the harp. I use it to return the favor."

"Return it to who?" Peter asked.

"Why, Tehus of course," was her reply.

Peter thought often about his parents. He was surprised at how much he missed them. He would often find himself staring out a window wondering if he would ever see them again, and then something would tell that he would. But that fear continued to come back.

Finally one evening, Edesha met with them and took them to the courtyard where the breakfast gazebo was. It was a warm evening when they went and lay under a tall weeping willow.

"If someone wanted to be a Servant of the Light, what would they need to do?" Peter asked.

"First of all, they would need to be a follower of The Way. But there is more to a Servant of the Light than merely following. A Servant is one that commits their life to the work of Tehus. They use all their abilities and efforts to further His glory. They are not ashamed; they are bold and strong. They are warriors for Tehus."

"So, is every single Servant a warrior?" Andrew asked. "I mean, what about Jubal? Is she a Servant of the Light?"

"I am glad you ask of Jubal. Jubal is a wonderful example of a Servant. Though she does not wield a sword against the shadows of Sheol, she lives her life for Tehus. There is more to being a Servant than fighting evil, sometimes it requires merely being a servant of your gifts."

Peter lay back in the grass with his hands behind his head and sighed. "Edesha, why did Tehus choose for me to find the Golden Book? Why didn't he choose Solomon, or you?"

Edesha sighed. "Sometimes, Tehus takes the simple things of this world and shames the wise with them."

"What does that mean?" Andrew asked.

Edesha picked up a seed from the grass. "Look at this seed." He held it up. "See how tiny it is? And yet this tiny seed, this simple seed, can become an enormous tree. Then someone with lots of wisdom can look at the tree, and look at that seed, and never understand how it is possible."

"Oh…" said Andrew. "So it's kind of like Tehus choose Peter to find this book and know these things because he is like the seed. Like the little thing that nobody else would think of choosing. But Tehus did, and he is going to use him to confuse somebody."

Edesha chuckled. "Something like that Andrew." Then Edesha laid a hand on Peter's shoulder. "Peter...when you looked in the Golden Book, was there anything else that you remember seeing?"

"Well, yes. I have been thinking about that for a while. I remember reading some type of riddle. Only bits and pieces of it have come back to me," he replied.

"That is what we need," Edesha said. "Try Peter, try to remember what you read. I want you to write it down as it comes to you. I will make sure there is some paper and an ink feather in your room."

Peter nodded. He stared up at the starry sky, and for the first time, really noticed the stars. "Wow, the stars are so bright," he said.

"Ah yes, that reminds me," said Edesha. "In Eden, we pass through seven seasons. During this season the stars are very bright. This is also the season in which we celebrate the Festival of the Stars."

"Cool, a festival! Where is it going to be at? What are we going to do?" Andrew asked excitedly.

"It is held at Edren. Unfortunately most of the town was burned in the battle, but the Square remained, and many of the surrounding shops and houses. It is a joyous time of celebration, but my favorite part is the fireworks."

"I love fireworks!" Andrew exclaimed.

Edesha laughed. "You will see many of them come two days. But I fear that I have some more things to attend to this evening, so I must leave you now." Edesha rose to his feet.

"Edesha," Peter said, "before you go, I have a question."

"Yes Peter, what is it?"

"Have you figured out what's going to happen to me? Am I going to stay here in Eden forever?" Peter asked with tears in his eyes. As much as he loved Eden, he missed his parents terribly.

Edesha turned and knelt down. "No my dear boy. We will make sure you return home and are safe."

Then he stood and walked briskly out of the courtyard.

* * * * *

The words were blurry, but they were there. Peter smoothed down the page and tried to understand the riddle forming before his eyes. The library shelves towered over him. He could still hear the rain pouring outside.

Deep in sleep, Peter watched himself and tried to remember what he was reading. Some of the words stayed, and when he woke, Andrew was still sleeping. It was still dark out, though the candle on the nightstand burnt softly. He pushed aside the covers and picked up the piece of paper, then began to write with the feather.

The gate that lies in land of dark
Holds a power not all may hark

It's secret is two, make sure both are known
If not, the one who attempts, will be unknown

The first secret is this:

If three are seen take one only
Only, take one wisely, for two will kill
Do not take three, for death will follow thee

Before you turn, beware
Remember two secrets must be known

The second secret is this:

And that was it. Peter put the feather pen down. He couldn't remember anything else. Finally he found sleep again.

* * * * *

The next evening, Edesha met Peter and Andrew as they were eating.

"There is something I would like to show you," he said. "Follow me."

The Master led them down stairs and through halls. Soon Peter and Andrew no longer knew where they were in the castle, and nothing around seemed familiar. Edesha stopped suddenly at the end of a very long hall. There stood two tall doors with golden rings hanging down as their handles. There was a single keyhole with a locking mechanism connecting the two doors. Edesha reached into his cloak and drew forth a silver key. He opened the doors and they stepped in.

At first the room was dark as night. The Master reached over in the dark and struck something like a match. Then Peter and Andrew watched as a small flame, it seemed, flew around the room. Every few feet it would light a candle illuminating the room a little more. After three candles were lit, they discovered that the flame was traveling across something like a string connected to every candle in the room. The flame traveled across the string until it finally dropped from the ceiling to a very large candle upon a table in the center of the room. When the flame hit that candle it seemed at first to burst, then settled down to a bright steady glow. Around the room were seven pillars. In between each, on the wall behind, a candle glowed. Down three stairs there was a large table with seven ornately carved chairs around it. One chair sat at the head of the table, opposite of the door to the room. The pillars rested directly behind each of the chairs. Wrapped around each of the pillars, at the height of a full-grown man, was a golden strand of leather securing a sheathed sword tightly to the pillar. All of the swords' handles were different except for the same symbol etched upon them: a golden tree bearing seven branches, barren of any leaves.

The Master walked to the opposite side of the room and sat at the head of the table, as the boys stood silently atop the stairs in awe.

"This is the meeting room of the seven High Servants of Eden." The Master extended a hand to each of the chairs. "Zebulun, Issachar, Asher,

Naphtali, Manasseh, Ephraim." Then the Master rested a hand upon his chest. "And Edesha, High Servant and Master of Edeneth, the head of the Seven."

The boys stood still in awe. When Edesha had announced his name he seemed to rise in power and stature before their eyes. "These are the Seven commissioned by Tehus to proclaim His will to Eden, and protect the followers of The Way from the evil of Sheol." The Master stood from his seat and went to the pillar behind. He reached and drew forth the sword from its sheath. The blade reflected the candle flickers of the room and glowed brightly. Peter noticed that it was a golden blade. "This is an old sword. My father wielded it long before I. Each blade about this room was formed in the seven years of awakening when the Light of Tehus was still strong. They have begun to glow again." Even as they watched, all the swords about the room seemed to glow a soft blue light. "The time is soon upon us when the Seven will gather and take forth their blades of power. A battle will soon take place that will decide the war."

The boys watched as the blue light of the blade illuminated Edesha's face. He swung the sword once or twice and then placed it back in its sheath.

"Come, I have one more thing to show you." After a short walk they came to yet another room the boys had not known of. Inside, they found many things of interest to young adventurous boys. A great number of suits of armor, and swords, and axes, and bows covered the walls. This was a darker room, except at the far end where a small table rested.

Peter Crossings And The Gate Of Abaddon

Edesha led them to the table and uncovered what lay beneath a green sheet of fabric. Two swords glinted in the candlelight.

"Here, these are for you." He handed them each a blade. The swords were made for their exact height, and though they seemed heavy, they were easy enough to wield. "May you never have to use these. But in case we are not able to hold off the shadows, you may have to defend yourselves in the end. These blades were also formed long ago, and the strength of Tehus still dwells in them."

Also laying on the table were two belts, which Edesha handed to the boys. "Keep these blades with you at all times." They fastened the belts to their waists, and slid the swords into the sheaths.

"Now come, night is upon us, and tomorrow we shall attend the festival." He led them out of the room and shut the door behind. The sound of the large, solid door echoed down the hall.

Chapter Ten

The Unexpected Visitors

The day of the festival had come. It was early morning when Philophos came and woke Andrew and Peter.

"Up, up! Get up!" Philophos' manners had not improved. They got dressed, made sure they had their swords, and then left the room.

They followed Philophos outside and around to the edge of the castle. A cart bearing many sorts of wonderful foods was parked there. A door was opened to the kitchen, and from it came Jatod, carrying bags of food in all four arms.

"Good morning boys!" he boomed tossing the sacks into the cart. "Are you ready for the festival?"

"Am I ever!" Andrew said. "Are you going to be there Jatod?"

"Of course I am! What would a festival be without

James Andrew Wilson

food?" Jatod ducked into the kitchen and came forth again carrying more food.

Peter and Andrew were asked to help load the cart, which they did very happily. After they had finished, Jatod took them into the kitchen where he had prepared a scrumptious breakfast for them.

They spent most of the morning going about chores in preparation for the festival. Everybody seemed a bit more joyful than before. They all went about their business singing and smiling.

Toward noon, everyone gathered at the front of the castle. There were at least twenty carts filled with all sorts of things, such as food, tents, chairs, and Andrew's favorite: fireworks. There were many people the boys didn't recognize. They did spot Solomon though. He was leading Jubal into a seat on one of the carts. Horses, the first animals the boys had recognized in Eden, pulled all of the carts. Peter and Andrew sat atop a packed cart of tent supplies as the convoy set out down a long road from the castle. They bounded down the road laughing and singing. It seemed no more than an hour when they reached the town of Edren, but it was slightly longer than that.

Peter and Andrew could see that a lot of the town was in ruin, but the area they went through was still intact. It consisted mostly of tall houses and brick roads. They came in through the main street where many people were already busily preparing things. They passed under a bridge connecting two of the tall buildings. Peter and Andrew heard giggling and laughing. They looked up to see a row of girls pointing and smiling at them. The girls quickly ducked

Peter Crossings And The Gate Of Abaddon

down when the boys saw them.

They finally came to the Town Square. Peter and Andrew hopped off the cart. The Square was actually a large circle with shops of all sorts surrounding it. Within the center stood a tall, ornately shaped fountain streaming forth pure water that glistened in the afternoon sun. Peter and Andrew were introduced to many people of the town whose names they hopelessly forgot.

Tents started sprouting up all over the road and the Square like wildflowers. Everyone was so busy and intent on their duties that Peter and Andrew soon felt that they had been forgotten.

"Hey Peter, while they set up, let's go take a look around," Andrew said standing from the edge of the fountain and dusting himself off.

"Don't you think we should stay here? What if someone comes looking for us?"

"Oh come on, I just want to go look at some of the shops."

"Remember what happened last time we went exploring?" Peter replied.

"Yeah I know, but Edesha didn't tell us to stay in one spot. Besides, we'll only look at the shops that are in the Square." Andrew smiled.

"Well...oh, alright, let's go." Peter stood, and they started exploring the town.

At first they just walked by the shops looking at their strange names. They had names such as: Calliwho's Creations and Cough Remedies, or Timber's Teeth Specialist (which Peter and Andrew thought must be a dentist), and many other peculiar sorts of names. Then they came to a store that they decided to enter.

"Mr. Sockeye's Swords. Well this might be interesting," Peter said as they opened the door into the shop.

Inside they found a surprisingly clean store with walls covered in hundreds of different swords and weapons. Some of them were thin and straight, others were thick and jagged with many spikes and sharp points. Suddenly a figure jumped out from behind the counter and in a flash there was a sword at Andrew's throat. A man not much taller than the boys with a long beard, wrinkled face, and a patch over his left eye, glared down his blade at Andrew.

Peter, surprised by his own actions, swiped back his cloak and in a flash drew forth his blade. "Leave him alone!" he said to the little man, pointing his sword to the plump belly.

"Aye! Forgive me little sir. I thought you was somebody else." He lowered his blade from Andrew's throat. "Ye can sheath your sword. I won't hurt ye, nor your friend," the man said holding up his arms.

Peter slowly sheathed his sword and wrapped his cloak back over it.

"Alright, now that we've got that settled, what be ye needin' today from Sockeye's shop?" the man asked as he hopped up and sat dangling his feet on the counter.

"Uh, we're new to this town and we were just taking a look around," Andrew said.

"Oh, I see. Well, my name is Mr. Sockeye, and this here is my shop. I apologize for all that, ya see…"

Peter Crossings And The Gate Of Abaddon

Mr. Sockeye leaned in close and whispered, "There's a very nasty person in this here town that has a truffle bit a problem with me, and I can't be too careful ya see." Mr. Sockeye leaned back and crossed his arms. "So…what can I help ye with then?"

As Peter and Andrew watched Mr. Sockeye, they realized that he was a Widdle, and a rather feisty one at that. "Oh, nothing really, we're just here for the festival today," Peter said.

"Aye! The festival, 'tis a joyous time. What part of Eden did ye come from?"

"We came from the castle Edeneth," Peter replied.

"Edeneth!" Mr. Sockeye exclaimed. "How did you two happen to be there?"

Peter hesitated, and wondered if he should tell Mr. Sockeye the reason he had come to Eden, when the door suddenly burst open. In came a tall person in a long black cloak. He nearly stepped on the boys as he stomped over to Mr. Sockeye and picked him up by the collar.

"We have some business to settle buddy," said the tall person.

"Uh, yes…yes…" Mr. Sockeye looked at Peter with pleading eyes. Peter wasn't sure what he should do, if he should help Mr. Sockeye, or leave him be. Then he thought of the terrible things that might happen to him, and he decided to help the Widdle.

Peter pulled out his sword and thrust it squarely at the cloaked figure's leg. "Ahhrgh!" The figure didn't budge but continued to hold the Widdle tightly in his grip. "What do you think you're doing?" came a terrible hissing voice from the cloak.

It turned and glared down at Peter. Even through the shadow that the cloak cast on the creature's appearance, Peter saw a horrific face with penetrating green eyes. When the face saw Peter, it dropped Mr. Sockeye, and stepped toward the boy.

Its voice changed to a calm soothing tone, "Excuse me, I didn't see you there."

Peter backed away, his sword still drawn. "Who, who are you?"

"No one special really. Don't worry, I won't hurt you." The figure stepped closer. It reached out a hand toward Peter. Then in an instant, four spiked hands grabbed Peter and hurled him high where they clenched him so hard he felt he would break.

"Let him go!" Andrew dove at the cloak and stabbed it with his sword. The cloaked creature shrieked a terrible scream, then turned and glared down at Andrew while still clutching Peter. Andrew shrank back in fear and let out a breathless word, "Aracite…"

"Arhh!" Mr. Sockeye came suddenly flying through the air with a large axe. He whacked the Aracite in the head and sent it falling to the ground. Peter fell from the death grip.

"Go! I'll hold him off!" Mr. Sockeye shouted to the boys. They stood quickly and rushed for the door. The Aracite reached out a hand and grasped Peter by the foot. It snarled and growled at him.

"Leave him be!" Mr. Sockeye shouted, crushing the axe down on the creature again. It hissed and screamed.

Peter and Andrew ran out of the shop and into the Square. They heard screaming from the shop, and as they turned back to look, the Aracite bounded out a window, spilling glass everywhere as it landed. Its cloak was shredded revealing its spider like body that was now wounded and bleeding.

Peter and Andrew ran. The Aracite bounded after them. They darted away and hid behind a pile of boxes. The Aracite came leaping over the boxes and stood with its back to them. They breathed deep and then dashed away as the Aracite turned and screamed after them. Just then, a tall muscular figure bounded in between the predator and prey wielding a brilliant sword.

"Stand back fiend!" It was Gaberilin. He spun his sword around and thrust it into the creature that fell to the ground shocked and wide eyed.

Gaberilin took his sword from the Aracite and turned to the boys. "Come quickly, follow me!" he said.

They followed him hurriedly back toward the fountain. The previous joy and commotion of the town was now replaced with a group of shocked bystanders. Everyone stood motionless as though they were in a trance. At the fountain they found Philophos and Edesha waiting.

"Peter, are you alright?" Philophos asked with genuine worry in his eyes.

"Yes, I'm fine," he replied.

"Stay near, we're not sure that that was the only one," Gaberilin said as he stood in front of them clutching his sword.

Peter looked up at the Master with frightened eyes. Edesha wrapped his cloak around Peter and pulled him tightly to his side.

"Go, you must leave!" Mr. Sockeye came suddenly up to the group. He was out of breath and wielding a blood stained axe.

Gaberilin stood tall and pointed his sword down at the Widdle. "Who are you?" he asked.

"I am Mr. Sockeye. I own a shop here, but that ain't matter. You's all got to leave now!" he said looking cautiously around. Most of the people of the town had already disappeared into the houses.

"Why?" Gaberilin asked. "What do you know about the Aracite?"

"I uh…" Mr. Sockeye stammered.

"Speak!" Gaberilin poked the Widdle's belly with his sword.

"I have been doing some dealing with the Aracites. But this one wasn't after the boy, well, not at first any how."

"You have been dealing with the Aracites?" Gaberilin moved closer to Mr. Sockeye. "In any other circumstance I would throw you in the dungeon this second, but tell me what you know first." Gaberilin grabbed the axe from Mr. Sockeye.

"I heard rumor of the Aracites looking for a boy during the festival," Mr. Sockeye confessed.

"How many?" Gaberilin asked slowly.

Mr. Sockeye hesitated. "Nearly a hundred or more. They says they would get him no matter what the cost be."

Gaberilin was furious. He threw the axe back into

Peter Crossings And The Gate Of Abaddon

the hands of the Widdle. "You will stay and fight! If you survive I will deal with you later."

"Jatod!" Andrew exclaimed. Jatod came up to the group just then with Mr. Timf following him.

"Everyone is heading back to the castle. We must leave now," Jatod said.

"No, we can not leave," Edesha said. "We would endanger the others if we followed them. The Aracites will kill whomever they must. Let us be the only ones they have a chance to."

"But how can we hold off a hundred of them?" Philophos asked.

"Trust in the Light!" Edesha said and he swung back his cloak. A bright blue light glowed as he withdrew his mighty sword.

Philophos hesitated. Then he threw back his cloak as well and drew forth a sword.

"We stand to the end. Protect Peter," Edesha said. Everyone backed around the two boys. Jatod stood with all four arms ready for battle. In his top right hand he wielded a cast iron pan, which left his other three hands ready to smash heads. Mr. Timf held tightly to his sword. Mr. Sockeye gulped, and clenched his axe. Gaberilin stood tall and mighty; looking intently for any movement. No one was in sight and the town stood motionless.

It appeared that the burnt and crumbled buildings beyond suddenly started moving. It was actually the dark shapes of Aracites scurrying through the wreckage. Then suddenly, three black-cloaked figures dropped from the sky to the ground. Peter and the others looked up and saw the roofs crawling with the black spider-like beasts. They were hissing and drooling as one by one they dropped to the ground below.

From nearly every rooftop surrounding the Square, the Aracites fell. The creatures took slow simultaneous steps until they were no more than three feet away from the protectors. The hideous beasts snarled and growled. They smelled rank and great drops of sea green drool slid from their lips.

"Give it up fools. We have come for the child," one of the taller ones said in a deep guttural voice.

Peter peered out from those surrounding him. He saw the Aracites circled around them and still dropping from the rooftops. He ducked back in and looked frightfully up at Edesha who stood upon the edge of the fountain. Edesha looked down at the boy.

"Trust in the Light Peter. Do not fear. When the time comes, take the leap, He will protect you," Edesha said. Peter was not sure that he knew what this meant, but he nodded his head and clenched tightly to his sword.

"Wait, take this," Peter said. He reached into his pocket and pulled out a folded piece of paper. "This is all I could remember of the riddle," he said handing it to Edesha. The Master took it, and with sad eyes placed it in his cloak.

Gaberilin let out a mighty shout and charged the Aracites. He dove into the black mess, slashing his blade with force. The others bounded in as well. Mr. Sockeye wielded his axe, crashing into the tar-like black skin. Mr. Timf slid underneath a pair of legs and came up behind the monster, then stabbed it in

Peter Crossings And The Gate Of Abaddon

the back with his small sword. The Aracites fought quickly and skillfully. They dodged most strikes, and gave many.

Edesha stood towering over Andrew and Peter. His sword shone like a great beacon as he swung it, sending Aracites flying in a great arc. The black figures kept coming.

Gaberilin had been forced to the edge of the Square. His back was to a wall, and all around him the Aracites moved in. He looked up and saw a windowsill right above him. Just before the Aracites could bound in and rip him apart, he scrambled onto the sill. The creatures below jumped at him. One grabbed him by the foot. He slipped down off the sill and dropped his sword into the swarm. The death grip of a dark hand pulled him down as he held on with all of his might to the windowsill. His fingers slid, and he fell. The Aracites covered his body and ripped at his clothes. Suddenly, they were lifted off him and thrown back into the sky. He scurried back to his feet as Jatod wrestled with the black ones, pounding them in the heads with his frying pan. His four arms had the strength to fend off one Aracite each to their own. He grabbed most of them by the heads and sent them flying, and crashing into walls.

Gaberilin found his sword. It was dented and stained from battle and much toil. Grabbing it up, he fought his way back toward the fountain.

The two Widdles had fought their way to Mr. Sockeye's shop. They went in quickly and shut the door.

"Here," Mr. Sockeye said through breaths, "take

this." He bounded over the counter and swiped a sharp object from the wall, then tossed the deadly looking axe to Mr. Timf.

Mr. Timf grabbed it by the handle and examined it. It had many jagged points and a long sharp spike at the top. Mr. Sockeye ran across the counter and grabbed another smaller axe in his other hand. He continued running across the top of the counter and then bounded out the window yelling and screaming.

Mr. Timf was surprised by his actions. He held tightly to the axe, crawled up onto the counter, and leapt head first out the window. As he flew to the ground, his axe met furiously with an Aracite, sending it to the dirt. The Widdles fought wrathfully through the creatures, breaking many of the enemy's bones with their mighty axes.

Peter and Andrew swiped at the Aracites with their little swords. The creatures had managed to scurry closer, but many of them were still flung back by the fury of Edesha.

All this time Philophos watched in horror, only wielding his sword once. He stood near to the fountain. Soon the Aracites came close to him and began reaching out for him. "Stay back! Get back, you— you, ugly beasts you. Get back!" Philophos swung his sword but to no avail. Soon he was being trampled by the Aracites. One of their long legs stepped down on his leg, breaking it at the kneecap. Philophos screamed and reeled in pain.

Gaberilin bounded in and flashed his sword through an Aracite. The circle around the fountain had grown much smaller, as there was now nearly no

Peter Crossings And The Gate Of Abaddon

room to stand. The Aracites crowded closer.

"Stand fast!" Edesha shouted, slicing cleanly through one of the beasts.

They fought and fought for what seemed like hours. The sun neared its last light when Gaberilin felled the final Aracite. All about the Square lay a massive heap of black bodies. They already stunk. The Widdles came to the fountain, crawling over the dead ones. Everyone was exhausted.

"We've done it," Gaberilin said, falling and sitting on top of one of the dead creatures. His sword fell to the ground. But then, as everyone looked at him, Gaberilin's face suddenly turned pale with horror and shock.

He reached down and swiped up his sword. "The boys! The boys are gone!" Gaberilin bounded around the fountain and then began to search the dead heap.

Everyone panicked and searched with him. Jatod stumbled over a pile of bodies and heard a noise. "Ahh, help..." it moaned.

He threw away an Aracite to find the beaten and bruised body of Philophos. "Over here!" Jatod shouted.

Everyone came and stood around. Philophos was not dead, but his leg was broken and he was bleeding badly.

"Oh, Philophos..." Edesha quickly sheathed his sword and picked Philophos up into his arms. Philophos screamed in pain.

"Quickly everyone! To the castle!" Edesha said as he crawled over the bodies.

"But what about the boys! What do we do?"

Gaberilin asked crawling after him.

"Yes, what are we going to do?" Jatod asked.

Edesha paused. "The enemy has no doubt taken them. We do not yet have the army gathered that is needed.

"But the Aracites will reach their city before the night is over!" Gaberilin said.

"That is why we must hurry! Come!" Edesha declared.

They finally crawled over the last few Aracites and made their way quickly to Edeneth.

* * * * *

They leapt high above the ground from tree to tree, flashing like black bullets. The Aracites bounded through the forest clutching their captives. They went, never ceasing, with great speed and dexterity. At first, Peter and Andrew had tried to struggle loose of the creatures tight grip, but finally gave up. The Aracites had them tightly bound in their strong hands.

Peter began to feel sick as he bounced up and down. He closed his eyes and tried to control himself. He remembered exactly when he had been taken. Philophos had just said something to the Aracites, and then in the blink of an eye, Andrew and him were swept away down a long alley, through much rubble, and then into an open field. It had not been long before they entered the forest. He wondered if any one had even noticed that they were gone.

The Aracites flashed through the night unheed-

Peter Crossings And The Gate Of Abaddon

ingly. After nearly two hours they came finally to the long end of Even Wood and into a wide expanse of barren land. After a short while the ground beneath them changed from long, dry, silky grass to cracked and broken dirt. This area was known as the Dead Lands. There were some places where the cracks were three or more feet wide and fell into unknown darkness. The Aracites leapt over these with ease.

They went on, no one speaking a single word. The cover of darkness, lit before by the brilliant stars, had begun to grow darker as they neared their destination. The air felt thick like smoke, and smelled of ash. Soon Peter and Andrew were coughing from the choking air. It would clear for a second in some areas, and they would gulp up the clean oxygen. After some time of this, the Aracites finally slowed, and then halted.

They set the boys down to their sides, still holding tightly to their cloaks. As the boys looked before them they saw what was know as Aracon. A great globe reaching nearly two miles high loomed over them. It was nestled between two monstrous mountain ranges. From within one of the mountain ranges, a great red smoke crawled over the sky. There stood the great globe city of the Aracites.

The two Aracites grabbed up the boys again, and darted toward the foot of the globe. They reached it quickly and jammed their claws into the sticky wall. Indeed, it seemed as though they were spiders as they scaled the outer wall nearing the top with great speed. When they stood finally at the edge of the great hole, and the very top of the web city, Peter could see for many miles. He looked toward the mountains of red smoke and saw over their peaks a very dark land. Blood curling screams came from the black land. Peter looked away from the dark place and down through a great opening in the globe. He saw within, a mass of smaller globes and long strands of web running throughout like a labyrinth. Then, before he could take another breath, the Aracites grasped the boys tightly and bound in.

They fell for a moment through the air passing by webs and globes until they landed abruptly on a long rope of web. It was barely wide enough for the Aracites to scale across it. They moved quickly across the web bridge toward a very large globe in the center. The entire city seemed to glow like it was a greenhouse. Peter began to sweat from the heat in the city as he bounced along in the clutches of the Aracite. All around him he could see the black shapes of Aracites crawling and leaping throughout Aracon.

It was not long until they came to the large globe in the center of the city. There was a small opening in the web, just large enough for the Aracites to slip through. Once inside, they found an amazing room, with a majestic throne that seemed to crawl throughout the entire expanse. Upon it sat the figure of a woman, cloaked in dark black with long hair the same silky, midnight color. Her face was beautiful, but the rest of her body was covered in the cloak. She smiled when the boys were brought into her chambers.

Her voice was soothing as she spoke, "Welcome, Peter and Andrew. Welcome to the Core of Aracon. This is my city."

Peter Crossings And The Gate Of Abaddon

She then looked at the two Aracites, "Leave us. I will call for you later." The Aracites bowed, and then ducked quickly out through the small door.

Her shimmering green eyes turned back to the boys. "Please, be seated." As she spoke, two small chairs crawled up directly beneath the boys. They sat on the web seats, which to their surprise were very comfortable. "There we are. Now I know whom you two are, but let me introduce myself. I am Queen Lebijez, ruler of Aracon, and lord of the Aracites."

Neither of the boys spoke a word. "I can see that you have not much to say. Perhaps then I shall ask of you a question… are you afraid of spiders?"

The boys sat silently. "I can see that we will have to persuade you to speak." Lebijez stood from her throne and revealed her surprising height. "No matter, we have many ways of making fools speak…" her voice hissed as she moved closer to the boys.

Chapter Eleven

Aracon City

Edesha sped up the stairs. "Summon Atris!" he shouted down to Gaberilin. "Tell her to send out the calling."

Gaberilin turned and ran quickly back out the door. He sprinted to the stables to see if by chance Atris was there. She wasn't. He bounded up the rickety steps in the corner of the stable to the small tower. Grabbing the long horn he blew into it. It sounded three times through the night. He blew it once more, and then rushed down the stairs. Gaberilin swiped a glowing torch from its spot on the wall, and burst out of the stable.

Atris could see the flickering of the torch as she dove down toward the cliff. She slowed herself and landed softly on the hard ground.

"Atris!" Gaberilin exclaimed. "How did it happen that you were here so quickly?"

"I was already on my way, the fireworks had not

James Andrew Wilson

yet gone off, I feared something had happened," the great bajet said.

"Something *has* happened, something terrible! The boys have been taken by Aracites! The Master has summoned you."

"What did he say?" Atris asked, quickly rising from the ground.

"He said to tell you to send out the calling," Gaberilin conveyed.

"I will return!" Atris promised, and then flew off with amazing speed into the night sky.

Gaberilin turned and dashed back into the castle. He ran up a flight of stairs and began calling for Edesha. Soon he found him. He entered into the room to find Philophos stretched out on a bed with the Master at his side. Also in the room stood Solomon, and Doctor Allamar.

The Master turned to see Gaberilin enter. "Gaberilin, did you find Atris?" he asked.

"Yes, I gave her your message and then she flew off into the night sky."

"Good. I need you to do something as well."

Philophos suddenly screamed. The Master turned and asked Doctor Allamar, "What is it?"

"It's broken all the way through. I will have to amputate it," Aramil replied.

"No, don't! It hurts!" Philophos rolled and yelled.

"Philophos!" The Master grabbed him by the arm. "Philophos listen to me! Doctor Allamar knows what's best, trust him."

"No!" Philophos reeled over in pain.

"If we do not amputate, you will die. You are

Peter Crossings And The Gate Of Abaddon

losing too much blood," Doctor Allamar said to Philophos.

Philophos looked about at everyone in the room. His face was dirty and tear-stained. He turned to Dr. Allamar and silently nodded.

"We will begin immediately." Dr. Allamar went over to a shelf and took down a small stick. He placed it between Philophos' teeth. Gaberilin and the Master left the room closing the door behind them.

Edesha walked quickly, with Gaberilin at his side. "I need you to gather the warriors together. Summon all the bajets, and prepare everyone. We will set out as soon as the others arrive."

"Where are we going?" Gaberilin asked.

"To Abaddon, but first, we must pay Queen Lebijez a visit."

* * * * *

"They will not speak! I have bound them in the cell." Lebijez stormed back and forth in her chambers.

"What would you like me to tell him?" A tall Aracite stood waiting for his queen's message.

"Tell Nefarious that we have the boys and they will not cooperate. We will deliver them to him at his request."

"I will deliver the message," the Aracite bowed. He did not leave the core but stood still with all his arms behind his back.

"What? What is it?" the queen barked.

"My queen, if I may ask. We have the boys, but what will happen when it is noticed that they are

James Andrew Wilson

missing?"

"We will deal with that when it comes! Get out of here! Deliver the message!"

The Aracite bowed again, and then departed. Lebijez strolled back and forth in the core. She lifted her hands and caused the webs beneath her feet to rise into the form of Peter. She screamed and from underneath her cloak shot forth a clawed hand through the web statue shattering it to bits.

"If I must, I will kill him myself before they have a chance to rescue him." She raised forth the image again and slashed it apart. "I will kill him!"

And then a dark thought came to her mind. "Ah, but maybe this could be good." She mulled over her dark intention. "Yes, this could be very good..."

* * * * *

"It's no use!" Andrew plopped down to the web ground exhausted. "If that stupid Lebijez hadn't taken our swords, we'd be able to cut through this."

"I guess there is nothing we can do but wait," Peter said sitting down beside Andrew.

"We have to do something though! What if we're trapped in here forever?"

"No, she can't kill us. Remember what she said back in there."

"Yeah." Andrew remembered the scene. "She wanted to know if Edesha was coming."

"And when we didn't answer, she threatened us again. She said *Nefarious* would make us speak. I think she's working for Nefarious."

"Oh I see," Andrew said. "So she can't kill us, or Nefarious will get her."

"Yep," Peter replied. "But there is still something I don't get. Why did she ask us if Edesha was coming? Don't they think he will? I mean; he is going to save us, isn't he?"

"Of course he is!" Andrew said. "He wouldn't leave us here to die."

"But remember what they were talking about. They said a battle on the enemy's turf would be near impossible to win."

Andrew sighed. "Do you think they will come for us Peter?"

"I hope so."

"Yeah… Even though we are trapped in some big spider city with all sorts of monsters all around us, and even though we are millions of miles from home in a completely different world, Peter, I'm glad we're friends."

"Me too Andrew." A small tear trickled down Peter's cheek. "I'm glad to have such a great friend…"

They sat for a while, neither speaking. They felt trapped and alone. They wondered if this was the last of them, and if they would ever make it home. They hoped they would, but they feared they would die in the Aracite city before anyone ever tried to save them.

* * * * *

She had flown unheedingly for many hours, darting across the night sky at amazing speed. She could hear the mighty falls, and smell the lush green valley. The majestic bajet began to descend and soon flashed by the powerful waterfall. She came to the oversized town and went directly to the most dominant house. She conveyed the proper message to the one within and then darted back into the sky.

Atris flew north for the remainder of the night. When she reached her next destination, the sun had just lifted. She told the inhabitants of the town the message and then set out again back toward the castle.

It was late morning when she arrived back at Edeneth. She came and rested on the landing and then fell over from exhaustion. Gaberilin rushed out of the castle and came to her side.

"Atris, are you alright?"

The bajet breathed hard as she spoke, "I have flown hard all night, but I'm fine. I just need to rest. The message has been delivered, they are on their way."

Gaberilin helped the bajet to the stables and provided her with a place to rest. He then rushed back to the castle. He told the Master of the news, and then set off again through Edeneth.

Gaberilin returned outside to the many numbers of men and bajets who had gathered during the night. There was a large area near the castle surrounded by a strong fence. The entire field was filled with men and bajets. Most of the men were awake and suited in flashing gold armor; others were just waking from their sleep and scurrying around for breakfast. The bajets stirred up dust with anticipation, and chomped on the food provided them.

Peter Crossings And The Gate Of Abaddon

Gaberilin walked amongst the group. He was clad in his fine gold armor, with a long blue feather streaming back from his helmet. These were standard colors for the warriors of Northern Eden. His sword was at his side, and his bow and quiver upon his back. He greeted the men, many of whom he knew by name.

After rounding the entire camp, he came to the Master, who had just exited from the castle. Edesha stood clad in white, with a gold belt secured around his waist. Upon his back rested a long blue cape that halted inches above the ground. At his side was his mighty sword, glowing brilliantly with a blue light. He held his tall staff in his right hand. His black hair rested neatly on the back of his neck and just above his shoulders. He appeared as a great beacon of hope, ready to take his army into the clench of death's grip and fight to the end.

"How are things going?" Edesha asked.

"Most have gathered," Gaberilin reported. "I count nearly seven hundred men, and near five hundred of the bajets."

"Some will have to double up on the bajets. The others will be here soon. Make sure the men are ready to leave at a moment's notice."

"Yes Master. How is Atris doing?" Gaberilin asked.

"She is fine. She will be ready to fly again when the others arrive."

Just then Edesha looked up into the sky to see six bajets descending quickly toward the castle. Upon their backs were grand looking people all differently clad.

"Prepare the men." Edesha turned and went quickly back into the castle.

* * * * *

Peter stood before the queen. "If you will not speak, then I will have to kill you!"

Peter tried to speak, but it seemed as though his jaws had been glued together. He tried to pry his mouth apart, but his teeth only ground tighter. Lebijez screamed a horrible scream and shot forth from beneath her cloak many spiked arms. They flew straight at Peter—

Peter's eyes burst open. He breathed deeply, sweat was pouring from his face. It was only a dream. He awoke to find himself still in the web cell. Andrew was curled up against the wall, snoozing quietly. Peter wiped the sweat from his face and stood to his feet. Suddenly there was a loud crash and the globe rattled back and forth. Andrew woke with a start. "Wha—who? What's going on?" he asked standing.

The boys looked to the side of the globe to see the shadow of an Aracite scurrying up it. Another one crashed into the globe, and the two crawled to the top. The web moved back from the top creating an opening the size of a manhole cover. The two spidery Aracites dropped in.

"The queen has requested you," one of the drooling figures hissed. It grabbed Peter, but as the other moved toward Andrew, Andrew kicked him sharply.

"Argh! Come here you little beast!" The Aracite growled and grabbed the squirming boy in his

Peter Crossings And The Gate Of Abaddon

clutches. They leapt out of the cell. The opening covered itself back up as the Aracites sped through the city back toward the core.

They came to the massive globe and entered into the queen's presence. Lebijez stood with her back to them, looking out a small opening in the core to her city beyond. "Leave us," she said to the two Aracites. The two left the boys and scurried out of the core.

Queen Lebijez turned to face the boys. She took three steps toward them as the small window behind her formed back into a solid wall of web.

"What do you want with us?" Andrew asked abruptly with an edge to his voice.

"Well, I suppose that is better than nothing. At least you're speaking now." Lebijez inched closer. "Now perhaps we can get an answer out of you."

Peter stepped forward. "The answer is no! We are not afraid of spiders, and we're not afraid of you either."

"Very well." Lebijez turned and sat upon the web throne. "But that was not the question I was looking for the answer to."

Neither of the boys said a word.

"Answer me now! Is Edesha coming to rescue you or not!" The queen stood from her throne and screamed.

The boys didn't answer.

Lebijez sat back down. "Alright then..." She took a long breath and smiled. "So you are not scared of spiders?"

"No! We're not! What does that have to do with anything anyways?" Andrew asked.

James Andrew Wilson

"Nothing really. It matters not how you feel about us, but I am glad that you do not find us frightening. That will make things much easier."

"What things?" Andrew's eyebrows were tightly creased.

"We have been gifted, as you have no doubt seen, with great strength. That strength is something that you can obtain."

"Why would I want that?" Peter asked crossing his arms.

"Do not take me as a fool, dear Peter. You and I both know that Nefarious will kill you."

"How do you know? What if Edesha rescues me first?" Peter replied.

"Ah, so he is coming to try and save you." Lebijez smiled cruelly. "Oh but don't you see, I want to help you."

Andrew's heart began to beat very fast as he watched Lebijez move closer to Peter. He did not trust Lebijez one bit. "Peter, don't listen to her," he pleaded.

Lebijez moved closer. "I can make you mighty Peter. I can give you strength you never imagined."

Andrew grabbed Peter by the arm. "Peter! Don't listen to her! She's lying!"

In a flash, there shot from Lebijez's cloak a black hand. It grabbed Andrew by the mouth and pulled him to the ground. Peter looked in horror at his friend, when suddenly another black hand grabbed him by the head and turned his eyes back toward Lebijez.

"He is of no use to you Peter. You can be anything

Peter Crossings And The Gate Of Abaddon

you desire without him. Let him go. Come with me." The face of Lebijez that had once been beautiful, seemed now very dark and horrible. Her eyes were fixed on Peter.

In that moment, Peter remembered what Andrew had done for him back in his world. How he stuck by him and helped him. How he had been a friend. Peter looked at Andrew trying to pry the black hand loose. He looked back to the horrific face of Lebijez before him.

"Choose now Peter, this may be your only chance," Lebijez hissed.

Peter took a deep breath, clenched his fists and spoke boldly to the queen.

* * * * *

Edesha burst open the two doors to the room and moved quickly in. Six figures, all clothed majestically, followed him. The candles were lit and the seven High Servants all took their seats. They were clad all in different attire of royal garments; except for the long capes that each of them wore. Upon the capes in fine embroidery of gold shone the symbol of the seven-branched tree. Each of them as well carried finely carved staffs. Everyone held these at their sides as they sat around the table.

"Fellow High Servants of the Light and The Way of Tehus, I believe that the time has come to end this war, or die trying. The seven blades have not glowed these many years, and now they glow even more brilliantly than ever before."

Indeed, as the High Servants watched the swords, they throbbed with light. "It is impossible to deny that the time has come," said Issachar rising from his chair. He was clad in a deep maroon cape, and his hair was a snow-white color. "We have all gathered here on this day without calling from any, except I believe, the very calling of the Light, and that of Tehus." Everyone nodded in agreement.

Naphtali, who was the only female of the group, stood to her feet. She wore a violet cape sewn of velvet. Her hair was a soft brown, straight and long. "This war is reaching more lands than we can contain. Scouting shadows have already passed the boarders of my wooded lands. We must set out immediately, with haste, if we are to reach Abaddon before night fall."

Manasseh, who bore a silver cape, spoke, "My cities have seen some of the shadows as well. We shall need to set out quickly, yes, but we must assemble the armies of the north first. Edesha, none of us were able to bring soldiers from our borders. The mere fact that *we* are here puts our lands in danger."

"My bajet has summoned the giants and the Widdles as of last night. I expect them to arrive any time soon. We have gathered together seven hundred warriors, and five hundred bajets. They are ready to depart upon my order," Edesha said.

"And the boy? What of him?" Asher asked.

"He has been taken by the Aracites," Edesha said calmly.

"How long ago?" Zebulun asked alarmed.

"The evening of yesterday," Edesha replied.

Peter Crossings And The Gate Of Abaddon

"We cannot wait for the giants any longer! We must leave immediately or he will surely be killed. Nefarious will waste no time."

"The boy is strong," Edesha said.

"But if the rumors I have heard are true, then the boy is the only one who knows how to loose the gate. You know that we cannot end this war without the power held there within."

Edesha then pulled a piece of paper from his cloak. "The boy has given us the location of the gate, and this." He spread out the piece of paper. "I had Solomon translate it for me. It is the first half of a riddle that contains the secret to opening the gate."

All of the High Servants listened as Edesha read aloud.

"The gate that lies in land of dark
Holds a power not all may hark

"It's secret is two, make sure both are known
If not, the one who attempts will be unknown

"The first secret is this:

"If three are seen take one only
Only, take one wisely, for two will kill
Do not take three, for endlessness will follow thee

"Before you turn, beware
Remember two secrets must be known

"The second secret is this:"

"Is that all?" Zebulun asked. "What is the rest of the riddle?"

"Peter has not remembered it yet. But I believe in time it will come," Edesha said.

"Our time is spent!"

"What else can be done?" Edesha replied. "This is our time to rise and fight."

"Edesha is right," said Issachar. "We must end this war now. Even my mountain villages, which I at one time thought were well hidden, have been discovered by the crimson eyes…one way or the other it must end. But the riddle, what is the answer to the first secret?"

And then Edesha pulled a rolled piece of parchment from his cloak. "This is a painting done by Ethral. It shows The gate of Abaddon, and upon it there are three key holes."

"I see, so that explains what the *three* are that the riddle talks of," said Manasseh.

"Well then the answer is obvious," said Issachar. "We are to use the first key hole. For the riddle says:

"If three are seen take one only
Only, take one wisely, for two will kill
Do not take three, for endlessness will follow thee

So it is obvious that we are to use the first key hole."

"But how do we know which one is the first?" questioned Zebulun.

Edesha examined the painting. The three key-holes were in a horizontal line. "It must be the one on the right. The gate was made by our people of old, and our words travel from right to left. The first must be the one on the right."

The seven conversed over this much more until they all finally agreed with Edesha. Then all the High Servants rose from their chairs. Edesha spoke with authority, "As the High Servants of the Light, the chosen of Tehus, let us take now our blades." One by one, each brought forth their swords. The blades glowed brightly as the presence of Tehus circled the room.

* * * * *

"I will never join you! My friend is more important to me than power." Peter stared into the glaring eyes.

"Fool! If I cannot persuade you, then I will force you!" She turned and stared at Andrew. "Both of you!" In a flash, Lebijez thrust the boys into the air. In the process of grabbing the boys, she tossed aside her cloak. It was then that Peter and Andrew discovered what dwelt beneath the queen's long clothing. It was the body of an Aracite, only twice the size. She walked on four legs connected to a large abdomen, just like that of a spider.

In one giant leap, she bound out of the core through a hole that appeared the instant before they would have crashed into the side. The hole covered back over as they landed atop it. Peter and Andrew struggled to free themselves from her choking grip, but the queen was even stronger than the other Aracites. She maneuvered through her city with

James Andrew Wilson

speed and ease. Her long hair waved back in a jagged stream, her eyes bulged with anger.

"I will make you join me!" She was furious as she leapt from web to web. Briefly she came to the top of a web globe that seemed to be making crawling noises. It sounded like millions of tiny feet scurrying about within. The queen stood upon the top of the globe, which seemed set apart from the rest of the city. She held the boys over the globe, and suddenly a hole formed beneath them. To their horror, the boys looked within to discover hundreds upon hundreds of tiny black spiders crawling all throughout the entire inside.

"One single bite," Lebijez said, "that's all it took to change me from a beautiful woman to the form I am now. At first I hated it; I hated everything about it. But after time, I learned to love it. I forced others to come to my house, where I would secretly place a spider near them. It was not long before I had formed my own band of followers, my own race. We came here and created our own city away from those pathetic life forms we used to be. Now we are feared throughout all of Eden and there are none who can defeat us!"

"I have seen the likes of you destroyed by mighty warriors!" Peter shouted.

"What? What are you talking about boy?" the queen hissed.

"I have seen the Servants of the Light defeat slaves of your race."

"They are not slaves! They have their own choices."

Peter Crossings And The Gate Of Abaddon

"But did any of them ever choose to follow you? No. They were all forced, just like you are forcing us to. They would never have chosen to follow you, they have to; they are slaves."

"No! You're wrong boy! You will learn to respect me and love me just like the others have."

"No Lebijez, I won't, never! I am a follower of The Way, and will never bow to the likes of you!"

Lebijez screamed and hissed and raised the boys into the air. But the second before she dropped them into the swarm of spiders, Peter kicked the wrist of the queen causing her to miss, and drop him beside the hole. Andrew though, fell straight for the swarm of spiders.

Lebijez screamed and grabbed her wrist. She looked at Peter who was slipping, and sliding down the side of the globe. "It's useless to resist boy!" She reached out a hand for him, but lost her balance suddenly and slipped off the globe. One of the spikes on her body scraped against the globe and millions of little black spiders scurried out from the gash. Andrew lowered his foot. He had managed to grab the edge of the hole and pull himself up just in time to kick Lebijez.

"Andrew!" Peter called as he slid down the slick web. Some of spiders were crawling toward him. Andrew ran to where he was, laid himself flat, and reached a hand toward Peter.

"Gotcha!" He grabbed his wrist and tried to pull him up, but the web was so slick that both the boys fell from the globe. They plummeted for a second before landing on yet another web globe. They stood hurriedly to their feet.

"Quick, we need to get back to the core and get our swords!" Peter shouted. They looked around the city, and then spotted the central core. They hurried across a long stretch of web searching for a path that would lead to it.

Meanwhile, Lebijez had fallen far before landing hard against the outer wall of the dome. She barked some orders at a couple of Aracites and they set out toward the boys.

Peter and Andrew found a long web that connected to the core. They carefully ran across the web as swiftly as they could. Three Aracites suddenly jumped onto the web causing it to shake. The boys almost lost their footing.

"Andrew, hurry!" Peter shouted looking back to see the Aracites bounding after them. They came to the core and dove in through the opening.

"Where did she put them?" Andrew asked as he searched about.

"I bet she hid them somewhere in the walls," Peter said running his hand along the web.

The Aracites appeared suddenly in the core. "Hide and seek, always loved that game," one of them taunted. "Game over! Come here kid!" An Aracite leapt at Peter, but Peter was able to dodge him causing the creature to crash into the wall slitting the web. From the wall fell two shiny blades.

"I knew it!" Peter said as he grabbed for his sword. The Aracite reached out and clutched Peter's leg.

Peter sliced the hand with his sword and darted

Peter Crossings And The Gate Of Abaddon

away. Andrew grabbed up his sword and dove out of the way of an oncoming Aracite.

"We need to get out of here!" As Peter said this, the globe shook back and forth as three more figures appeared outside the swaying structure. Their shadows crawled for the entrance.

Peter and Andrew turned and jabbed their swords into the wall. They quickly cut a small hole just as the other Aracite bound toward them. It crashed through the hole, ripping the web even more.

"Come on!" Peter stood in the hole, looked down at the maze of webs far below, and then jumped. Andrew followed and the boys fell through the city.

They managed to miss all the stray webs and land at the very bottom of the city. The landing was hard, but the mass amount of web caused the ground to be like a giant mattress. They also had managed to land close to a part of the web that dipped down like a bowl. So they slid when they landed, instead of hitting abruptly.

"Look over there!" Andrew said rising to his feet. He pointed to a hole in the outer web that seemed to have light coming from it.

They dashed after it. When they came to the hole they looked in it to find a torch softly glowing. It illuminated what appeared to be a long dark tunnel leading away from the city. Without hesitation, Peter grabbed the torch and ventured into the darkness. Andrew followed, and as he did, he turned to see the black shapes of the Aracites crawling all through the city.

"They're looking for us Peter," Andrew said as

they descended further.

"I know, let's just keep going."

"But how do you know this leads anywhere better?" Andrew's voice echoed through the tunnel.

"I don't." They continued into the unknown.

Chapter Twelve

Into the Heart of Abaddon

They descended deeper into the darkness. The tunnel wound through the blackness like a snake. The walls were hard like stone, and cold like ice. The flickers of the torch danced on their faces, but the overpowering darkness consumed much of the light the flames gave. Peter led on. He didn't stop or turn, but charged forward without ceasing. The ground was hard and jagged, causing them to stumble along the way. At first they descended into the tunnel, but soon they found their calves were sore from ascending. They were rising now, not toward light, but into ever increasing darkness. The echoes of the scurrying Aracites in the city far behind were drowned out in the claustrophobic atmosphere.

"Peter, it's hard to breathe." Andrew reached out for Peter's shoulder, and then fell to the ground

James Andrew Wilson

clutching his chest.

"Come on Andrew," Peter said in-between deep breaths. "We've got to keep going." He pulled Andrew up.

"But it's not going to end. We're just going to keep going until we run out of air."

"No we aren't! Come on!" Peter pulled Andrew further. They trudged on as fast as their tired legs would allow. There was the continuing fear that the Aracites would discover where they had disappeared and come after them. But this fear only caused them to continue on, hoping somehow that they would exit into a place of safety.

A clicking sound suddenly echoed through the tunnel. The boys halted. They could hear a scurrying noise coming from further up the tunnel. It sounded like it was moving toward them, very fast. Peter frantically searched the enclosing walls for a place to hide. A hole, or crack, or crevice, anything! He ran his hand along the wall until he found a place where it curved under to a small indention.

Peter grabbed Andrew and dove down into the dark cubbyhole. The boys fit snugly and had to force themselves to breathe quietly. It felt as though they were wrapped tightly in a blanket and about to suffocate.

"Peter, the torch!" Andrew whispered. "Put it out."

The torch was still glowing softly outside the hiding spot. Peter hadn't noticed that he had dropped it. He struggled to free himself from the tight enclosure. The scurrying sound grew louder.

Peter Crossings And The Gate Of Abaddon

"Andrew, I'm stuck!" Peter ripped at his legs trying to free them. Andrew pitched in and together they were able to shove his legs free. He reached out with his foot and smoldered the flames, diminishing the entire tunnel to a thick, overwhelming darkness. Peter pulled his legs back in and wrapped his arms tightly around them.

The boys sat as still as they could, listening to the ever increasing noise of the scurrying. The *click-click-click* of what sounded like spikes clashing against the walls began to hurt their ears.

Thump! A large object came suddenly and crashed before them. They could not see a thing, but heard the hissing and snarling of some sort of large creature. They could smell its stench, like that of mold, and knew immediately what it was.

"What was that?" the Aracite snarled. It searched around and found the smoldered handle of the torch. "Hmm… how did that get here?" It began to run its long spiked hands along the walls. Something touched Peter's knee. Every hair on his body stood on end. The hand moved down to his foot. As quietly as he could, Peter reached in his cloak for his sword. The hand grabbed his foot. He whipped forth his blade and slashed into the darkness.

The Aracite recoiled and screamed. Peter shoved himself from the hole and slashed into the air. The Aracite jumped away. The boys could hear it sniffing as though it was searching for them by smell. Peter lunged toward the Aracite and thrust his blade forward. He felt the sword stab something, and then it dashed away quickly back toward the city, clicking

James Andrew Wilson

its claws against the walls.

Andrew rolled from the hole and stood to his feet. "Peter, Peter? Are you there?"

"Andrew, I'm here." Peter walked back to Andrew and bumped into him.

"Peter, that was an Aracite."

"Yeah, I know. I think I wounded it, but it ran back toward the city." Peter sheathed his sword. "We need to hurry, before others come." Peter started walking.

"Wait, Peter." Andrew reached out and grabbed his cloak. "Why was the Aracite coming from that way, and not from the city?"

Peter thought for a second. "I'm not sure Andrew."

"Neither am I, and that is what scares me. Peter, what is on the other side of this tunnel?"

"I don't know. All I know is that we have to get away from that city."

"But what if we're going someplace worse than that?"

"What choice do we have Andrew? What else can we do?"

Andrew didn't say anything. It was the first time he had heard Peter shout at him as if he was angry.

Peter sighed, "Andrew, I'm sorry. But really, what else can we do?"

"You're right Peter, come on, let's go."

The boys hurried on through the tunnel. Peter led with Andrew holding tightly to his cloak. After some time they started descending again. The slope became steep very quickly and they had to walk with their feet sideways so as not to slip.

"Look Peter, there's light ahead!" Andrew pointed down to a small glowing red light at the end of the tunnel. As they neared it, they began to sweat. Along with the light came a terrific heat. The air thickened like smoke and the boys found it even harder to breathe than before. And then there was a loud rumbling and shaking that sent them to the ground. They slid down the rest of the tunnel clawing and reaching in attempts to slow down. Finally they plummeted out of the tunnel into a smoky red air and onto a broken black ground.

They stood slowly brushing the soot-like dirt off themselves. "Peter, where are we?" Andrew asked as he looked about at the landscape.

"I'm not sure Andrew, but it doesn't look good."

* * * * *

"Prepare for departure! The giants have arrived!" Gaberilin ran quickly to the back of the camp where his bajet waited. A brilliantly carved saddle sat upon the back of Aroh. "Aroh, we're going to meet the giants!" Gaberilin said as he swung himself onto the bajet. The two rose from the ground and flew quickly away.

At the bottom of the great hill that Edeneth sat upon, twenty or more giants had just waded into the river. Upon each of their backs were at least ten Widdles. Some of the Widdles had slid themselves into the giants' pockets; others sat upon their shoulders, while still others merely clung to the giants'

James Andrew Wilson

clothes. In four large strides all the giants crossed the river.

Gaberilin descended to the front of the giants and leapt off Aroh. He came up to the foot of the leading giant. Gaberilin's head reached only to the giant's knee. Folds of skin on the giant's massive forehead looked like piles of blankets at the foot of an unmade bed. The arms were very large and covered with thick brown hair. "Welcome to Edeneth fair giant!" Gaberilin shouted up to the entirely enormous head. The giant looked down at Gaberilin and smiled.

"Thank you good sir, glad to be here," he said in a booming voice. "The bajet, Atris, summoned us the night of last and we have come in haste."

"And I thank you for that, for this is a time of haste!" Gaberilin replied.

"Indeed! We have brought the Widdles with us as the bajet requested."

"Thank you for coming quickly, my Master will no doubt desire to speak with you immediately. If you would be so kind as to wait here beneath the hill of the castle, he shall meet with you shortly."

The giant nodded and then sat down slowly being careful not to crush any of the Widdles. As the giants sat down to rest, Gaberilin leapt again onto the back of Aroh and sped back to the castle. Edesha had just come forth with the other High Servants when Gaberilin landed again amongst the camp.

"Master," Gaberilin said running up to him, "the giants have arrived and await your greeting at the foot of the hill.

"I will speak with them at once!" Edesha mounted

Peter Crossings And The Gate Of Abaddon

Aroh and sped away down toward the giants. He landed before them and dismounted. "Galmas! Welcome to Edeneth!" Edesha said to the lead giant.

Galmas looked down at Edesha. "It is a pleasure, and a pleasure as well to see you again old friend."

"The same, although I would have preferred it under better circumstances. I would enjoy to talk more with you, but we must set out in haste."

"I understand, we are ready at your command," Galmas said.

"We will leave shortly," Edesha said rising into the saddle again. "Be strong mighty ones!" Aroh flapped his wings and ushered the Master back up to Edeneth.

"Prepare Atris for flight," Edesha said to Gaberilin as he slid off of Aroh. "And make sure the other bajets in the stable are saddled and ready as well."

"Yes Master." Gaberilin nodded and went quickly away toward the stable.

Just then the door to the castle opened and out came two armor clad Widdles. Mr. Timf and Mr. Sockeye came up to Edesha. They were wearing matching armor and both carried a large double bladed axe.

"Sir," Mr. Timf bowed, "Mr. Sockeye and I would be honored if we could join our people in this battle." Mr. Timf sniffed (his nose was running again).

"I thank you, but you are not required to battle," Edesha replied.

"We will stand with our people to the end," Mr. Timf said.

"Yes, and besides, I have to make things right. I shouldn't have been dealing with those Aracites.

James Andrew Wilson

They were looking into having me make some weapons for them. I never did get them finished. Oh my… I am sorry," Mr. Sockeye confessed.

"I forgive you, and honor you for desiring to set things straight. You may join the battle, and in fact, I would like you two to be the leaders of your people."

"You, you mean it?" Mr. Timf asked.

"Yes, but this will be a brutal battle, I want you to understand that," Edesha said leaning hard on his staff and staring the Widdles in the eyes.

"We understand!" they replied.

"Very well, the mighty bajet Frenwar will be yours. He will carry you well."

The Widdles bowed low and thanked the Master again. A few moments later, Gaberilin came riding on Atris with seven other bajets following. They all landed and Gaberilin dismounted.

Edesha came up to Atris and laid a hand on her white neck. "Are you rested enough old girl?" he asked stroking her long feathers.

"I am ready Master," she nodded.

The other High Servants mounted onto their bajets, and with the help of Gaberilin, the Widdles crawled onto the back of Frenwar. All the warriors double checked their armor and then mounted their bajets. Some sat two to a bajet, while others sat alone atop the mighty flyers. All the warriors were clad in glistening gold armor, with helmets atop their heads, round shields at their backs, and long sheathed swords at their sides. Some also carried bows, and others carried maces.

The door to the castle once again opened and a

Peter Crossings And The Gate Of Abaddon

lady dressed in streaming white came forth. She held a golden harp in the cleft of her right arm. Jubal walked gracefully toward the battle-ready army. All heads turned and watched as she started picking the strings. Her slender hands moved dreamily over the harp. An unexpected wind came suddenly and moved her long hair through the air. The silky white shall of her dress drifted on the breeze. She sang a mesmerizing song in her dreamy voice wishing the warriors farewell and the blessing of Tehus.

When she had finished, all the warriors removed their helmets and bowed their heads. Edesha gazed mournfully at her. She had grown even more beautiful in his eyes after learning how she had become blind and her sad story. He cared deeply for her, but more than that…he loved her. He slid off of his bajet and came up to her. "My dear Jubal," he said in a tender voice. Then he touched her soft cheek. "My dear sweet Jubal…" but there was nothing further that could be said, or needed to be said.

Jubal reached up and grasped his hand. She held it tightly and then released it. "Go, do what you must. I will be praying for your return."

Then Edesha bowed before the lady. After he arose, he mounted again onto Atris. "Farewell my dear Jubal…farewell."

With that, Atris lifted from the ground only to have all the others rise and follow. A mighty wind roared from all the strong wings of the bajets. The company set out toward the giants and the Widdles.

Mr. Timf and Mr. Sockeye greeted the Widdles, many of whom they had known before in Widdleville.

James Andrew Wilson

The Widdles were very pleased to have two so well dressed leaders. The giants rose scooping the Widdles once again onto their backs and into their pockets.

"Come, the time is upon us. We travel to the end of the war!" The Master led the army toward the dark land. At the head of the group, the seven High Servants flew quickly upon their bold bajets. The warriors followed in a valiant storm of quickly flying wings. At the rear, the giants hurried along the terrain. The army moved with great speed toward their destination.

* * * * *

Within his tall, dark tower, Nefarious cowered over the glass ball. He scanned the entire expanse of his black land. His dark minions were doing their job, for a change. But this was different than before, with the boy so near he knew they would soon see some type of rescue effort. No matter, he was well prepared.

The volcanoes had been erupting very frequently. He had managed to construct many fire weapons, and the number of shadow warriors were many. There would be no chance of losing this time. The plan was perfect. They would be completely trapped in the Petra Passage when they came...if they came.

"They'll come," Nefarious reassured himself. He couldn't let this one slip; he had to be prepared for anything. As soon as the boy was in his grasp, he would win. And fortunately, the boy was already on his way.

"As long as Lebijez leaves him alone, he will be

Peter Crossings And The Gate Of Abaddon

---

all mine." Nefarious laughed to himself. "It seems though that it was too easy. But really, how easy was it?" He moved aside his cloak and looked down at his body. "Was this all worth it? Will it be worth it when I have won?" He knew it would be, it had to be. Ultimate power. What else could truly satisfy?

He gazed back into the ball. He scanned the surrounding mountains watching the devourers perched high in their cliffs, licking their lips. Then his gaze moved toward Aracon. He could just barely see the globe over the mountains. He looked down the face of a tall cliff to the opening of the tunnel. *Wait!* What was that? He looked closer. Could it be? Nefarious saw two small figures just coming forth from the tunnel. They fell to the black ground, then they stood and brushed themselves off. The two figures looked about their surroundings. Nefarious whipped away from the ball and dashed for the doors.

* * * * *

"My queen," the Aracite bowed, "Nefarious requests that you deliver the boys to him immediately."

"We don't have the boys anymore fool!" Lebijez barked.

"What do you mean?"

"I mean that we lost them! They're gone, hiding somewhere that we can't find!" Lebijez screamed and pulled at her black hair.

"Queen, I think that perhaps I know where they are."

"What? What did you say?"

"In the tunnel, on my way back to Aracon, I was attacked by something in the dark. Perhaps it was the boys." The Aracite showed the small stab wound on his leg.

"You fool! Why did you leave them there?" Lebijez grabbed the Aracite by the throat.

"I, I didn't know what it was! I couldn't see anything in the dark!"

"Argh!" Lebijez threw him to the ground. "You had better hope that they are still there, for your sake. Follow me!" Lebijez crawled speedily out of the core. She gathered many Aracites and they bound into the tunnel.

"I'll get you boy," Lebijez hissed as she sped through the murky hole.

* * * * *

Peter and Andrew stood in shock as they looked upon the broken land. Not far to their right, an enormous volcano protruded from the black ground. It spilled searing lava from its peak, which ran down its sides like millions of long fingers. Around the foot of the volcano a moat of lava had formed. It leaked down into the cracked land causing it to glow with red intensity. The volcano puffed thick red smoke into the air.

The boys looked across the rest of the land. It seamed to go on for miles: black, broken land glowing blood red from the lava. They could see thousands of dark figures moving about, crawling over the land like ants. Away to the distance they could see what appeared to be a tall tower, surrounded by lava.

"Peter, I think I know where we are," Andrew said slowly.

"So do I Andrew. Abaddon."

"We should turn back Peter." Andrew began to back away toward the tunnel.

"No! Andrew, we can't go back!" Peter turned and shouted. Sweat was pouring from his face. There was a small stream of fresh blood trickling down his cheek from a recent scratch. His hair lay matted about his head and it appeared wet from the sweat. Yet, there was a strength in his green eyes that Andrew had never seen before. The dark land loomed before him, but he wasn't afraid of it. He knew what he had to do. "Andrew, we can't turn back. I saw a vision in the pool at Patmos."

"What did you see Peter?" Andrew asked.

"I saw myself…only I was different. I was brave, and I was fighting Nefarious. If we turn back, evil may rule Eden forever. Andrew, we have to continue on."

Andrew looked to his friend. He swallowed hard. His throat felt so dry and parched. He was exhausted, but he couldn't leave his friend alone. "I'll follow you Peter," he said.

Peter pushed aside his torn and battered cloak. It was frayed and ripped at the ends, but it still bore its strong blue color. He drew forth his sword. "Come on Andrew." Peter stepped forward.

Andrew drew forth his sword and followed. At first it was fairly easy to navigate the cracked land,

James Andrew Wilson

---

but it soon became exceedingly difficult. None of the fowl creatures had noticed them yet for many of them were still far off. They kept their heads low as they leapt across the cracked surface.

They stopped upon a large chunk of battered ground. It rested on the bank of a small gushing river of steaming lava. Away down the river, some dark shapes were slopping the lava into a large cart. Peter and Andrew ducked down behind a large piece of broken rock. "We have to jump across," Peter whispered to Andrew.

"But it's at least seven feet across!" Andrew replied in a hushed voice.

"Come on Andrew, I know you can do it."

"So do I, I'm just not sure if *you* can. You were never very good at sports back at school."

Peter looked across the river. A large piece of flat ground was directly across. He knew that if he didn't make it, he would disintegrate into the lava. But he had to try; he had to do it. "I think I can do it."

"I'm going first. Let's hope those things down there don't see us," Andrew said.

"If they do, just run," Peter said. Andrew peeked out to make sure the creatures weren't watching. Then he crawled back onto the chunk of rock. He only had room to step three times before he leapt. He sheathed his sword and rubbed his hands together.

"Okay...okay, I can do this." He charged forward. One step, two steps, three, he leapt. Peter watched as Andrew flew over the river and landed easily on the other side. Andrew turned and waved for Peter to follow.

Peter Crossings And The Gate Of Abaddon

Peter swallowed hard. He sheathed his sword and crawled onto the chunk. He took a couple of deep breaths and turned suddenly to see three dark shapes shifting down the riverbank grasping fiery swords. They were screaming something horrible at him.

"Peter, hurry!" Andrew shouted whipping forth his sword. The creatures neared and their screams intensified. Peter stepped back. He took one last breath and then ran forward. He came to the edge and jumped with all his might.

* * * * *

The army traveled with un-halting speed. Edesha led the group silently. He hadn't spoken a word to anyone the entire time. Gaberilin found this odd and finally decided to speak to him. He flew up to his side. "Master, is there something bothering you?"

Edesha looked to Gaberilin. "I feel that we must make a change of plans."

"In what way?" Gaberilin asked.

"Once we reach the Dead Lands, I want you to take a force and lead them to Aracon."

"But Master, where will you go?"

"I will take the rest and lead them to Abaddon. I feel that Peter may already be in greater danger than we had supposed."

"Do you feel that he is in Abaddon already?" Gaberilin asked.

Edesha thought for a second. "Yes, Gaberilin. I feel that he has escaped the grasp of the Aracites and is in the dark land."

James Andrew Wilson

Gaberilin looked down in thought. "I will do as you command." He bowed his head and then fell back.

Atris continued forward with determination. "Do you really believe the boy is already in Abaddon?" she asked.

"Yes Atris. I also feel that we will encounter a strong force of evil when we reach the land."

"I am ready Master, do not worry about me," Atris said.

Edesha looked toward Abaddon. They would reach the Dead Lands within the hour; from there it would not be long. The company continued on.

* * * * *

Peter could feel the burning hot lava at his back. He had landed the jump, but was tottering back and forth on the edge. His foot slipped and he fell back.

"Gotcha!" Peter felt a tight grip at his wrist. Suddenly he was pulled back up onto his feet.

Peter breathed deep. "Thank you Andrew," he said between breaths.

"No time for that, hurry!" Andrew turned and leapt away. Peter looked back up the river to see the shadows floating after them. Then as he watched, the shadows shifted and morphed into hideous beasts that bounded after him. Peter whipped forth his sword and dashed after Andrew.

They leapt across the protruding chunks of black land. "Andrew!" Peter shouted. "They're shadows!"

Andrew jumped to a big piece of ground. "What are?" he asked.

Peter Crossings And The Gate Of Abaddon

"Those creatures. They're the true forms of shadows!" Peter said landing beside Andrew.

"You're right!" Andrew exclaimed looking over Peter's shoulder at the monsters scurrying after them.

"Andrew, watch out!" Peter shouted pushing Andrew down as a creature flew over their heads and crashed behind them. "They're all over!"

The shadow creatures suddenly started appearing all around them. They were crawling out from between the cracks of lava. At first they would squeeze forth as a vapor of shadow, then they would change instantly into the grotesque figures.

The shadows surrounded the boys. They crept closer to them. Peter and Andrew looked to each other in fright. "Peter! Look!" Andrew pointed to Peter's sword.

Peter gazed at the blade; it was glowing. Then Andrew's small sword started glowing. The blue light about their blades grew brighter. The shadow creatures cowered down and hid their faces. The boys started swinging the blades in an arc around themselves.

"Stay back shadows!" Peter shouted to the cowering creatures. But suddenly, the swords dimmed.

"What's going on?" Andrew asked looking at his sword in bewilderment. Then the air grew even thicker and darker than before. Their blades felt cold and heavy. The shadows crept closer, drooling and hissing. One of the beasts reached out and grabbed Peter's leg.

"Leave them alone!" Many of the shadows surrounding them were suddenly thrown to the side. All the creatures turned and gazed fearfully at the oncoming shape. The circle of shadows parted to allow a tall hooded figure a straight path to the boys. The hooded shape walked quickly up to Peter and Andrew. The boys could not see the face, but the voice was powerful.

"Do not fear boys. They will not harm you."

"Who are you?" Peter asked.

"We mustn't speak here. Come with me, I will take you to a safer place." A pale hand extended from the dark cloak. The hand seemed frail with long chipped nails and bony fingers. The knuckles were large and knobby.

Neither Peter nor Andrew desired to go with the cloaked figure. They looked about at the many shadow creatures who seemed frozen in a trance and unable to attack. What other choice did they have?

Peter heard a ghostly voice in his head, "Come with me Peter. Don't worry; you'll be safe. Trust me Peter. I will protect you."

Peter swallowed hard and sheathed his sword. Andrew reluctantly followed. The boys stepped forward and reached out toward the hand. They were suddenly swept up into the arms of the cloaked figure. It turned quickly and dashed across the dark land with such incredible speed it seemed they were flying.

Try as they might, Peter and Andrew were unable to keep their eyes open. A strange dizziness came over them and they soon fell into a trance of sleep.

* * * * *

Peter Crossings And The Gate Of Abaddon

"Gaberilin!" Edesha shouted back. "Halt the army, we have reached the Dead Lands."

The seven High Servants came and formed a circle. "Something has happened to the boys," Issachar said solemnly.

"Yes, I have felt that as well," said Edesha. "I have decided to split up the army. We will make an attack on Aracon, while the remainder will come with me to Abaddon."

"I will go to Aracon. I have been there in times past," said Issachar.

Zebulun and Asher agreed as well to go with Issachar. The others stayed with Edesha.

Gaberilin came up to the circle. "The army is halted."

"Very well." Edesha explained the numbers he desired to be divided. Gaberilin orchestrated the division and soon the two groups were ready.

"Gaberilin, once you have gotten through the city, descend into Abaddon over the northern Petra Mountains," Edesha said. "I will be going through the Petra Passage. The air is too thick and poisonous for the bajets to navigate through, so we will be charging in on foot."

Gaberilin nodded. "Master, may Tehus guide you."

"You as well. Now go!" Edesha whisked away toward the dark land with a great army following. Gaberilin, atop Aroh, flew quickly toward the globe city of the Aracites.

Atris whisked through the sky. They descended from the clouds to see the dry and cracked Dead

Lands spanning on like a barren desert. The jagged peaks of the Petra Mountains rose like spikes into the red air.

"Fly Atris, fly with all your might!" The mighty bajet burst through the air with a great host following.

Just beyond the mountains, a numerous and fierce army of darkness was gathering. The army of Light was expected.

Chapter Thirteen

Nefarious

When Peter finally opened his eyes he was shocked at what he saw. He found himself in a large, dark, round room. Snapping torches lined the walls. Their smoke disappeared into the dark corners of the room. He was lying prostrate on a cold hard ground. Andrew was beside him, still asleep. Peter nudged him a little and he woke with a start. "Wha-huh?" Andrew sat up quickly. He looked about at the dark room. "Peter, where are we?"

"I'm not sure." Peter gathered himself up and stood slowly to his feet. Before them sat a slender pillar with intricate carvings crawling over it. Peter stood fully to see what sat upon the top of the structure. A crystal white ball was nestled into its stand upon the flat top of the pillar. Peter's eyes did not gaze long upon it though. Away behind the pillar was a large chair the size of a throne. It was dark like the rest of the room and had spikes protruding from its back. Upon the throne sat the still, cloaked figure that had rescued them from the shadows. The figure's face was hidden in darkness. It leaned upon a pale hand and seemed to be watching Peter intently.

Peter tried to peel his eyes away from the figure. He began to sweat with nervousness. His breath became quick and short as the cloaked shape sat dead-still watching him. Peter suddenly flashed his cloak aside and reached for his sword. Where the handle should have been there was nothing but air. His sword was gone.

His eyes wide with terror stared at the cloaked figure. He couldn't speak from fear, and his knees began to tremble. He fell to the hard ground and clenched his fists together.

Suddenly his breath came back. All his pain and fear diminished and his sweat stopped pouring. He heard a deep sigh come from the dark shape upon the throne. Peter and Andrew stood to their feet. They watched as the cloaked shape rose from its throne and floated through the thick air. It landed opposite the ball.

Two pale hands emerged from the darkly draped figure and rose to its hood. The bony fingers gripped the edges of the cloak and slowly pulled it back. A stark white face appeared from the hood. Its features were long and frail. The eyes sat droopily in their sockets. They were dark eyes...hollow eyes. The hair was thin and long, it lay matted and twisted into knots upon the chalky white scalp. The hands returned to their hiding.

"Peter Crossings and Andrew Hatch." His voice

Peter Crossings And The Gate Of Abaddon

was sharp and stinging to the ears. "Obviously I already know who you are. Let me introduce myself."

A hand emerged again from the cloak. It moved slowly through the air. Peter and Andrew suddenly found that they were rising from the ground. They hovered effortlessly above the floor as the figure rose to their height. They sat suspended for a moment, no one speaking a word. Peter was amazed at the feeling of being weightless, but he was too suspicious about the strange circumstances to really experience and delight in it.

"As you can see, I posses powers beyond normal humankind. Do not be fooled though, I know the strength of the human mind. My mind has just been, well how shall I say, enlightened. I shall tell you more, but please, come and sit." The three began to drift through the air until the boys were set down before the great black throne. The pale hands moved and from the corners of the room shot two black chairs that ended up at the back of the boys' knees. The boys sat, although it seemed that their bodies were forced into the stiffed back chairs.

"Ahh, now that is much better," the strange figure said sitting down upon the throne. "I trust that you have enjoyed your time thus far in Eden?" The boys didn't answer. "I have lived in this wonderful land for many a year. I remember the first time that I saw a bajet. I was only five and the great animal scared me so much that I hid in my bedroom the remainder of the day." He laughed a surprisingly gentle laugh. "Oh what wonderful days I had growing up in Eden. My friends and I would often go and visit the giants.

Have you seen the giants?"

Peter found himself feeling a bit more trust toward the odd person. "No we haven't," he replied.

"Oh, that is too bad, perhaps you will get to meet them before your visit is over. Oh, yes, you will return where you belong in due time, be sure of that."

"How, how do you know?" Peter asked alarmed at how much this person knew of him.

"Peter, my dear boy. Do you honestly think that we would take you away forever? Of course not dear lad! You will be safe and happy soon enough, I guarantee it. But about the giants, we had the most wonderful times in the valley. We would swim in the great lake beneath the falls, we would climb the cliffs, and oh it was delightful." He paused suddenly and sighed a deep long sigh. "But now things have changed." He raised his hands and looked at them in disgust. "I have grown old. So old in fact that I can no longer spend time with those I used to call friends. I say used to, because I have not seen them for so long, I have forgotten them. I wouldn't notice them if they were to walk in here and tell me who they were. Oh, for the happy days again."

"That's awful!" Andrew exclaimed. "It's just not fair, why don't your friends come and visit anymore?"

"They don't like what I have become. Look at me! I have withered to a worthless pile of bones barely strewn together. The truth is, I'm lonely." He hung his head down low letting his knotted hair fall about his face.

Peter began to feel compassion for the old figure.

Peter Crossings And The Gate Of Abaddon

It didn't seem fair that everyone had forgotten about him and shunned him. "Is there anything that we can do to help?" he asked.

Beneath his ratted hair a devious smile crept across his face. It vanished as he turned his gaze upward. "Actually there is—oh, but you wouldn't…"

"No really, what can we do?"

"Oh it is too much to ask."

"Come on! Tell us! We really want to help!" Peter was now standing to his feet pleading.

The old white face let out a long sigh. "I would enjoy company. That is, to have somebody to talk with. Somebody that would stay with me in the few remaining years I have and be a, well, be a friend."

Peter sat back down. He started to remember how it felt when he didn't have any friends. He hid it, but he really desired deeply for a friend. He could feel this anguished person's pain. But to stay with him for years? What about Edesha, what about Gaberilin and the others? What about his family? What about his home? What about his life?

"Oh bother, I knew it would be too much to ask. Well, perhaps we can at least share *some* time together."

"I'm sorry," Peter said. "I just, I have, well…"

"Friends. I know. That's what everybody has, friends. But look at lucky me. I'm nobody. No friends, nobody."

"Oh come on Peter, why not stay for a bit?" Andrew asked.

Peter looked at Andrew, and then back to the pale head. "Wait a minute," he said, "you still haven't told

James Andrew Wilson

---

us your name."

"Oh, well I'll be, you are right. You see, I haven't had visitors for so long I have forgotten how to be polite. My name is," he seemed to hesitate, "Riousafen."

And then something happened to Peter. A flash of visions, or maybe memories came to him very quickly. He remembered Solomon talking in the castle. The sight of that shape in his dream, the one with hollow eyes, flashed. And then he saw his parents. And finally a strong memory came. He was reading the Golden Book, and he remembered what it said:

> The gate that lies in land of dark
> Holds a power not all may hark
>
> Its secret is two, make sure both are known
> If not, the one who attempts will be unknown
>
> The first secret is this:
>
> If three are seen take one only
> Only, take one wisely, for two will kill
> Do not take three, for endlessness will follow thee
>
> Before you turn, beware
> Remember two secrets must be known
>
> The second secret is this:
>
> To discover the answer to the first
> Knowledge from Beyond must be known

One who has read many words will know
Once the key is turned, the power forth will burst

"Riousafen? Hey Peter, isn't that who Solomon was talking about?" Andrew snapped him back out of visions.

Riousafen appeared surprised by this. "You...you have met Solomon?" he asked.

Peter looked to the pale head. "Yes we have, and he told us what you did!" he exclaimed.

"What do you mean?" Riousafen asked with a look of concern in his eyes.

"He told us that you tried to kill him, and that you are very evil," Peter replied.

"Kill him?" Riousafen seemed shocked. "How could he have said that? Listen to me Peter and Andrew, Solomon has done a terrible thing. He has lied about me. I never tried to kill him, I tried to protect him."

"Protect him?" Andrew questioned. "From who?"

"From somebody very evil. His name is Edesha. We used to be friends before he became evil. He was the one that tried to murder Solomon! I tried to stop him, and succeeded, but Edesha murdered his wife. Then he brain-washed Solomon, and made him believe that I was evil. They sent me away and told me never to return. So I came and lived here and have grown old. They have all abandoned me..."

"Lies!" Peter stood from his seat and shouted, "You're lying!"

"Peter? Whatever do you mean?" Riousafen asked, the nervous look in his eyes again.

James Andrew Wilson

"Edesha is no longer your friend, not because you are old, but because you are evil! I remember you from the library. You read the Golden Book and have done many evil things."

"Evil? Peter I am just an old—"

"No you're not! You have been lying to us and deceiving us this entire time. I'm not sure what you want from us, but you're not going to get it!"

Riousafen frowned and his eyebrows arched down. He looked quickly to Andrew. "Andrew, what do you think about what your friend is saying about me? You know that I am telling the truth. Remember on Patmos? I sent someone to you, didn't he tell you?"

Andrew stood to his feet. He looked at Peter, and then glared back at Riousafen. "I believe Peter. I have felt really weird ever since you brought us here, and I don't like it. I don't think you're telling the truth either."

The chairs suddenly shot away from beneath the boys and crashed into the corners. Riousafen stood from his throne and stared down to the boys. His eyes darkened and his stature seemed to grow larger. "Oh but I have been telling you the truth." His voice had now changed to a dark, deep, booming sound. He and the boys began once again to rise into the air. "For you see, I was indeed friends with Edesha long ago, but I left their weakness for a higher power. Look at what I have become!" He raised a crooked hand to the shadowy ceiling. "I have become amazing! My power has far surpassed that of Edesha! He can no longer win."

Try as they might, the boys could not move an

Peter Crossings And The Gate Of Abaddon

inch. It felt as though they were tightly bound with strong constricting cords. They were lowered to the ground upon the opposite side of the ball from Riousafen. "And as for my name," he said, "my name is Nefarious! I am ruler of this land, and of the shadows that haunt you! Finally I have you! Finally I have won!" Nefarious reeled his face back and bellowed a cruel laugh. "Now, all that's left is to watch my victory take place. And then," Nefarious glared at Peter, "then I will kill you! If you will not join with me, you will die!"

Peter struggled in the invisible cords that seemed wrapped around him. "I will never join you Nefarious! You're just like Lebijez!"

"What? What are you talking about?"

"Lebijez tried to make us join her. You two are just the same, you're both evil!" Peter shouted.

Nefarious growled. "Lebijez..." He glared hard at the boys. "You say you will never join me, so be it. After you see your precious friends fall, perhaps you will think differently!"

The room immediately shrank to darkness. All the torches were snuffed out as though dark hands were crawling amongst the walls putting out the flames. The boys' heads were forced to turn and stare at the ball. Nefarious reached a milky white hand over the ball and it started to glow. Shapes started forming in the haze. Suddenly, a brilliant image exploded above them. It was as though they were watching a giant TV. It portrayed a very dark and jagged mountain range. There was a long canyon scratched into the mass of peaks. The image zoomed in closer to the canyon. At first the canyon seemed empty and desolate, but soon they heard a loud roar of shouts and screams. From both sides of the canyon a mass of figures hurried toward each other. A tangle of shadows flooded the canyon from one side, while a horde of armor clad figures spilled in from the other.

"Edesha!" Peter shouted. At the lead of the armor-clad army, Edesha charged extending his brilliant staff forward. There were three others around him who also carried staffs. These four seemed to glow with a powerful light. Behind them ran a mass of soldiers all hefting a sword and shield and some grasped maces.

As the shadows neared the Servants of the Light, they would change from their vapory shadow form into the gruesome, snarling true shapes that they were.

"Attack!" Edesha shouted flashing forth his sword that was so brightly illuminated it nearly hurt Peter's eyes. The other three bearing staffs whipped forth swords as well. Edesha came in contact with the first enemy. The shadow screamed and jumped at him only to be blown back to the ground with fierce intensity. All the dark warriors and the warriors of the Light slammed together into a fierce battle.

Then Peter saw many large shapes crawling up around the canyon on the wide sides. They were enormous, and from their backs fell many small shapes. Then Peter realized that they were giants, and they were carrying Widdles. Many of the Widdles were equipped with crossbows, which they steadily fired

Peter Crossings And The Gate Of Abaddon

into the swarm. Some of the stout Widdles took axes and plummeted into the heart of the battle swinging wildly. Peter suddenly saw a face he recognized. Mr. Timf bounded off the back of a giant and stood battle ready, clad in brilliant armor. He waved for a group of Widdles to dive into battle after which he dove in swinging a giant two-headed axe.

Then some of the giants leapt off the canyon walls into the mess. They crushed some of the shadows beneath their enormous feet. Many of the shadows were wielding crude looking fire-blades with which they stabbed harshly into the giants' legs. The shadows crawled over one of the giants and managed to cause him to fall to the ground. He was immediately covered with the ant-like monsters.

Another sort of creature appeared suddenly on the battlefield. Small, gnarled looking shapes that crawled like beetles started appearing from holes in the mountains. Peter recognized them as the same type of creature that had bitten him at the castle. They spilled out of the dark tunnels onto the canyon walls.

"Argh!" Nefarious growled. "Wretched devourers."

Some of the devourers snapped at the giants, while many others bounded into the fray and seemed to bite at anything. They savaged mostly over the slain bodies of the shadows. Like vultures they watched for a shadow to fall and then rushed for it and fought fiercely over it like dogs.

Many of the shadows were falling left and right, but many of the warriors were being slain as well. A group of shadows had managed to clear a path

James Andrew Wilson

---

through the soldiers and stood now forming a circle. They lashed out and slashed at the warriors with their cruelly shaped swords.

Edesha led the group with power. Shadows were flying from his fury in a wide arc. He swung his sword with power and might. From time to time he would extend his staff and ignite a shadow into flames. The other staff bearers did this as well. Mr. Timf clashed his axe against many evil ones and fought furiously, screaming most of the time.

Then some larger creatures fell like drool from the mountains. They were devourers, but much larger, nearly the size of the giants. The giants turned and wrestled with these furious creatures. The giant devourers snapped and spit at the giants, crawling around them with a great amount of spiked legs. The giants overcame many of these enormous monsters.

A great sound of clicking came suddenly to the battlefield. Crawling along the wall of the canyon with great speed, a large number of Aracites entered into the battle. A large Aracite bounded in and spewed web across the warriors trapping many of them against the walls and to the ground.

"Lebijez!" Nefarious exclaimed. "What is she doing there?"

Lebijez led her army of the fierce Aracites into the battle. The Servants of the Light fought with all their might, but the forces of evil seemed too numerous. The battle raged on for what seemed like eternity. Peter and Andrew watched intently every second.

"Come on Edesha, come on," Peter whispered to himself.

"It seems as though your friends will soon find their death. I wonder; have you reconsidered my offer yet?" Nefarious asked tauntingly.

"Edesha will win, and you will fall!" Peter shouted.

Nefarious laughed. "We shall see boy!"

Peter watched hopelessly as one by one the warriors fell in number. Many of the Widdles were trampled by the oncoming slaughter. Most of the giants still remained, but they were beaten and wounded badly from the devourers. Mr. Timf swung unheedingly, swiping the shadows away in a great circle. But he was struck suddenly from behind and fell to the dirt. Peter and Andrew gasped. Another Widdle slew a shadow to the side and came to the body of Mr. Timf. He knelt beside him for a second and then rose in fury swinging at all the dark shapes. Even Edesha seemed to be panicking. The shadows were moving in closer and closer around him. He swung with all the strength left in him. It seemed as though the shadows would triumph.

A brilliant flash of light suddenly shot across the canyon. Every head turned to see a mighty array of shocking white bajets with armor-clad riders swooping into the canyon. Upon their lead sat Gaberilin swinging a tall sword through the evil hordes.

"What is this?" Nefarious grasped the ball with both hands. "No. No!" The view of the battle suddenly shifted upward and there they saw an amazing sight. The dark smoky air was clearing and the bajets were spilling in. Then the boys noticed that great white hands were pulling the black smoke aside.

James Andrew Wilson

They remembered when Atris had shown them the cloud people. She had said they were coming to Abaddon to do something about all the fowl air. The Yafna all pulled at the blackness and soon there was a great gap in the air and the sun shone down brightly into the canyon.

"Gaberilin!" Peter and Andrew shouted. The mighty warriors swept across the canyon dividing the shadows like flies. All the Aracites were quickly slain except for Lebijez who scurried swiftly up the canyon wall. She screamed terribly and then disappeared into a dark tunnel yawing in the mountainside. Edesha seemed to regain strength and furiously crashed through the shadows.

A large black shape flew across the canyon and landed before Edesha. "Macthon!" Nefarious shouted. "What are you doing?"

Nefarious and the boys watched as Macthon and Edesha clashed in battle. The sun illuminated the Master's staff and he shot a flame toward the massive creature. Macthon fell to the ground. He tried to regain his feet but Edesha swiped forward his sword first.

"No! This can't be! This can't be!" Nefarious backed away from the ball, clawing at his dark cloak. The ball diminished with the last image that of Edesha standing over the dead Macthon.

Nefarious was cringing and screaming wildly. He was now on the ground ripping at his hair, eyes bulging.

"You've lost Nefarious!" Peter proclaimed. The boys were now free of their invisible restraints and

Peter Crossings And The Gate Of Abaddon

walked slowly toward the pathetic figure.

Nefarious stopped all of a sudden. "Oh my boy, but no. I have not lost." He stuck a hand within his cloak. "For you see, I have the reason you are even here in Eden. The reason you were taken from your pathetic life and placed in this land." Nefarious slowly pulled his hand forth. A long blue ribbon spilled to the ground from the object he clutched in his bony fingers. It was a key, a large golden key. "I have the key to the gate. The one thing that can seal me away, that can seal away the shadows, that can seal away all evil. I have it!"

Peter immediately dove forward reaching for the key with Andrew closely following. Nefarious darted out of the way and stood above the boys. "No, no, you can't have it. For you see, I do win!" Nefarious thrust the key back into his cloak.

"Now I will do what I should have done before." Nefarious reached back into the air and screamed. Part of his cloak ripped as two pale wings shot out from his back. "See what I have become?" he roared. "I have given myself to Sheol, and in return I have been given power! I have become brilliant!"

"No Nefarious," Peter said rising to his feet, "you've become a monster."

Nefarious pierced his gaze at Peter and screamed. "Monster or no monster, you will still die!" Then with a flap of his wings he grabbed the two boys under his arms. He rose from the room to a high window and exited into the thick air.

There seemed to be a constant roar sounding through the red smoke. The noise only increased as

James Andrew Wilson

Nefarious rose higher following the reach of the tall dark tower. Peter and Andrew could see far below a large moat of burning hot lava surrounding the tower base.

They came to the top of the tower and Nefarious threw the boys down before him. There were many short spikes surrounding the edge that fell to impending doom. "Take a good look at it. This is the last thing you will ever see."

The boys stood and looked about at the dark land of Abaddon. It was withered and cracked and black as a raven's feather. The land seemed to be constantly moving with streams of lava that spilled from the many volcanoes poking high into the thick air. To Peter's right there seemed to be an even greater darkness. An enormous hole was gouged into the land and gaped its unending darkness like fowl breath. The amazing pit spanned far across the land engulfing much of it in utter emptiness.

"This is my land! This is what I rule!" Nefarious seemed delighted in the wasted ruin.

"There is nothing here but death Nefarious," Peter said turning to face the evil lord.

"Only death for your friends, and for you. I would never have imagined that a boy could cause so much trouble."

"Some people are meant to do great things," Peter said boldly.

"Like me! I am meant to win," said Nefarious. "I will re-write history as the one who broke the prophecies. I will set straight the order of this land and show that Sheol is supreme. And none will stop

Peter Crossings And The Gate Of Abaddon

me, especially you!" Nefarious moved forward quickly and grabbed the boys. He thrust them high into the air and moved slowly toward the edge.

"You could have been great Peter. You could have ruled and become mighty like me. But you chose to be weak, and the weak must die. There is only room for one power." He came to the spikes and started to extend the boys outward. "I have been waiting for this moment for—"

Suddenly Nefarious arched his back and let out a blood-curling scream. He shook the boys violently and then dropped them just on the inside of the spikes. They watched as Nefarious staggered back and clutched at his sides. He tore his dark cloak down the front to reveal an amazing blue light. Nefarious reeled in pain as he grabbed the glowing objects from his sides and lashed them out from his body throwing them to the ground. They were the boys' swords.

Peter and Andrew watched Nefarious as they stood quickly and grabbed their swords. Underneath his long black robes, Nefarious bore a tattered and torn white garment. It was so ripped to shreds that it barley hung on his body. There were black stains covering it and holes all over it. His pale head looked frightfully at the boys. Their swords seemed to be on fire.

Without hesitation, Peter attacked Nefarious. Nefarious turned to the side causing Peter to cut through the left wing. It fell from his body and flopped onto the hard surface. Nefarious screamed in pain and backed away.

James Andrew Wilson

"No, never!" He reached into what remained of his cloak. "I must win. You can't have it." He pulled forth the key with the long blue ribbon. "If I can't kill you, I will kill it. I win in the end, I always win!" Nefarious slowly scooted back. "Remember that boy. You will always loose." He came to the spikes and halted. "I am lord over all, and always will be. The Light will go out and darkness will rule Eden forever." Nefarious' eyes widened as he clutched the key tighter, turned, and dove off the great tower.

The boys watched as the long blue ribbon disappeared over the edge. In that strange moment, a far off voice seemed to sound in Peter's head. It was the voice of Edesha, "Trust in the Light…When the time comes, take the leap…He will protect you…"

Peter took a deep breath. He looked quickly to Andrew who appeared confused and scared. Peter swallowed hard and looked at the spikes. He sheathed his sword. Then he ran full force and dove over the edge.

Chapter Fourteen

Farewell to Friends

Nefarious plummeted toward the bubbling lava. He twisted round and round from the unevenness of his wings. In the chaos and confusion of falling, the key slipped from his grip. It fell along side him for a moment, then he fell faster and it shot up behind him, the long blue ribbon flailing back in the wind. Nefarious twisted over and reached up for the key. It was out of his reach by only an inch.

Peter darted down after him. He had mere seconds before he splashed headlong into the burning lava. The blue ribbon flapped in the air. He sucked his arms to his sides and fell quicker. Stretching out his arm, he was barely able to grab the frayed end of the long ribbon, but he was about to splash into the searing moat. Out of nowhere, it seemed, he landed suddenly on a surface that felt like a large feather mattress. The last that Peter saw of Nefarious was his body splashing into the lava and quickly disappearing beneath it.

James Andrew Wilson

"Hold on my dear boy!" Peter grasped Atris by the feathers and scooped the key up into his hand.

"Atris! Where did you come from?" Peter asked, his heart thumping so fast he was afraid it would knock him off the bajet.

"All that I was told was that I was supposed to fly as quick as I could toward Nefarious' tower."

"Well you got here just in time!" Peter wrapped the ribbon around his hand three times and sucked the key tightly to his palm. "We have to go and get Andrew, he's still on the top."

Atris rose quickly to the top of the tower where Andrew was standing and cheering loudly. "Peter! Atris!" He was waving his hands high.

Atris landed beside him and Andrew crawled up behind Peter. "Did you see it Andrew? Did you see me?"

"I saw the whole thing man! You were awesome!"

"And Nefarious is gone, never to be seen again." Peter let out a deep long sigh.

"It's not over yet Peter," Atris said as she rose from the tower.

"What do you mean?" Peter asked.

"There is still some very important business to attend to with that key."

"You're right Atris. Take me to the gate!"

"I will, but first of all, we need to pick up somebody." Atris darted through the sky, which already seemed less red and smoky. The jagged Petra Mountains came into view and Atris descended quickly toward them. They soon came to the long canyon where the battle had taken place. Atris landed softly

Peter Crossings And The Gate Of Abaddon

and the boys leapt off her back.

They stood among countless slain shadows. A battle weary person came up to them. He was tall, dark haired, and held a mighty staff. "Edesha!" Peter ran forward and hugged him. Edesha wrapped an arm around the boy.

Peter pulled his face back. Tears were trickling down his cheeks. "I took the leap, just like you said. I was so scared Edesha."

Edesha knelt down in front of the boy and placed a strong hand upon his shoulder. "You believed, and you triumphed. Now what have you got to show for it?" The Master stood back and smiled.

Peter let a smile creep at the corner of his mouth as he extended the key outward. Edesha smiled again and closed Peter's hand over the key. "Come, it is time."

All three mounted onto Atris. The bajet called loudly and then rose quickly into the air. She flew with great speed over the dark land.

Peter looked down at the desolate scenery. There wasn't a hint of green, or life anywhere. His thoughts drifted back to Nefarious. He thought it was sad that Nefarious was so blind. That he couldn't see the awfulness of what he had become, and of the land that he ruled. Just as Nefarious had attempted to deceive Peter, he obviously had been deceived as well. And then he threw away what life he had left, and thought that he would still win. Peter felt sadness for Nefarious, and wished that he could have helped him somehow. That he could have showed him these things and taken him to a better place. But that wasn't

James Andrew Wilson

possible now, Nefarious had chosen and he was gone.

Peter wasn't sure if Andrew or Edesha had said anything during the flight, but his thoughts snapped back to the situation when Atris began to descend. The flight became bumpy as they neared the enormous gaping hole. A mighty wind rushed forth that smelled like the mustiness of a forgotten cave deep in the earth. Atris maneuvered through the harsh winds and finally landed.

They crawled off of Atris. "Peter, we believe that we have discovered the answer to the first riddle." Edesha walked with Peter to the gate. Just like the painting by Ethral, there were three keyholes in a horizontal line. "The answer seems to be rather obvious that we are to use the first key hole, which would be this one." He pointed to the one on the right."

"Why that one?" Peter asked.

"Because that is the way of our words. We read from right to left. This would be the first one. But, do you remember what the second riddle is?"

"I do. I remembered it while I was in Nefarious' tower.

"The second secret is this:

"To discover the answer to the first
Knowledge from Beyond must be known
One who has read many words will know
Once the key is turned, the power forth will burst"

Peter tried to understand the riddle. "What does it mean by Beyond?" he asked.

"That is what we call your world," replied Edesha.

Peter Crossings And The Gate Of Abaddon

"I am not sure I understand the answer to the second riddle."

"I do!" Andrew exclaimed. "It's really easy. You said the first one would be on the right because that is how you read in Eden. But not us, we read from left to right!"

"Yes, that's it!" Peter exclaimed. "That is the answer to both of the riddles. So the key must be used in the first lock, and that is the one on the left."

The boys looked up to Edesha. He sighed loudly. "Very well then, go ahead Peter."

"Me? You want me to open it?" Peter asked fearfully.

Edesha looked down at the boy. "Yes, it seems that Tehus has chosen to give you the knowledge to opening it, therefore you will be the one to follow through with it."

Peter's hands were sweating as he turned back and gazed at the enormous gate. It stood alone with the great gaping hole on the other side. There was no fence surrounding the hole, just a dark emptiness. The gate was very tall and made of black iron. Huge hinges were clamped to two enormous pillars on either side of the structure. Peter took a step toward it. He felt like one feels when they finish reading a good book and then their friends are gone and have disappeared back into the pages. No more adventures, no more laughs, no more tears, only the concluding page.

He came to the foot of the tall structure and looked straight up at it. The keyholes were low enough that he could reach up and insert the key. He unwrapped the ribbon from his hand and raised the golden key upward. He inserted it into the left keyhole.

Suddenly the ground began to shake and crack. From the cracks there arose dark shapes. Shadows quickly surrounded them, and when Peter turned back to look, they spanned on as far as the eye could gaze.

"Turn the key Peter!" Edesha shouted pulling forth his golden sword ready to stand to the end.

Peter turned back around. With all his strength he twisted the key.

* * * * *

Jubal stood on the balcony feeling the wind against her face. Tears streamed down her cheeks. She was not singing, and that saddened her even more.

Solomon sat in his chair beside a crackling fireplace. He held a large book in his hands, but it was not being read. He waited, and thought...

Philophos was alone. He thought of himself and his cowardly heart. He lay in bed staring at the ceiling. Perhaps the end was near; perhaps it had already come.

Miyo sat at his desk; a large map was sprawled out before him. He was not studying it. His eyes were closed and he found that there was nothing left to do.

Jubal raised her face toward the night sky. Her words lifted with the wind and traveled into the unknown. Tears fell off the balcony and plummeted toward the earth below.

* * * * *

Peter Crossings And The Gate Of Abaddon

"Turn the key Peter!"

Peter turned back around. With all his strength he twisted the key.

The gate burst open. An overwhelming wind gushed out from the pit blowing Peter back. There was a very loud howling sound echoing through the air. The ground rumbled and shook like an earthquake. The sky darkened and then there was a giant crack of lightning that shot through the gate into the pit. Suddenly Peter and Andrew heard what sounded like millions of screams all at once. They watched in horror as thousands and thousands of glaring red eyes were sucked in through the gate. All sorts of things were flying into the gate as though it were a giant vacuum swallowing all darkness. This went on for nearly three minutes until the last pair of eyes was thrown into the pit. Then the doors to the gate moaned as they began to scoot across the dark ground. They moved magically together with a loud clang. Hundreds of black hands reached out through the gate's bars. Peter remembered the night that seemed so long ago when the shadow had come into his room and reached out toward him.

An amazing light exploded then from the gate. A ring of light shot back and surrounded the gigantic hole. Then millions of beams of light shot to the center of the circle where they formed a giant glowing ball. The ball then fell into the pit sucking all the shadows down with it. The screams ceased and the ground settled.

Peter blinked three or four times and then gazed back up at the gate. It was securely closed and now the iron was a glistening white color. Peter felt a heavy weight in his hand and looked down to see the key, now shining brightly with a clean, new looking ribbon fastened to it. Peter stood to his feet and looked at the Master. Edesha stood gazing up at the closed gate. Then he turned his head and looked at Peter. He sheathed his sword and a calming smile appeared on his face. "It is finished."

Andrew ran to Peter and tackled him to the ground. "You did it Peter! You sealed the gate and all the shadows and everything! You did it!"

"No Andrew, *we* did it."

Andrew stood up and wiped his fist on his shirt. "Well, I guess I did have something to do with it." Everyone laughed.

"Well Atris, I think it's time that we returned to the castle." Edesha crawled up onto the bajet.

"Do you think we should bring them too?" Atris asked loud enough for the boys to hear.

Both the boys looked franticly to Atris and then up to Edesha. "Well, I suppose we should bring them along. No use leaving them here all alone. Besides, what would a celebration be without Peter Crossings and Andrew Hatch?"

"Celebration?" Andrew asked excitedly running and jumping onto Atris. "I'm coming."

"Peter, how about it?" Edesha asked with a big smile.

"Oh you go ahead, I think I'll stay here," Peter replied seriously.

Atris, Andrew, and Edesha all looked bewilderedly to Peter. "Yeah right! Of course I'm coming!" Peter ran and jumped behind Andrew. Everyone laughed again. Atris rose slowly from the ground and turned away from the gate.

As they flew back toward the canyon, Peter looked over his shoulder. The gate sat motionless. He whished it was able to wave, or say good-bye, or something. It just sat there, holding the hordes of evil with unbending power. Peter turned back and looked thoughtfully at the key still in his hand. It was all over. Sure there was still going to be a celebration, but then he would surely return home. He was sad, but at the same time, the thought of home sounded very good indeed.

* * * * *

Neither Peter nor Andrew remembered much of their return back to the castle. It was very late into the night when they had finally reached Edeneth. They didn't remember how they had climbed up the long stairs to their room, or how they had crawled into their beds. There wasn't a sound to be heard as they lay bundled up in the luscious covers staring at the ceiling.

Neither one could sleep. Peter was thinking about all their adventures, while Andrew was wondering what type of food would be at the celebration. Yet, they eventually did drift into sleep, and a very deep one at that.

When they finally woke up, it was because of a loud knock on the door and a familiar voice calling. "Peter, Andrew! Hello, I do say, are you in there?"

James Andrew Wilson

Peter immediately recognized the voice and crawled quickly out of bed. He scooted across the floor and opened the door. He stood staring straight into the eyes of Miyo, who was very well dressed and leaning on a shiny black cane. "Peter dear boy!" Miyo grabbed Peter's hand and shook it. "Wonderful to see you again!"

"It's good to see you too Miyo," Peter said yawning. "What time is it?"

"Well past lunch I must say," Miyo said examining his pocket watch. "Yes indeed, half past one for sure, or so it would be said in you world. Anyways," he tucked the watch back into his breast pocket, "I have been requested to make sure that you two are properly dressed and present at the field very promptly." Miyo scooted in quickly past Peter and proceeded to the wardrobe.

"Now let's see…" Miyo reached into the wardrobe and pulled forth a set of clothes that Peter had nearly forgotten about. Miyo held up his yellow t-shirt, and in the other hand a pair of blue jeans. "Alright, now, put these on."

Peter changed into his clothes and felt quite strange wearing them. He had never seen his shirt so free of wrinkles, and his jeans so new looking. Miyo then handed him his tennis shoes. Peter slid into the molds of his feet and tied them. They seemed foreign, but he had to admit that they felt comfortable.

Miyo was able to drag Andrew out of bed and convince him to put his worn jeans and long over shirt back on. They both washed their faces but didn't bother to comb their hair, for neither one of

Peter Crossings And The Gate Of Abaddon

them enjoyed doing so. Rather they ran their fingers through it, and licking their hands, stuck the few stray hairs down flat.

"Now let's see." Miyo investigated both of them before declaring that they were ready. "Very well, let us be off now." The boys followed Miyo out of the room and down the stairs. The castle seemed empty, all except for a few torches softly glowing in the halls. They came finally to the two doors leading out to the field. Miyo opened them and the boys exited into the pleasant atmosphere.

Outside, under the slowly setting sky, a party was taking place. There was a whole bundle of dancing and music and games and laughing and shouting and most of all, food. Andrew immediately noticed the very long rows of tables with mountains of food covering them. He wasted no time but made his way quickly through the crowd and began testing all of the delicacies.

Miyo had disappeared into the crowd nearly as soon as they had arrived, leaving Peter all to himself. He looked about at all the happy people dancing and rejoicing and wished he were one of them. As he stood in thought taking in all the commotion, someone suddenly spoke his name.

"Peter, my dear boy! How pleasant it is to see you safe again." Peter looked up the gray cloak to see Philophos leaning heavily on his right side upon a crutch of sorts. "I hear you had a grand adventure."

Peter was a bit taken back by the apparent niceness of Philophos. "Yeah, sure did," he replied. They stood in silence for a moment, each one studying the other. Finally Peter spoke, "Philophos, what happened?" he asked pointing to the crutch.

"Oh, this?" Philophos stood on his left foot and shook the crutch. "Those awful Aracites are what happened." Then he scooted his cloak aside to reveal, where there should have been a leg extending from his knee, a shiny golden peg that reached directly to the ground. "Doctor Allamar did the operation. It was not the most pleasant experience I've had, I must admit, but neither was getting it broken."

The site was quite odd to Peter, and he nearly felt woozy to his stomach at the thought. He decided to change the subject, "So, where is Edesha?"

"I was wondering the same thing. I suppose the Master is still in the castle. It's strange that he hasn't come out yet…" Philophos leaned back on his crutch and flopped his cloak back over his peg leg. "Well, I applaud you Peter Crossings, you have had more courage than I." Philophos bowed his head and then hobbled off swinging his crutch back and forth like a pendulum.

Andrew meanwhile was very busy picking bits and pieces of the mountains of food and placing them quickly into his mouth. He moved along the enormous stretch of tables rather swiftly until he bumped into a large object that felt very much so like a tree.

"Why hello there little one!" the great tree boomed.

Andrew looked up to see the hard weathered face of Jatod. Jatod smiled at the boy before him who looked very much like a chipmunk whose mouth is so full of nuts it just might explode.

Peter Crossings And The Gate Of Abaddon

"Jah-od" Andrew managed through a mouth full of food. He clenched his eyes together and swallowed.

Before Andrew spoke, Jatod clamped a big hand on his shoulder. "Give yourself a minute lad. Now there we are."

"Jatod!" Andrew exclaimed.

"Well, I'm glad to see you too!" Jatod chuckled. "How do you like the food?"

"Oh, it's great!" Andrew said grabbing another morsel and consuming it. "So did you hear about what Peter did?"

"Yes I have, that is why we are holding this celebration. Where is Peter anyway?"

Andrew looked around, suddenly remembering that he had left Peter. He saw a stage with a band playing many instruments and happy people hopping about. There were Widdles, and others dancing merrily before the stage, but no Peter in sight. "That's a good question Jatod. I don't really know where he is."

"Well you better be off to find him then! The Master should speak soon, better make sure he's here."

"Yeah, I'll go and look for him." Andrew grabbed a few more items of food and hurried through the crowd. He called for Peter many times, and was nearly positive that he had looked everywhere, but Peter was nowhere to be found.

Peter was in fact nowhere near the party. His curiosity about Edesha had grown so much that he decided to go and look for him. He had no idea where he might find him, so he just began walking through the enormous castle. He had not gone for more than a minute when he heard something echoing softly through the castle walls. Stopping for a second, he cupped a hand around his ear and listened. The faint plucking of a harp and a soothing voice touched his ear. Peter quickly started forward again, following the music.

He finally came to the source. He stood before yet another door he had not yet seen in the castle. It was slightly cracked and so he peeked in. There was a great window at the far wall, and another in the ceiling.

Peter watched as Jubal stopped playing her harp and Edesha came before her. She was seated in a large chair so Peter could not see all that happened. But he could see that Edesha knelt before her and said something as he held her hand.

Peter bumped the door slightly causing it to creak. Edesha stood suddenly. "Oh, Peter, please come in," Edesha beckoned.

Peter scooted in blushing. Edesha turned to Jubal and kissed her hand. Without a word she gathered her harp and stood. She smiled and nodded her head, then turned holding her harp in one hand, and clutching the chair in the other. She walked slowly, reaching for the door, and then exited closing it behind.

Edesha stood with his hands behind his back looking down at Peter. He was dressed in very elaborate attire mostly consisting of emerald green and gold. "I thought you would have been at the celebration," he said.

"I was," Peter replied, "but I couldn't find you anywhere, so I came looking."

Peter Crossings And The Gate Of Abaddon

"I see." A glimmer glistened in Edesha's eye. "There is something I want to show you."

Peter watched as Edesha walked to a small table. There was a maroon sheet over it with a box shaped hump in the center. The Master rested a hand on the table and waited for Peter. Peter walked slowly toward the table, shifting his eyes from Edesha to the table.

"Go ahead and uncover it," Edesha said.

Peter reached out cautiously and grabbed the silky sheet. He pulled it back until it fell off the object beneath. Peter stared in awe at the revealed box. It was a glass box carved with extremely intricate golden shapes, symbols and pictures. Peter could see a glistening object through the clear glass and he knew exactly what it was. The key.

"This is where the key to The Gate of Abaddon rested for nearly two hundred years until it was taken."

"Did Nefarious take it?" Peter asked.

"Yes. It is time that you knew the truth about Nefarious." The Master sighed. "Riousafen as he used to be called before his corruption, was well known within Edeneth. He was the bearer of one of the seven swords. Nefarious was a High Servant of the Light."

"Nefarious? But how did he get the key?" Peter asked. He had noticed that there were no locks, or lids on the glass box.

"The box is sealed with a great power that can only be changed by a High Servant. All the High Servants must commit themselves entirely to the order of the Light. Riousafen made the same vow, but he turned away from it seeking his own gain. He took the key on a dark night and fled quickly toward the evil land. Over the course of ten years, Riousafen became Nefarious. He had to have wings seared into his body, and an unseen restraint bound to him. Through his blindness, he believed that he would still be all-powerful. Even his deceitfulness could not match that of the very essence of evil: Sheol. Evil took him and mangled him to a withered shape that was more evil and darkness than flesh and blood. In the end, his greed overcame him, and he destroyed himself."

Peter stood silent. He thought about the last few dreadful moments before Nefarious had taken that leap to his death. "There is something else though," Peter said. "You said the Golden Book was written in Eden words, so how was I able to read it?"

"Tehus must have revealed it to you, just like he allowed you to see through the invisible cloak. He seems to have blessed you with secret seeing eyes. His plan was for you to know and it was never thwarted. You have learned many powerful things Peter, but I think the thing that you will take back with you is the most important of all."

Peter knew exactly what Edesha meant. "You're right, I never would have defeated Nefarious without Andrew."

"A true friend you have in Andrew Hatch. Our life will go on and we will go through the ages of our world, but yours will now be much different. You have learned what it means to be a friend and to have one. To trust, and to be bold."

"I've learned so much," Peter said looking at the

Peter Crossings And The Gate Of Abaddon

marble floor. "I'm not sure I want to go back home Edesha."

The Master knelt before the boy and placed a hand on his shoulder. "Your time here is over now Peter. There are others back in your world who need you. You still have a life ahead of you at home, and it is waiting. Be bold, and go after it. You have accomplished your mission here, now it's time to go home."

Peter nodded. He tried to hold back the tears. "Edesha...thank you." Peter wiped his eyes and stood straight. He took a deep breath. "I'm ready."

The Master stood and walked slowly toward the door. Peter looked once again at the key. Then he took the sheet and covered it back over. He followed the Master and soon they were back at the field.

"Peter, Peter!" A red haired boy with many freckles emerged from the jolly crowd. Andrew ran to Peter and shook him. "Where have you been man? I've been looking all over the place for you!"

Peter looked up to the Master. "I've been with Edesha."

"Oh, well you should a' told me." Andrew pulled his hands back and slid them into his pockets.

Peter and Edesha laughed. "Well at least you didn't starve, I can see," Edesha said noticing the cream filling smeared over Andrew's face.

"Nope, sure didn't," Andrew smiled.

Edesha chuckled again. "Come you two, follow me." The boys followed Edesha as he wound his way through the crowd. They were stopped many times to talk with those at the celebration. Peter was very happy and surprised to bump into Mr. Timf, for he

James Andrew Wilson

thought the Widdle had died in the battle.

"Nope, didn't die. Just had a good nock on the head for sure. But I has a strong noggin'. Ah, Peter lad! I am glad to see that *you* are well. You have had many an adventure for being such a youngin." He patted him on the back.

Andrew convinced them to go through the food line. They all ate happily filling themselves rather well.

Finally they came to the stage where Edesha asked the band to stop playing. The boys followed the Master up three steps onto the wood planked platform.

"Fair people of Eden!" Edesha said raising his arms to the crowd. Everyone gave their attention. "Tonight we rejoice because of the bravery of two young lads." Andrew nudged Peter and smiled. "A great battle has been won, and The Gate of Abaddon has once again been sealed on the evil of this land, thanks to Peter Crossings and Andrew Hatch." The crowd roared and cheered and clapped. Andrew took a bow, and Peter just watched all the Widdles and taller people cheering for him. Edesha said some other things, but Peter couldn't stop thinking about this new feeling. Before Eden, he had hardly even been noticed, but now he was being hailed as a great hero. The feeling was overwhelming.

"So it is a bitter-sweet privilege to announce the farewell of these two brave boys. In the short time that they have been in Eden, they have changed our world for years to come." Everyone cheered again. Edesha then turned to the boys. "Peter, Andrew, we would like to send you with some gifts on your way home for all that you have done."

"Alright!" Andrew readily accepted.

Just then Miyo came up on the stage. He was holding two items, each were wrapped in a forest green fabric and bound with golden strands of leather. They were not very large, but they seemed heavy. Both the boys received the gifts, one each. Andrew immediately started to unwrap his, but Miyo quickly stopped him instructing to wait until he was back home. The crowd laughed.

"It is also with a great honor that I would call Solomon and Jubal to come forward," Edesha said.

The boys watched as Solomon appeared from the crowd and Jubal as well. He led the lady up the stairs and brought her to the side of Edesha.

"I shall someday leave this castle, but I will not go alone." Then he turned to Jubal and took her hands into his. "With the blessing of her father, Jubal and I have become engaged to be wed."

The crowd erupted in cheers, and Solomon smiled broadly and clapped as well. Andrew and Peter also thought they made a good match. Jubal was over-whelmed and began to blush, so Edesha directed the attention to Solomon. "My dear friend, and soon to be father has one last thing to say to the boys."

Solomon came nearer to the boys and began to speak. "At one time in my life, I was fearful. I doubted and many evil things happened because of it. But these two boys, they have shown great courage and bravery. It has been my honor to know them. And so Peter and Andrew, as you travel back home remember this: even when we feel small, or weak, or as though we do not have the strength, there is power to be had in the trust of the One mightier than we." Then Solomon bowed.

The Master smiled and then placed two fingers in his mouth and whistled. Out of the evening sky a call sounded, and the brilliant white feathers of Atris glistened as she dove down and landed upon the stage. Gaberilin was upon her back, and he hopped off when they had landed.

"Peter, Andrew, it's time," Edesha said. The crowd was silent, and suddenly Peter whished that nobody was watching, for a tear trickled down his cheek. Andrew hurriedly ran to Atris and gave her a great hug, but Peter slowly made his way across the stage. He looked up at Edesha. Edesha smiled a calm soothing smile. His eyes glimmered. "Go on Peter," he said calmly.

Peter sucked in all the tears and walked over to Atris. At the side of the saddle there was a pouch into which they slid their gifts. Gaberilin grabbed Peter and placed him on the back of the bajet in front of Andrew who had already climbed on. "Farewell Peter, may Tehus guide your flight home," Gaberilin said. "Oh, I almost forgot something." Gaberilin reached into his pocket and pulled out a shell attached to a strand of leather. "This Trans-Portal Shell is for you." He placed the shell around Peter's neck.

"Hold on boys," Atris said, and then she called and rose from the stage. Peter looked down one last time to see Edesha waving. He saw Gaberilin, and

Peter Crossings And The Gate Of Abaddon

Miyo on the stage. Solomon and Jubal were waving as well. Mr. Timf was waving from the crowd. Jatod was waving with all four arms. Philophos did his best to wave without falling over, but it proved useless. Peter felt bad afterwards, but he chuckled a little when Philophos lost his balance on his peg leg and toppled over into a group of Widdles. Peter waved until everyone was out of sight, and then he turned back around.

"Homeward bound," Andrew said.

Something suddenly dawned on Peter. "Andrew, how long have we been gone?"

"A long time."

"How are we going to explain where we've been all this time?" Peter asked frantically.

"I don't know. I didn't even think about it."

"Me either, at least not until now. Oh man, my parents are probably worried sick!" Peter sighed loudly.

"Ah, come on Peter. They'll understand if we just tell them that we've been in Eden fighting shadows and Aracites and finding hidden islands and flying on bajets," Andrew said sarcastically.

"Yeah, right," Peter replied, but then he had to laugh.

Chapter Fifteen

It's Only the Beginning

And so it happened that Peter and Andrew left Eden. Atris had flown with ease through the evening sky. Neither of the boys had much to say, they were both caught up in thought, and soon found themselves to be rather tired. Andrew started to doze off in the calm breeze. He found himself nodding his head forward and bumping into Peter.

"Andrew, hey, wake up," Peter said nudging him.

"I—I'm awake." Andrew yawned loudly.

"We're almost to the Portal Sky," Atris said. "Hold on tight."

Soon they were riding on the wind like waves of the ocean. The majestic purple sky reached over the mountain range spilling a calm haze over the triangular peaks. Atris alighted onto the cloud and the boys slid off her back. They looked out upon Eden

James Andrew Wilson

---

and remembered all the adventures they had in the strange land.

"You best be going now," Atris said. "But before you leave, I must tell you this. You are never to tell of the portal to anyone except your parents, though they may not believe you. Make sure you never come through the portal either, unless the need to do so is too great. There is evil still in your world that would come to ours if it knew how."

The boys agreed to this and then turned to leave. "Wait, don't forget your gifts," Atris prompted.

"Oh yeah!" exclaimed Andrew. They gathered their gifts and then turned back around to leave. Just before they entered the portal, Peter turned and gazed over Eden. He could see the purple fingers of the Portal Sky reaching back toward the sea far away. The beautiful stars were etched across the glowing canopy. The entire land seemed at rest and filled with joy. He thought that he could even hear the faint plucking of Jubal's harp far off in the distance. Peter exhaled a long breath, stepped into the white haze, and then the world of Eden was gone.

* * * * *

The boys crawled up out of the trapdoor in the stage. They had made their way through the hall of faces and even chatted briefly with Ethral.

"Ah, you're back I see," he had said. "I trust your visit was colorful." And as you know, it was very colorful.

So they made their way across the stage and to

Peter Crossings And The Gate Of Abaddon

---

the door leading out of the auditorium. But before they exited out the door Andrew said, "Hey, let's see what these things are." He was referring to the gifts.

They opened them to find the two swords that Edesha had given them. If they hadn't been so excited, they probably would have thought more properly and wrapped them back up, but instead they placed the sheaths on their belts and then exited the room.

"Mr. Crossings! Where have you been young man?" Peter was suddenly staring into the unwelcoming, wrinkled face of Mrs. Frudie. "You're late for class, and we are all waiting for an explanation for why you missed last class!" Frudie slammed her hands to her hips. "Well?"

Peter felt utterly confused. He had been gone for *weeks*. But why was Frudie only accusing him of missing one class? Andrew peeked out from behind only to duck back when he saw Frudie. "Hatch! I see you, come back here!" Frudie grabbed Peter by the ear and Andrew by his bushy red hair. "All right you two, I don't know what you've been up to with those toy weapons, but it's over now. Put them into your lockers and then straight off to class with you!"

She shoved them down the hall and waited like a vulture for them to try and dash away. "Peter, what's going on?" Andrew whispered as they came to their lockers.

"I'm not sure." Peter turned the numbered knob and peeled open his locker. The boys slid their swords inside and went to grab their books.

"Uh, Peter, what class are we going to?" Andrew asked.

James Andrew Wilson

Peter arched his head back and peered at the clock that had always been conveniently placed above his locker. There was more than one occasion when he had to check the time to figure out what class he was going to. He figured that he forgot simple things like that because he would always much rather be somewhere else. The clock read 2:15.

"Social Studies, last class of the day," he said.

Andrew started the dig for his books. "But which day?" He found his worn and scribbled on book.

Peter then remembered that all this time he had been wearing his watch. He looked down at it now. "September 12th," he said. "It's the same day!" Although neither of the boys were sure if they believed it yet.

"Maybe your watch got messed up when we went through the portal," Andrew guessed.

"We'll see," Peter said as they shut their lockers and walked toward the classroom. Frudie the vulture had disappeared off into the school somewhere to find somebody else to pester. The boys found the class and could hear the muffled speaking within. They looked hesitantly to each other and then cracked open the door.

The teacher stopped speaking and turned his eyes to Peter and Andrew, as did the rest of the entire class. All eyes sat motionless upon the two boys. Peter looked about at the other kids who all just stared as though he were a ghost. Peter started to sweat in the aggravating silence. He swallowed and started for his seat. There was a clatter in the back corner as the frightened image of a boy with black spiked hair scur-

Peter Crossings And The Gate Of Abaddon

ried back, tripping over his chair. Peter watched as Judas Fitzgerald stood and ran to the back corner of the room staring wildly as Peter approached.

"Stay away from me Crossings!" Judas shouted pointing a shaking finger. The entire class watched as for the first time ever, Judas showed fear. "Do— don't come any closer!"

Peter cautiously stepped forward and pulled his chair out. He sat slowly down onto it, watching Judas carefully. Judas was sweating as his eyes stared horrified at Peter.

"Mr. Fitzgerald, please sit down!" The strange feeling in the room disappeared at the teacher's voice. Judas flashed his eyes to the teacher. "I'm not asking you Judas," the teacher said.

Judas looked cautiously at Peter and then started scooting along the wall. He finally came to his desk and sat down again. "Very well. Now, Peter and Andrew, I would like to see you directly after class for an explanation." The boys nodded and listened as the teacher continued rambling on about something at which they were clueless.

For the first few minutes, Peter tried to listen, but he finally let his eyes travel. They scanned across the green chalkboard until resting on the top right corner where a single word and number were inscribed. Pale white chalk seemed to voice the revealing truth in an eerie way. "September 12th," Peter whispered to himself. "We haven't even been gone for but a few hours…"

* * * * *

"It was all my fault!" Judas Fitzgerald confessed through streaming tears. "I told Peter to pass the note, I shouldn't have," Judas sobbed.

Mr. Wiggy folded his arms and sighed. "Thank you Mr. Fitzgerald, that will be all I'll need from you."

"Re—really?" Judas asked, shocked. "Thank you, thank you!" Judas grabbed his backpack and dashed out of the classroom door.

"Peter Crossings," Mr. Wiggy whistled as he stared at the boy through thick glasses, "although you didn't write the note, you still shouldn't have been passing it. Next time, bring it up to me after class and I will deal with it."

"Yes sir, I'm sorry sir," Peter said with his hands clasped behind his back.

"Alright then, that will be all, you can go."

Peter grabbed his bag and made his way toward the door. "Oh Peter," Mr. Wiggy called, "I almost forgot, happy birthday."

Peter nodded and then it hit him. It was still his birthday! Although he had been gone in Eden for over a week's time, he hadn't been gone from home for even a day. The words of his mother drifted back through his ears. "We were thinking, if you'd like, that we could invite some of your friends from school over and have a birthday party this evening. How does that sound?"

Peter adjusted his bag and dashed out into the hall. He ran through the few remaining kids until bursting out into the sunshine. A mile long line of busses and mostly mini vans cluttered the streets surrounding the school. Peter cupped a hand over his

Peter Crossings And The Gate Of Abaddon

eyes and searched the expansive front yard of the school. Hundreds of kids were laughing and playing, while still others stood in lines at the buses. Then Peter spotted what he was looking for. He leapt down the stairs and flashed through the crowd.

Andrew was just crawling into the front seat of a blue car when Peter crashed into him. "Wait, Andrew!"

"Peter, what are you doing?"

"Today is my birthday party, my mom wanted me to invite some friends. You're the only friend that I have and I want you to come," Peter gasped.

"Cool! But I'll have to ask." Andrew ducked his head into the car. "Mom, this is my new friend—"

"Peter Crossings," his mom suddenly said. "I know who he is, his mom and I have been trying to get you two together for months."

"What?" Andrew asked surprised.

"Yeah! You probably don't even know it, but the Crossings are our neighbors."

At first Peter and Andrew weren't sure they heard right. "You mean, we have been living by them all this time?" Andrew asked.

"Yes sir, we sure have." his mom replied smiling. She also had red hair.

"No way! This is so cool!" Andrew turned and gave Peter a high five. Then ducked his head back in the car. "So can I g—"

"Of course you can go! Just have Martha give me a call when the party's over."

"Alright! Thanks mom!" Andrew threw his bag into the car and shut the door. "Well, let's go man!

James Andrew Wilson

Peter and Andrew wound their way through the crowd. Peter searched the sidewalks for the van. Finally he found it and breathed a deep sigh of relief to see the white mini van purring by the curb. His mother was waving happily from inside. Immense joy spilled over Peter at the sight of his mom. He had missed her so much.

"Well hello Andrew!" Martha said as the two hopped in the side door.

"Hello Mrs. Crossings. Peter invited me to his birthday party tonight, I hope it's ok."

Martha looked more surprised than she had ever been in her life, and in fact, she was. "Of course it's ok!" She smiled at Peter through the rearview mirror. He blushed and smiled back.

* * * * *

"Wow, you really do like to read," Andrew said as he ran his hand along the rows and rows of books.

"Yep, I sure do," Peter said as he plopped down on his bed.

"Have you read all of these?" Andrew asked examining the spine of a book.

"Yeah," Peter said solemnly staring at the ceiling.

"What's up man?" Andrew asked turning from the bookshelf.

"I don't get it Andrew. We were gone in Eden for at least a week, but here, it has only been a few hours."

Andrew came and sat on the edge of the bed. "Remember Solomon was talking about that. The times are different." Then he sighed. "And now it's all gone, just like it never happened."

"But I remember it all so well. I remember Edesha and Philophos, and Gaberilin and Mr. Timf. I remember Jubal and Miyo. I remember Edeneth and everything, like we'd been there forever. But we will never see Eden again."

The boys sat quietly for some time pondering over all these things until Andrew dug in Peter's backpack and pulled out his sword. Andrew pulled the blade from the sheath and a folded sheet of yellowed paper suddenly fell to the bed. Peter reached over and picked up the paper. After unfolding it he read out loud.

Dear Peter Crossings,

World's apart we are, at least that is what some might say. But for you, the truth is clear. Although our lives and existence may be as a dream to the other, we have shared that dream for a short time. With your parting from our now renewed land, I shed tears of many meanings. In the years to come, may you grow in strength as you realize the power of life and the hope that we can give, or take away. As you discover the road set before you, may the strength of Tehus guide your way. Even if the hordes of darkness rise about you, never forget the Power of the Light. There is a greater strength in our world, and in yours, in which you will find victory. We will never forget the bravery that you have shown and given.
A Servant of the Light,
Edesha-

Thank you...

PS, I had Solomon write this for me, he can write in your words. I am learning how to now, but I'm not very good at it yet.

Peter folded the ornately scripted letter back up. He took a deep breath and sighed. "Well, it's over."

"No Peter, it's only begun. Like Edesha said, in the years to come, may you grow in strength. We've learned what it means to be brave and be a friend, now let's be friends. I have so many cool things to show you. I have to catch you up from not having any friends for so long."

"And I have to let you read some great books."

Andrew hesitated. "Yeah, but I don't think that any of them will compare to the adventure of Peter Crossings and The Gate of Abaddon!"

Peter smiled. He liked the sound of that.

"Peter, Andrew! Come on up for cake!" Martha's voice sounded from the kitchen.

"Alright!" Andrew said speeding up the stairs.

* * * * *

The spotted gray and white hair lay over his wrinkled face. He dropped tears into his withered hands and sobbed. All around him there was ruin and decay. He was always too weak; he had always been too weak. But now it was too late, there was nothing he could do to change the past. His leadership had proven faulty, and the kingdom had suffered because

Peter Crossings And The Gate Of Abaddon

of it. Now there was no chance for redemption…

Unless…unless the past *could* be changed. But he couldn't do it; he had already failed too many times. If he were to go back he would only fail again. But, perhaps there was one who could go back. One who had proven himself before and showed his strength. It was time for the young hero to return, only to change the past…

* * * * *

Lightning cracked in the night sky sending Peter Crossings straight up in bed. Sweat swam off his forehead and down his cheeks. The sky cracked again. From behind the closet doors a glimmer showed. Peter slowly pushed back the covers and stood to his feet. His slow breaths sounded thunderous against the muffled pelting of the rain as he scooted toward the opposite side of the room. Lighting lit up his room again shocking his face with a pale light.

"Peter, Peter come in!" the walkie-talkie on the nightstand crackled. "Peter, Peter are you there?" Peter dashed over and grabbed the device into his hand.

"Hello? Andrew?" he said.

"You're up too?" the walkie-talkie replied.

"I just woke up, what's going on?"

"I'm not sure. There's a big storm outside."

"Yeah, I can hear the rain, it's loud…"

"Wait!" Andrew said. The device fell silent for a moment. Peter sat in the evening glow, waiting. He was wide awake.

"Peter?"

"Yeah, I'm here," Peter replied.

"I think I know what's going on." Andrew's voice was shaky.

"What? What's going on?" Peter asked.

"Peter, go and look in your closet."

Peter looked to his closet. He set the walkie-talkie down and stepped lightly to the sliding doors. His sweaty palms scooted the door aside. As soon as it cracked open a brilliant blue light spilled out. Peter shielded his eyes as he opened it further and reached in. He knelt and found the weapon leaning against the wall. A small layer of dust drifted off of it as he grasped it by the handle and pulled it forth. The blade glowed with such a bright light that Peter's mind raced back to the horrific events right before Nefarious had plummeted off the dark tower. It had been three months since then.

"Hello? Hello? Is there anybody there?" Peter whipped from the closet and looked to his dresser. There atop it sat the Trans-Portal Shell Gaberilin had given him. The voice came from the little shell again. "Hello, is there anybody there? Please, somebody answer…"

Printed in the United States
18101LVS00001B/52-255